BILLY LOVE'S WOLFPACK

DR. JEAN WOLF

ISBN 978-1-387-30031-0

Printed in the United States of America

Dedication

This book is dedicated to the memory of my amazing mother, Margaret Wolf, dress collector and costumer, whose assortment of vintage 1920s and 30s clothing inspired my descriptions. The opening chapter depicts the lavender linen dress with the gigantic bow, which Billy Love wears to her fifteenth birthday party. In subsequent chapters, I dress my women in everything from drop-waist frocks to beaded flapper dresses, all found in my inherited collection. The dresses are carefully labeled with the year they were manufactured. Priceless.

Margaret Wolf

July 1, 1928 - Dec 19, 2011

Acknowledgments

I am grateful for my extended family of Wolfs, as this book, although a novel, is loosely based on some of the personalities of my own family. My grandfather really did have two rhinoplasties in the thirties, and he almost bleed to death with the second revision. And generations of Wolfs lived in Darmstadt, Germany before immigrating to the United States. I want to thank my first cousins who have supported me and given suggestions throughout the process: Mary Martin, Patricia Filer, Anne Harrison, Bob Zeller, and Lynn Grask. We are a tight-knit group of relatives. I consider us a wolfpack. Throughout my research for the book, they weighed in with their own thoughts, helping me make my story richer.

Thanks to Alice Myers, owner of Beaverdale Books, for finding my Beta readers, Betty Salmon and Mary Yungeberg. Betty and Mary provided important feedback that enriched my writing.

I am indebted to Jody Masterson, who helped format the book early on. Her computer skills are highly appreciated. Pam Barton, who designed the fabulous cover art and gave me advice about family trees and maps, is a true friend, indeed.

Carol Bodensteiner gave me great guidance on how to navigate the publishing world. My husband, Tom Logan, supported my journey, and put up with my daily updates on historical research tidbits.

Finally, I never could have published this novel without the funny, witty and insightful Terrie Scott. As my editor, her encouragement, detailed critiques, and feedback, was phenomenal. For my first novel, I got extremely lucky, or maybe, it was meant to be. Terrie is the best.

WOLFPACK FAMILY TREE

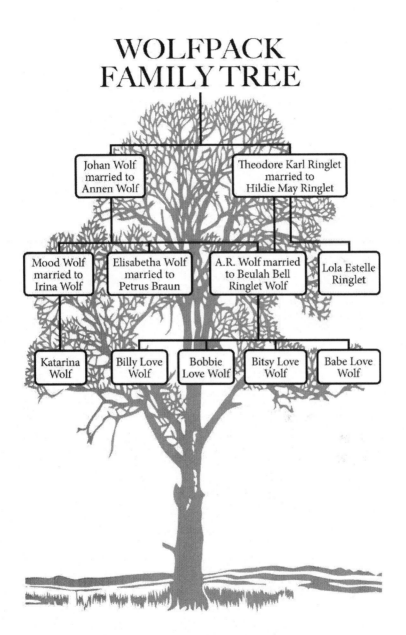

Johan Wolf married to Annen Wolf

Theodore Karl Ringlet married to Hildie May Ringlet

Mood Wolf married to Irina Wolf

Elisabetha Wolf married to Petrus Braun

A.R. Wolf married to Beulah Bell Ringlet Wolf

Lola Estelle Ringlet

Katarina Wolf

Billy Love Wolf

Bobbie Love Wolf

Bitsy Love Wolf

Babe Love Wolf

For the strength of the Pack is the Wolf,

and the strength of the Wolf is the Pack.

~Rudyard Kipling

Chapter 1

15th Birthday

Oklahoma, USA
1928
Billy Love

I awoke this morning feeling older and more sophisticated. A small family party is planned to celebrate my coming of age. My mind meanders back over the years. I have questions. Why in the world would my mother and father name me Billy Love Wolf? First, Billy is a boy's name and I am definitely not a boy, but I am boyish, especially in the context of my adoration for the rodeo. Billy Love is a pretty good rodeo name, I figure. I heard there was a boy named Billy Wolf in Tulsa, too.

I have been teased about my name by my classmates, but I will show them. For I also am a first chair viola player in the high school orchestra. And we received excellent marks last year at the state competition. I reckon Billy Love will become known as a world class strings player. Already, I am playing concerts in Tulsa. Later tonight, I will rehearse Debussy's Sonata for the flute, viola and harp at Maize's house. Of course, since she plays the harp, it is best that we practice in her parlor.

I am the oldest girl of four, so I have to be the responsible one. My sisters have crazy names too. Bobbie Love, Bitsy Love, and Babs Love (Babe). Bitsy Love and Babe Love are twins so they get a lot of attention, especially when you hear their names called. Identical, they are somewhat whiney. I call them the whiner twins; if they whine enough, they get their way. They fight a lot too, and our mother Beulah Bell is always refereeing. "Girls, stop bickering right now," she admonishes on a daily, sometimes hourly, basis. The twins tend to ignore her.

Bobbie Love hates physical activity, so she considers the rodeo a filthy hell hole. We really don't have anything in common. She has a group of snooty friends, and she cut her hair in a bob last year. Our parents were pretty upset about that, but it took the attention off me for the moment. She can't carry a tune either!

I think about the rodeo. We have a great one here in Enid. My father, A.R. Wolf (the A stands for Adolf and the R stands for Rubin), owns and operates a vast cattle ranch. You can understand why he prefers to go by A.R. He is a bit evasive about his past; even I, his first born, think him a bit shady.

We have horses on the ranch. I have been riding since I was three. Actually, I have my own horse named Lobo Love which is somewhat a play on words. Lobo means wolf, so it translates as wolf love. Clever huh? I have done some barrel racing, but am becoming a bit bored with that. You can only round so many of those containers. I hold the fastest time in the county, so I reached my goal.

I really want to ride bulls, but mom and dad are adamant that is not something young women of a certain social standing should do. We live in Oklahoma for goodness sakes, the home of the first bull riding woman. She no longer rides, but she is giving lessons and I am determined to learn from her.

"Billy Love, you need to get ready for the family party," mother yells up the stairs. "They will be here in an hour."

"Mother, I will be down shortly. Do you need help?" I respond. "No, just put on a pretty dress and get down here. Your Aunt Lola Estelle will probably regale us all with her fancy stories about the nightclubs of Tulsa." Mother's tone is sharp with disapproval. I think her jealousy of her sister is ridiculous.

I washed my long, thick, dark brown tresses last night and put them wet into pin curls. As I brush my hair today, it falls in waves down my back. My lavender linen dress is laid out on the bed. It is beautiful. When we purchased it two months ago, I thought it was perfect. The dress is trimmed with ecru lace and it falls to my mid-calf. A giant bow ties up the back. Yet, now that I am fifteen, it seems babyish. But I have no choice. There is nothing else suitable in my closet. I shut my door and hurry downstairs.

4

My grandparents are stepping out of their automobile--
Theodor Karl and Hildie Mae Ringlet, my mother's parents. Lola
Estelle emerges out of the back seat. Here in Oklahoma, everyone
goes by their first and middle names. It is tradition.

I adore my Aunt Lola Estelle. She is eight years younger than
mother, and she never misses a party. Mother is stuck on the ranch
with four kids and is quite envious of her glamorous sister. Lola
Estelle was one of the first women in Tulsa to cut her hair and raise
her skirts to the knee. And, she has glamourous flapper dresses that
are one of a kind. Her olive skin, dark brown hair and eyes are
matched with pale gold, tangerine and mint green sleeveless frocks
that shimmer with hand applied beading. When I go to Tulsa, she
lets me visit her closet and try on the dresses. She also has a white
lacquer table where she sits to apply her makeup. I like to watch
her transform herself to go out and take command of the social
scene.

"Hello, my darling Billy Love," Lola Estelle calls out. "Happy,
happy birthday," she continues. "Why I believe you are old enough
to go with me to the Spirit Club next winter."

"Lola Estelle, what are you thinking? She is still a child," my
grandmother says in an irritated voice. I am a bit scared of my
grandmother. Hildie Mae can be mean. We are all wary around
her. But I am not going to let her ruin my day.

Lola Estelle looks like a movie star. She has on a ruby colored
dress with matching shoes and purse. She has brought a bottle of
vodka with her. "I see you have come with an adult gift, Lola
Estelle," A.R. exclaims, as he enters the parlor. "Let's go onto the
porch and have a smoke before the party begins," he remarks as
my mother glowers at him from the kitchen.

My father smokes pipes and he has quite a collection from
which to choose. "A.R., you know how to entertain your sister-in-
law don't you?" Lola Estelle exclaims. "I brought my own smokes.
A pipe does not interest me in the least." I watch them enter the
porch and light up. My father is an imposing figure. He leans
against the porch post, takes the pipe in his mouth and inhales

5

deeply. His hair is a thick dark brown, which he slicks back with pomade. He has on cowboy boots. In profile, he has a square jaw with a prominent nose. I think he is ruggedly handsome. The acrid pipe smoke drifts through the screen, connecting with those of us remaining in the house.

My three sisters noisily trample down the stairs. Bobbie Love tries to avoid the twins. "You two are so annoying," she says loudly. The twins have on matching short sleeved cream-colored dresses with five evenly spaced horizontal vanilla satin ribbons encircling the entire dress. Ribbons tie back their blonde hair. They are impossible to tell apart.

"Bitsy Love and Babe Love come see your grandmother and show some respect," Hildie Mae toots as she pats them each on the head. "You girls are 10 now, and you need to quit being rowdy. It is not becoming young ladies." I see Bitsy Love and Babe Love roll their eyes at each other, then slip away into the kitchen.

We are waiting for my dad's parents to arrive. They are always late. Johan and Annen Wolf came to Oklahoma straight from Darmstadt, Germany. Neither one speaks English very well, and Annen reverts to German often. My grandmother wants to teach me German, but I want nothing to do with it: too guttural.

Johan and Annen Wolf do not use their middle names. Germans like to keep things simple. Away with the fussiness - they really hate all of the sisters having Love for their middle names. And Billy and Bobbie are boys' names in their eyes. Bitsy and Babe, those aren't even names.

Johan and Annen live in a separate house on the ranch. Johan came over to Oklahoma from Germany in 1893 and got a huge of parcel of land. I am not sure how or why, but I might ask him someday.

Father's parents have arrived. My heavily frosted cake sits regally on a white porcelain stand. Its sweet smell fills the kitchen. Let's get the party started.

Chapter 2

The Singer

Darmstadt, Germany
1928
Kat

My given name is Katarina Rosa Wolf but I am known as Kat. Kat—I like that the name implies I am a feline, light on my feet. It might be a stretch, but I think of my voice as a purr, steady but soft and emotive. The purr needs to become more of a roar. Today, I have my first official voice lesson with the great cabaret star Miss Anita Gunderson.

I am an only child and my father, Moody Wolf, has raised me alone. My mother, Irina, died in childbirth with me. She was Russian. My father has hinted that her family was forced from Russia by Czar Nicholas II. I think they were cousins of the czar and were considered traitors. I am not very interested in all of that. It was seventeen years ago.

My father is an alchemist at the Merck laboratories in Darmstadt. He works hard, but he is so old-fashioned. For a year, I have begged him to let me take lessons. It really is the only path I have ever wanted. The teachers at my gymnasium have given me solos and praised my voice, but it is not enough. I need to develop the smoky, nuanced voice of a jazz singer. And, Anita Gunderson epitomizes the jazz singer. I am a natural alto and so is Miss Gunderson.

Anita Gunderson lives in Munich, almost 3 hours from Darmstadt. I got up at 4am today to prepare. "Katarina, let's go!" Papa commands. Papa always calls me Katarina, never Kat. In one short year, I hope to move to Munich, get my own apartment, and sing in a cabaret. Papa does not know of my intentions and I won't tell him until I am 18, when he can't do anything about it.

My mother, Irina, was blue eyed and blonde. I have blue eyes, but my hair is dark, with streaks of ginger. Today, I have pulled my hair to one side and added an ivory clip to hold it place. I feel excited to meet my teacher in my glamorous new dress. Papa let me purchase it last week. It is not a flapper dress—Papa would never allow that (just wait until next year). It is a tangerine, light weight jersey with a scalloped neckline, drop waist ribbon belt and asymmetrical beige lace overlays on the skirt. It hits modestly at the ankle.

Papa is like his name, Moody. I never know what his tone will be. He doesn't like to have fun, I know that much. Just last week he complained, "Those cabarets all over Germany are going to destroy all morality."

"Oh, papa, how can you say that? They are fun and the talent is so great."

Papa fought in the first war and has seen lots of suffering. He was a medic and carried the morphine to administer to wounded soldiers. Many of the soldiers died of massive injuries, but the morphine at least dulled the pain. He is now in charge of overseeing the morphine production at the Merck laboratories.

"I took the day off, I hope you appreciate it," Mood (as he is called by most of his friends) gripes.

"Oh, Papa, you are the best," I reply, as I smooth my skirt, giving him a big cheesy smile.

Miss Anita Gunderson gives lessons at her home, a small, but richly furnished cottage in the middle of Munich. She is 23 and started singing in Munich cabarets when she was 18. We are at her arched front door. "Papa, can you leave me and go to the café while I take my lesson?" I implore.

Papa stomps off, reluctantly, and I stride confidently to the door. I lift the heavy brass marker, but before I can bring it down, it suddenly opens. Standing before me, Miss Anita is the most elegant woman I have ever seen. She is tiny and delicate. She has on a taupe silk dress with a deep V of taupe lace on the neckline and lower sleeves. The dress has a dropped waist belt, and she has a dramatic matching silk scarf that runs across her throat and down the back of the dress. Her hair is so blonde, it is white—her eyes, a deep turquoise.

"Katarina, come on in. I am interested in hearing your voice," Miss Anita coos. I am intimidated, but I nod at her slightly as I step through the door. I hope that my face is not red - I just might break out in hives.

I have some sheet music tucked under my arm that I hope to sing for her. I tried to find some jazz music that Miss Anita herself might have sung in the clubs. I settled on "Life as a Dreamer," the alto version.

"Come over to the piano, Katarina," she says. I follow her, and stand behind her as she sits down in front of the keys. "The first things you will do every day between now and the next lesson are important warm ups. They will strengthen your vocal cords and help your pitch. First, stand up as straight as you can; then pull your shoulders back. Next, put your hand right below your rib cage. There is a muscle there called the diaphragm; every time you breathe, the muscle pushes the air over your vocal cords. To make your voice project clearly you will contract the muscle as you sing notes. Try it now," Anita insists, sternly.

This is not what I am expecting. Just teach me how to be a torch singer, I think. But, I need to do what she instructs me to do. I stand up straight, throw my shoulders back and suck in my stomach. "Good," she says. "Now sing a note."

"AAAAAH," Wow, I think. Those techniques do make a difference. Middle C is strong.

"A good start Kat. The next step is vocalizing. I have a set of scales you must practice every day. They will help you to expand your vocal range and make your pitch better."

I thought my pitch and vocal range were already good? I am an alto after all. Now, I am annoyed. "I brought some sheet music I could sing for you. It is "Life as a Dreamer," I offer.

"Kat, you must go home for a month and complete these exercises. If I think you have progressed enough, I will let you sing it at the next lesson. Not everyone can become a cabaret singer—I will only teach those who can become the best."

"Thank you," I say, dejectedly. I wonder what Papa will say when he finds out the lesson consisted of singing one note? I will make something up.

Papa has arrived and is strolling up the sidewalk. I want to go home and get started. I have a year to turn into a topnotch torch singer.

Chapter 3

The Cabaret

Munich, Germany
1928
Elisabetha

I was born Elisabetha Eva Wolf, but then I married Petrus Braun and became Liz Eva Braun. Elisabetha is too much to pronounce every time. Petrus even said so at a very early stage in our relationship. We were not blessed with children, so for the past ten years, we have been immersed in the art and culture scene here in Munich.

Most people are unaware that the German cabarets started in Munich, not Berlin, but they did, in the Schleswig District. The area is teaming with artists, writers, singers and actors. Why, at any given moment, you could pluck someone off the street and put them on the cabaret stage with a great entertainment result. The people of Munich are very liberal, so political plays in cabarets are common as well.

When I was two years old, my parents suddenly left Darmstadt and arrived in Enid, Oklahoma in time for the Cherokee land grab. Grab is what I call it, since my parents Johan and Annen Wolf now live on a large ranch outside Enid. I was left behind, to be raised by my mother's sister. What prompted my parents to leave was never revealed to me, but my aunt hinted they had some legal problems. My brother A.R. Wolf oversees the ranch now. He was born a year after my parents arrived in America.

From what I have read, Oklahoma is one vast dusty ranch. Culture is probably non-existent. I am German through and through and will always live here in Munich.

I have little contact with my parents. However, I believe they feel guilty, because in 1925 they invested a large sum of money into our cabaret, *The Garden*. Petrus and I named it *The Garden* because it reminds our customers of lushness, greenery and, of course, Eden.

Petrus is cleaning and making some repairs at *The Garden* today and I am meeting with Miss Anita Gunderson, the famous torch singer, to book her into our cabaret. We are meeting at the upscale restaurant Hessen House, which looks like a Swiss chalet.

Nervous, I arrive more than 30 minutes ahead of time, and go straight to the wash room. Looking in the mirror I see a small woman, about five feet tall with olive skin, and brown eyes and hair. Of course, my hair is bobbed. In profile, I see a fine boned face with bow-like lips, a cleft chin, and a sharp nose. My dress is black silk, conservative, but expensive.

I return to the table just as Miss Anita makes her way into the restaurant. "Hello, my darling Liz!" she exclaims across the room. She is wearing a wool, camel colored fingertip cape with scrolling appliques on the bottom and collar. Her skirt is brown suede and a brown veiled hat tilts perfectly on her gleaming blonde hair.

"Miss Gunderson, please join me," I exclaim, feeling like the plainest person in the room. "Petrus and I are so pleased that you are going to sing at our cabaret."

"It is a great time to be in Munich is it not? I have heard your nightclub is thriving every night of the week. What time do you get to bed?"

"Sometimes as late as 6am. I have gotten used to sleeping during the day. It does mess with your circadian rhythms, though. Petrus takes the early evening shift until 10 and then I came in and stay until all of the acts are finished. If there is a rowdy crowd, my security staff may have to escort people to the door."

We place our orders and continue the conversation. "Would I be the headliner act?" Anita coyly asks.

"Of course," I reply.

"A private dressing room? My own makeup stand?" Miss Gunderson persists.

"Yes, to both," I concede.

"One final request. I need five front row reserved seats."

"Done."

I do wonder about the rumors I have heard about Miss Anita and her romantic relationships. She has been linked to a number of slick men around Munich. Her latest is Casparus Bunz, a stockbroker who escorts her to and from the cabarets where she is singing. He is in his early 30s and has no intention of staying in a relationship more than a few months. Perhaps Casparus and his buddies will take the five seats.

"Do you mind if I smoke a cigarette?" Anita queries. She is pulling out her black slender holder and preparing to light the cigarette. Not really asking for permission, I would say. As a courtesy, I shake my head no. She waves her right hand dramatically and sucks hard, then elegantly puffs out smoke rings.

"Do you know why smoking is good for a singer like me?" she asks, and then answers her own question. "Because it makes my voice lower, more sultry, perfect for a torch singer." I smile at this ridiculous comment. Miss Gunderson thinks highly of herself.

"You can come by the Garden to rehearse around 3pm tomorrow. Our pianist, Friedrich, will be there too. Will you bring the sheet music so that he can practice? Also, how many songs will you sing?" I exclaim, wanting to be organized and efficient.

"That rehearsal time will be perfect. Around 10 songs. I am adding a new song called "Life as a Dreamer." A new vocal student brought it to me last week. She wanted to sing it for me, but I only had her sing one note, and then out the door she went to practice vocalizing for a month. She left the music, I played it, and now I will sing it in my act."

I think to myself—so typical of Miss Anita Gunderson, torch singer, who wants the torchlight exclusively on her. Poor student—I wonder who she is.

Chapter 4

Howling Wolf Ranch

Oklahoma, USA
1929
Billy Love

I am finally taking my first bull riding lesson today, after a year of begging my parents, Beulah Bell and A.R. I am sixteen now and I am a strong, flexible and balanced athlete.

Just now, I found out that I won't even be getting on a bull for the first three lessons. That notion seems ridiculous.

Father found me a teacher. She was the first woman bull rider in Oklahoma. In 1915, at the Tulsa Rodeo, she actually stayed on the bull a full eight seconds, beating out four men. She did have some injuries; the bull kicked her in her lower back and moved her spine. That injury ended her career.

Her name is Margaret "Mugs" McCall. With a name like Mugs, you don't need a middle name. I read about her in the Tulsa newspaper. She has many interests. To make ends meet, she sews rodeo clothes and costumes. She owns one of those treadles sewing machines that you operate with your feet. In addition to lessons, I will have her make me some pants and other clothes needed for competitions. I will not be wearing a skirt I know that—too constrictive. Mugs is a little like me, a renaissance woman. We both like bull and horseback riding; I play the viola, and she is a costumer.

The stock market crashed nine months ago, and it is a grim landscape here in Oklahoma. Our family got lucky or smart, I am not sure which. Mother's father, Theodor Karl who retired from banking in the summer of 1928, sold all of his stock, took the cash and invested in real estate. He advised my father to do the same thing. My father then expanded the ranch, renaming it the Howling Wolf.

I overheard my father telling my mother, chuckling, "Beulah Bell, thank goodness I took the advice of your father and got out of the stock market. Heh, heh, heh."

Like I said before, father can be cruel, a little sadistic. He laughs at other people's misfortunes. He also invested in his sister's nightclub, *The Garden,* in 1926. It is owned by my Aunt Liz and Uncle Petrus Braun--- cabaret is booming in Munich today.

My Aunt Lola Estelle is planning a trip to Germany next year, and has invited me to go with her. She has been corresponding with my Aunt Liz. I have yet to inform my parents of my intention to travel with her to Munich. No need to get them worked up, when it is so far away.

I am meeting Mugs in the largest of our barns today. I am a bit nervous, but excited at the same time. As I enter the barn, I see her in the far corner standing next to my dappled horse Lobo Love. Mugs is sturdily built, yet she has a delicate pointed nose and crinkly blue eyes. When she was a child her hair was dark, but by 30 it was gray, and by 40, completely white. Her hair is braided down her back. No bob cut for her.

"Hi, Billy Love, come over here and let me get a look at you," Mugs declares. "I need to see if you are physically fit to ride. I stand before her as she looks me over from head to toe. "Show me your flexibility."

I promptly bend over and place my hands flat on the barn floor without bending my knees. "Good, now I need to assess your muscle strength. Squeeze both my hands as hard as you can." "Ouch," she yells. "Now push both of your feet against the palms of my hands as I try to resist."

"You managed to push me back several feet, well done," Mugs exclaims. "I know you have great reaction times because of your barrel racing. Now, climb up on Lobo Wolf. I want to see how you sit in the saddle."

I wonder why Mugs is wasting my time with all of this. I am ready to proceed with bull riding, not horse riding, but I climb up and sit up straight in the new saddle, breathing in the leather smell.

"Billy Love, here is the first lesson of the day. It is fundamental to bull riding. Your stomach muscles must be developed into steel so that you can lean into and really ride a kicking bull. You will also need to learn to ride with one hand on the rein and the other in the air," Mugs says dryly.

"Your first lesson is done. Before next week, Billy Love, I want you to run two miles every day and complete 100 sit ups. Then, you must ride Lobo Wolf every day for an hour using one hand on the reins, leaning forward into the saddle at galloping speeds."

"But I can already do that on my horse, Mugs," I protest. "Well, we shall see next week when you demonstrate your technique for me," Mugs smirks.

"Bull riding is dangerous and you need to be strong and practiced on a horse before you climb onto that two-ton animal," Mugs continues, "if you do everything I ask and do it well, next week I will let you ride a steer calf.

"You won't be riding a bull until I know you can handle the horns. In rodeos, you don't get to pick the bull you will ride. Some of them kick harder than others, and some twirl more in trying to buck you off," Mugs lectures.

I think to myself, why, Mugs is trying to scare me. I will be ready to ride that calf next week. I will show her.

Father comes into the barn, talking to his ranch manager, Erikray. I overhear their conversation.

"Erikray, I hear Hitler has taken over Munich as the headquarters for his filthy Nazi party. He has moved into an apartment for his personal residence. What is to become of Germany as he rises to power?" he opines. "The Weimar party is doing nothing to stop him."

Erikray nods his head, but says nothing. "Mugs, how did my daughter do today?"

"Very well. I gave her some homework. Next week, I might put her on a calf," Mugs replies. Father smiles slyly and departs the barn with Erikray in tow.

I pull my face - Father still thinks of me as a little girl. I am determined to be a great bull rider!

"Mugs, I have a request of you. Will you make me a pair of jodhpurs for riding? I saw in a magazine that the great Coco Chanel designed a pair. She put leather down the inside thighs and seat to prevent skin irritation," I implore.

Mugs nods her head, "I will have them ready when you climb on that bull. And in return, you will play the viola for me. Wagner." I am delighted.

Chapter 5

Eva Braun

Munich
1929
Elisabetha

The stock market crashed all over the world in 1928, but its demise has not affected our cabaret, *The Garden*, here in the Schleswig district of Munich. I guess people need parties and entertainment to forget their financial woes, which is fine with me.

I am thankful to my brother A.R. Wolf for investing in *The Garden* back in 1926; having cash to operate has boosted our reputation as a top nightclub. Theodor Karl and Annen Ringlet also invested. Their daughters are Beulah Bell, A.R.'s wife, and Lola Estelle.

Lola Estelle, I am told, is quite the glamorous flapper woman. The finest in Tulsa. We have been corresponding and she plans a trip to Munich in 1930. She has not told her sister yet, but she plans to bring her niece Billy Love with her. Of course, Billy Love is also my niece, just on the other side of the family. If I know my brother A.R. he will try to prevent Billy Love from coming to Germany. We will see next year.

In *The Garden*, Fritz and I were able to create an intimate and glamorous space. The stage is round and there are platforms for several levels of seating. Gold chairs arch around each of the tables; clad in crisp, white linen table cloths and dotted with tea lights.

There are three dressing rooms in the back of the cabaret. Each has its own table and mirror, along with makeup supplies and costumes. At the back of the lounge, there is a gilded bar stocked with every kind of liqueur you could imagine. Those prudes in the United States prohibiting alcohol, how ridiculous. Just another reason to stay in Germany.

My husband, Petrus Braun and I, are meeting with his brother, Fritz Braun today. Petrus and Fritz look a lot alike. Six feet tall, with blonde hair and blue-gray eyes, they epitomize the Aryan look favored by Adolf Hitler.

We are connecting at *The Garden* prior to its opening in the evening. "Fritz, come on in," Petrus yells.

"Thank you for meeting with me. I have some very disturbing news regarding my daughter Eva," Fritz blurts out, as he looks around the cabaret to make sure no one is eavesdropping.

"Oh? This is your middle daughter? Isn't she just 17?" Petrus queries.

"Yes, she just finished at the convent school and is working for a photographer, but not just any photographer," Fritz says, forcefully. "Adolf Hitler's photographer, Heinrich".

"Oh my!" I exclaim. "That is alarming." Petrus scowls and pounds his fist on the table.

"I am getting us a drink," Petrus says, as he pushes back from the table and heads to the bar. Fritz leans forward and grabs both of my hands. His hands are clammy.

"It seems Adolf himself has taken a fancy to her. He is 40 years old, for god's sake. What can he possibly want from a 17-year-old girl?" Fritz exclaims, angrily.

"Hitler just secured an apartment for himself here in Munich, as he is making Munich the headquarters for the rising Nazi party." Fritz continues. "My wife and I are distraught and Eva's sisters are disgusted. Eva is still living at home, but she goes out frequently, almost every night. She tells us nothing about Adolf, even when we pointedly ask. I have repeatedly warned her that she is in danger. She obviously doesn't listen."

"What can we do to help?" I ask. Petrus returns to the table, slams down brandies housed in glass sniffers. He pushes one toward Fritz, another toward me.

Fritz drains it and retorts, "Eva needs a distraction from Adolf. She adores jazz. Perhaps she could come to the cabaret periodically and you and Petrus could talk with her, try to find out what he wants from her - why she wants to be with him."

"Hitler abhors the cabarets, so he would not likely come with her. She needs to see boys her own age," Fritz argues. I silently nod my head in agreement, tasting the bitter brandy slide down my throat.

I know Fritz does not have a lot of money. "Perhaps I can take Eva shopping for something suitable to wear to the cabaret. It will be modest for a 17-year-old girl," I propose.

"Next week I will take her shopping. Let her know. We shall meet at Lindtz, the department store."

****

Eva Braun rushes to meet me at the department store. She is late, and a little disheveled. Blonde and blue-eyed like her father, she calls out, "Oh, Lizbetha, I was modeling for Heinrich and the time got away from me."

"It is so kind of you to take me shopping and inviting me to *The Garden* tonight," Eva proclaims.

Together, we pull several gowns off the rack and enter the dressing room. "How are your sisters?" I ask, to start our conversation. "Oh, you know, they are boring and they snoop into my life," Eva replies. "Let me try this dress on first. I love the color and the neckline." The dress is a midnight blue velvet with a deep V neckline and a full skirt. I think to myself, good choice. But my niece is being evasive. Clearly, she is not going to reveal she is seeing Hitler almost every evening.

"Zip me up?"

I oblige. The dress fits perfectly. "It looks like you have a dress on the first try," I announce. "No need to look further. Should we go look for matching shoes?"

"Thank you so much again," Eva gushes. "I am so looking forward to tonight at *The Garden*. Will there be a jazz singer?"

"Why yes," I reply. "I just auditioned a new girl. She moved to Munich last week and got an apartment. I have a feeling she could become famous with her sultry alto voice. She will be accompanied on the alto sax," I grin.

Eva Braun claps her hands. "Marvelous, what is her name?"

"Katarina Wolf, I will introduce you. She goes by Kat. I think you might become friends."

I do not tell Eva that she might become more than a friend; a tool perhaps, to find out more about her relationship with Hitler. I also do not reveal that she is my niece or that her father is my brother, Moody Wolf.

"See you tonight around 9 o'clock," I say dryly. "Don't be late or you will miss Kat."

Chapter 6

In The Mood

Munich and Darmstadt Germany
1929
Kat

Tonight, will be the most important time of my life, for I am singing at *The Garden*. How far I have come in one short year. Miss Anita Gunderson's coaching and techniques stretched me well beyond where I thought I could go. I now have a repertoire of sultry songs fit for a night club. My voice projects clearly across any room.

Miss Gunderson tells me I have perfect pitch. Unfortunately, for Miss Gunderson, she is vocally flat. Her career as a torch singer may be over, as she has received few bookings over the past two months. Her jealousy of me is apparent. She abruptly canceled any further vocal lessons last month.

"Kat, I am marrying Casparus Bunz and moving to Berlin, so there will be no more lessons for you. I hear the cabarets in Berlin are more glamorous and well attended than here in Munich. I will revive my career in Berlin."

I think, good luck with that. How did she get Mr. Bunz to marry her? Who really cares, I am ready to start my own career.

My papa, Mood Wolf, has come around and finally admits that I have talent. He still is mostly against me singing in the cabarets, but he has been keeping a secret.

A few weeks ago, Papa informed me, "Kat, I have a sister Elisabetha Braun who is much younger than me. She and her husband live in Munich. They own *The Garden* cabaret."

"Papa, why did you not tell me this? I have an aunt in Germany? For 18 years, I thought it was just you and me, here in Darmstadt."

"My parents abandoned her when they moved to the United States. She was raised by her mother's sister. I have had little contact with her—I thought it best to leave her alone. When you persisted in becoming a singer, and I saw and heard how hard you worked, I felt the need to reach out to her. I wrote Elisabetha a letter and she responded. Here read it yourself."

Dear Moody,

I am ever so thrilled that you contacted me. I want to invite you and Katarina to our home in Munich as soon as possible. I want to get to know you both and audition Kat to sing in the club.

Your description of her vocal talent is impressive. Have her bring the sheet music for "Life as a Dreamer." Petrus and I have no children, so we are excited for our family to expand.

Love, Liz

"Oh Papa. I am forever grateful to you. Thank you, thank you, thank you."

Now, here I am seated at my dressing room table in *The Garden*. Bessie Falkner, *The Garden*'s costumer and makeup artist, is applying pancake makeup, false eyelashes, and ruby red lipstick. My hair is in a chignon. Papa has not conceded on a bob cut, not yet, but soon I will cut off my curls. My dress hangs in the corner.

It is a true flapper dress, topped with a pure white boa. It dazzles with sapphire beading over the entire sleeveless bodice. The skirt is layers upon layers of blue chiffon. The drop waist is encircled with rhinestones and a matching rhinestone clip keeps my chignon in place. Blue satin shoes will adorn my feet.

Bessie helps me into the dress. I keep staring into the mirror. Is this really me? Papa will probably faint. Thank goodness, Aunt Liz took me shopping at the department store. She is already like an older sister to me.

As I slip on my nylons, then my shoes, I hear Aunt Liz. "Kat, every man in the place will be courting you. Turn around and let me look at you."

I turn around slowly and smile at her. I think about meeting her for the first time and singing for her. She took me to *The Garden* to audition. What a beautiful club. Aunt Liz has mentored me in every way, including performance skills—how to talk to an audience, the use of a microphone, body language, gestures. She even worked with me to coordinate my singing with the alto sax player, Buddy and piano player, Franc.

"Kat, after the show I want you to meet someone. She is about your age, maybe a year younger. Her name is Eva Braun, Petrus' brother's daughter. I think she might become a friend," Liz exclaims.

"Oh, that would be lovely," I say, distracted. "How long before I go on stage?"

I think about the songs I prepared for tonight. All of them fit my sultry alto voice. Since it is my first night, there will be only four songs: "Falling in Love Again," "As Time Goes By," "Someone to Watch Over Me," and "I Want to Be Loved By You."

Petrus Braun calls out, "Ladies and gentlemen, please welcome to the stage our new torch singer, Kat Wolf."

I make my entrance slowly, gliding onto the stage, boa flung around my neck. The lights are bright, but I can see every table is full of patrons. "I am extremely pleased to be at *The Garden*," I croon. "Boys, take it away."

The tenor sax and piano accompaniment synchronizes perfectly with my vocals. After each song, the applause from the audience grows stronger and louder. Finally, at the conclusion of "Someone to Watch Over Me," there are people on their feet, yelling and clapping. I bow and see my papa, Mood Wolf, grinning and hugging his sister, Liz.

I pulled it off and then some, I think. I return to my dressing room, and find roses already encased in a vase, along with a note. I read it and start to cry - I grab a tissue to stop the mascara from running down my cheeks.

My darling daughter,

You were stunning in every way tonight. Your voice, your performance, your timing, your dress, your hair.

Love, Proud Papa.

Liz and a blonde woman in a dark blue gown appear in the doorway. "Outstanding performance Kat," Liz exclaims, reaching out to hug her. "I want you to meet Eva Braun. I told you about her earlier."

Eva steps forward. "Congratulations. I loved your act. So sophisticated and mesmerizing."

"Why, thank you. Perhaps we can get to know each other and share a drink after I change my clothes," I reply.

"For sure." Eva turns to leave the dressing room, when a man in a brown belted uniform pushes his way into the room. His look is surly as he strides across the room to reach the women.

"What are you doing here?" Aunt Liz says, with alarm.

"I am here to escort Miss Braun home," he says, as he places his hand firmly on Eva's upper arm.

"But I am not ready to go home yet. It is only 10 pm and Kat and I were going to have a drink," Eva replies, forlornly.

"I have my orders to get you home safely. Let's go."

"Sorry Kat. Aunt Liz will give you my telephone number. We can get together soon." Eva seems resigned.

Eva and the man leave, with his hand placed roughly on her back, guiding her out the club door. The patrons stare.

"Who was that? Why was he so threatening?" I say, scared.

"He is a brownshirt, otherwise known as one of Adolf Hitler's thugs who protect him," Liz shouts.

"What does Hitler have to do with Eva?"

"I will tell you tomorrow. Tonight, let's just have a party to celebrate."

Chapter 7

Rodeo

Oklahoma, USA
1930
Billy Love

My father A.R. is obsessing over the happenings in Germany. Who cares what is going on overseas? I have a great life making music, riding horses and preparing for the Enid rodeo, where I will make my bull-riding debut.

He rages to his father, my grandfather Johan. "Did you know Hitler used the pseudonym Herr Wolf to avoid recognition in 1923? He has also named his headquarters "Wolf's Lair." I hate the association with our own last name—it is an insult."

Johan nods, but stays silent. My grandfather is a bit odd. I don't really know what he did in Darmstadt, Germany before coming to Oklahoma in 1893.

We are headed to First Lutheran Church in Enid. Getting the whole family there on time takes gigantic effort. Bitsie Love and Babe Love quarrel over the hair brush—knocking over a vase, where it shatters on the floor. Bobbie takes an entire hour in the wash room and ignores our constant yelling and knocking on the door.

My mother, Beulah Bell, insists we eat a hearty breakfast. On Sundays, she prepares a massive batch of cinnamon rolls. Many of the hired hands come by for her infamous pastries. This pushes us back even later in our effort to get to church services.

I have been ready for an hour. My dress is a simple light blue satin with mother of pearl buttons up the front of the bodice. I pull on matching gloves.

"I am walking to church," I yell. "I will be in the second pew on the left side." I slam the front door and walk rapidly toward the church. It is tough being the oldest child; for once, I would like to be irresponsible.

I stride into the narthex at First Lutheran. It is the biggest protestant church in Enid. I settle into the second pew. Why do we have to sit on these hard, wooden seats? A little cushioning would be nice.

The service is about to start. Where is my family? There is commotion in the back of the church. Beulah Bell has Bitsy Love by the arm on her right side and Babe Love on the left. Both of the twins are scowling and trying to pull away. Mother pushes them into the pew and seats them on either side of her so that they can't physically fight.

Father enters and sits between Bobbie Love and me. Pastor Jim Bob Anderson emerges through a side door and steps up to the podium.

We stand for a hymn, then the pastor reads a series of scriptures. There is a lot of fiery language - and use of the words heaven and hell.

When the main sermon starts, I ignore the message and think about the rodeo next week when I will be bull riding for the first time.

I hear the twins whispering loudly to each other behind my mother's back. "I hate you!" Babe Love exclaims. Mother takes the back of her hands and slaps them each on the upper arm. "Stop that right now." Mother is always slapping at us. The twins actually have bruises from so much slapping.

Pastor Jim Bob is looking at our family. Did he actually stop the sermon? I go back to thinking about the rodeo. After thirty minutes, father leans over Bobbie Love, speaking loudly, "Beulah, I may never come back to this church. If he can't get the point across in 20 minutes, I may have to walk out."

"SHHH, we will talk about this at home." Pastor Jim Bob, having clearly heard my father's rant, concludes the sermon within a minute.

＊＊＊＊＊＊＊＊＊＊＊＊＊＊

"Mugs, I cannot thank you enough for all the bull riding lessons the past year. And now I have the best riding costume too," I say.

Standing in the barn, preparing for one last word of advice from Mugs before departing for the Enid Rodeo, I look down at myself. "OH, MY," I look fine.

I have on gray jodhpurs with black suede on my inner thighs and buttocks. The suede will protect my skin from chafing as I ride the bull. My long sleeved black shirt is edged with gray piping. On my feet are black snakeskin boots. I have a silver and turquoise belt encircling my waist and my hair is braided down my back in two rows. I pull on a broad brimmed black hat.

"Now, Billy Love, remember what I have told you to do when you are bucked off. Do not put your wrists out to break the fall. You will instantly snap the bones in both wrists. That will be it for riding bulls and probably end your viola playing."

"Try to land on your side, protect your head with your arms, and roll away from the bull. The rodeo hands will get the bull away from you."

"I feel strong and ready. Riding three different bulls has given me the skills to adjust to different levels of kicking, bucking and twirling."

"The goal is to stay on for eight seconds," Mugs instructs. "If you are bucked off before that count, you will receive zero points."

"Let's go now, I want to look the bulls over and listen to the gossip about each one. The rest of the family can come later. Unfortunately, my Aunt Lola Estelle will not be in attendance. She hates dirt and smelly large animals."

Mugs and I arrive at the Enid Rodeo on the outskirts of town. It is a small rodeo compared to the Tulsa Rodeo but still, it is my first. Honey mesquite trees are scattered everywhere on the property — I take in their earthy distinct smell as I contemplate my newest adventure.

There are six riders today. All men but me.

I climb the first rung of the bull pen to look at the six bulls. All of them seem to weigh around 1500 pounds. Their names are as imposing as their stature: Cyclone, Demon, Bruiser, Rocky, Hurricane, and Viking.

Mugs knows the nuances of all of the bulls. She shares the information with me. "Cyclone is smart and can sense a rider's moves. Demon has a nasty personality; he throws back his head toward the rider. Bruiser changes direction so quickly, the rider is thrown off. Rocky bucks hard. Hurricane is muscular and athletic, just like the riders themselves. Viking is named for the size of his horns."

"All bull riders to the arena to select their bull," the announcer blares.

The six of us line up and draw a slip of paper from a bowl. "Bruiser," I say to Mugs.

"Okay, remember what I told you about him. He is a twirler."

My family has arrived and is sitting in the stands. Bobbie Love appears annoyed. Bitsy Love and Babe Love are yelling, "Go Billy Love, go Billy Love," like they are cheerleaders at a football game. Mother and Father are stoic, frowning, worrying.

"Don't know why they let a girl on a bull," Calvin Clare Legend mutters to the boy beside him in the lineup. Then, he clucks his throat loudly, and lobs a giant gob of mucous at the tip of my snakeskin boot.

"Gross, Calvy Claire."

"Don't call me that. I go by C.C."

I pretend I did not hear him and stride quickly toward the bull pen. Bruiser has the two ropes already in place. The first rope is behind his front legs. I will grab it with my right hand. The back rope is called a flank strap. It is tightened to encourage the bull to kick. Underneath Bruiser attached to the rope is a bell which also annoys the bull and make him swirl and buck.

I am the first to ride. The flankman takes Bruiser to an enclosed wooden pen at the entrance to the arena. He tightens the flank strap. Bruiser snorts and shakes his head back and forth.

"Ladies and Gentlemen, Billy Love Wolf, riding Bruiser," the rodeo voice announces.

Mugs shouts "Go get him," as I climb down onto Bruiser's back. I wrap the rope around my hand tightly, mumble to myself and nod at the flankman.

I throw my left arm into the air. Bruiser charges out of the gate, his head shaking violently and thrusting his back legs into the air. One second passes, I hug bruiser's torso. He slices the air, and twists in the opposite direction.

Two seconds. I grip the rope. It is cutting into my hand. I lean to the left to compensate for his turn to the right.

Bruiser really wants me off his back. Three seconds. Bruiser thrusts his head back and forth and with one last blast of his hooves, I feel myself being propelled in the air toward the dusty ground.

Land safely, I think. With a thud that jars my entire body I land on my left side and quickly roll away from Bruiser. He is corralled and led away.

I stand up quickly and pat myself down. Nothing broken. I followed Mugs' rules. I dust myself off and wave to the crowd. They are standing and applauding.

I just finished my first bull ride!

Mugs hustles me out of the arena. "Great work, three seconds. Next time you can shoot for five."

"Oh no, I am going for the full eight. I want to be a bull riding star."

I watch the other five riders. None of them reaches the eight seconds needed for points to be scored. Calvin Claire comes closest at five seconds.

"Looks like a girl can compete with the boys now, doesn't it Calvy Claire?" I say to him with a wide smile.

****

"Billy Love, I am sorry I missed your bull ride," Lola Estelle laments. We are sitting in my aunt's tiny, but glamorous apartment.

"Really, Aunt Lola Estelle? You hate being around large, snorting animals, let alone sweaty people, bad smells and lots of blowing dust," I blurt out, followed by laughing.

I look down at the carpet swirling with red roses. Lola Estelle has on a pink satin robe. She is sitting at her makeup table, preparing to go out to the Tangerine Club.

"Now that I am seventeen, I want to go with you to the clubs," I lobby. "After all, I graduated high school".

"Your parents forbid me from escorting you to the nightclubs. They think I am a bad influence. However, Billy Love, my graduation gift to you is a trip to Munich, Germany. Your father's sister, Elisabetha, lives there. And, she owns a cabaret called *The Garden*. We can stay with her.

"Your parents will let you go, reluctantly, as I know A.R. is terribly worried about the rise of Adolf Hitler in Germany. I think he feels guilty that his own father abandoned Elisabetha when she was just two years old. You know he invested in her nightclub."

"No, I was unaware of that situation, but if his guilt gets me to Germany with you, great."

"Start packing. We leave July 10th."

I think to myself, two great adventures this year, rodeo bull riding and decadent cabaret partying in Europe. All grown up; now, I need the wardrobe to go with it.

"Aunt Lola Estelle, does your graduation gift include shopping for dresses?"

"Of course."

Chapter 8

The Opera

Munich, Germany
1930
Elisabetha

"Billy Love Wolf, let me get my arms around you. Why, you are a solid mass of muscle," I proclaim, as Lola Estelle and Billy Love arrive at the Port of Munich.

"Pleased to meet you, Aunt Liz. This is my aunt on the other side of the family, Lola Estelle," Billy Love says. "My father brings greetings from America.

"Let's drive through the city on our way home. I will point out some landmarks for you."

"Aunt Liz, I have never been out of Oklahoma, let alone the United States. I want to see everything," Billy Love is quivering with excitement.

I am amazed at this young woman. Petrus and I are childless and I am eager to establish a relationship with her. How lucky that I will have two nieces, young women, in my life now. Kat Wolf and Billy Love Wolf. I am impatient and eager to introduce Kat and Billy Love to each other. Kissin cousins.

I wonder how my brother and his wife came up with Billy Love's name. I will ask her when I get to know her better. I understand her sisters have unusual names also—Bobbie Love, and the twins Bitsy Love and Babe Love. Those names are a mouthful.

A.R. telephoned me last month. He is adamant that I watch Billy Love's every move. "I am very concerned about Hitler and the Nazi's rise in Munich. He is a murderer. Did you know his headquarters is called the Wolf's Lair?" he raged at me.

"I will watch over her, but remember the Weimer Republic is strongly in control," I answer.

I did not tell A.R. that my husband's niece, Eva Braun, was seeing Hitler. No, A.R. most likely would insist I put Billy Love back on the boat for Oklahoma immediately.

As we drive to Petrus' and my home, I point, "Billy Love, here is the Konigsplatz, a square of buildings with a grassy, broad lawn in the center. The plaza once was the cultural center of Munich. The buildings consist of an ornate gateway, a collection of Greek and Roman sculptures, and an antique museum."

I fail to tell my guests that many of the buildings within the Konigsplatz are now occupied by Nazi party members.

"Petrus, here are our guests," I call out as I enter the small, two story house.

"Billy Love and Lola Estelle, you will share the bedroom in the back hallway. Go ahead and get freshened up. We are meeting Kat for dinner. She is not singing tonight, so we can all get to know each other."

I hear the women talking. "Aunt Lola Estelle, shall I wear one of my pretty frocks to dinner? I love them so," Billy Love implores, as they settle into the room with twin beds and freshly painted yellow walls.

"Yes, I believe the yellow dress highlights your beautiful dark hair. The embroidery detailing of daffodils makes it even more attractive," Lola Estelle instructs. "I am dressing down tonight. I will save my flapper dresses and headbands for our visit to *The Garden* next week, to hear your cousin Kat sing."

As Billy Love and Lola Estelle descend the stairs, I notice how striking they appear—Billy Love in yellow and Lola Estelle in a black velvet ruffled jacket and long skirt. They will receive attention by young men at the restaurant. I have selected the Osteria Bavaria, an Italian restaurant that specializes in seafood.

"Kat will be meeting us at the restaurant, shall we depart?"

****

"Good evening, I am Bernard. Can I show you to your table? A young woman named Kat is already seated."

"Yes, thank you Bernard," I say, graciously. Kat is sitting quietly, looking out the window at passers-by. Her dark hair, recently cut to chin length, shines with the dark red streaks throughout. She, too, has dressed conservatively tonight. Her frock is royal blue, long sleeved, falling to mid-calf. She turns toward us. Her brilliant blue eyes crinkle with glee.

Kat stands up and throws her arms out to Billy Love, "It is so exciting to meet my cousin who I did not know existed until last year," Kat squeals, in a high pitch voice an octave higher than her natural voice.

"Likewise," Billy love exclaims.

I watch as they hold each other away from each other. If their eye colors were not so different, Billy Love's chocolate and Kat's sky blue, they could be twins. They are each around five foot five, with petite frames. "Everyone, let's sit down."

Petrus and I sit together on one side of the table facing the back of the restaurant. Kat, Lola Estelle, and Billy Love sit facing the front door. We catch up. Billy Love talks about the rodeo bull riding and playing the viola in the Tulsa Orchestra. Kat talks about her singing lessons with Miss Anita Gunderson. She tells the very funny story of how Miss Gunderson is vocally flat.

We are all having a wonderful evening. All of a sudden, I look across the restaurant and I grip Petrus' thigh tightly.

Petrus looks at me glaringly and whispers, "What are you doing?"

"Over in the far corner to your right, don't look!"

"Eva is having dinner with Hitler. What is she doing out in public with him? Fritz will be furious."

No one is paying them much attention, but I notice two brownshirts sitting at the table next to them, shielding them from the restaurant patrons.

"Kat," I say quietly, Eva Braun is having dinner with Adolf Hitler. Do not acknowledge that you know her in any way."

Kat can be a superb actress. She took up the conversation with Billy Love and Lola Estelle as if Eva was with a common suiter. "So, Billy Love, you have twin sisters who are whiners?"

Petrus and our entourage quickly leave the Italian Restaurant. What will we tell Fritz?

****

"Eva, Petrus and I are attending Mass at St. Peters Cathedral today at 5pm. Would you like us to pick you up?"

I think about the dinner out last week; picturing Eva with Hitler. Eva leaning forward into Adolf's space, attentive, laughing. When I told her father, Fritz, about the whole situation, he was very angry.

"Liz and Petrus, what can we do to discourage Eva from seeing him?" Fritz implores.

"I will take Eva to church and then invite her over to the house to meet Billy Love. Kat will be there too, and we will try to find out why she continues to see Hitler. Maybe we can figure something out."

"Billy Love, do you want to go with us to mass today?" I call up to the bedroom.

"No thanks, I am Lutheran, not much interested in religion, period," Billy Love responds.

"Alright, I am bringing Eva, Petrus' niece over for tea after Mass. Kat is also going to be here."

Lola Estelle is out for an evening stroll when I arrive home with Eva Braun in tow. Billy Love is lounging on the sofa, listening to opera on the radio. Kat has not arrived yet.

"Billy Love meet Eva Braun, Petrus' niece."

Eva grabs both of Billy Love's hands. "Delighted. I understand you are from the wild, wild west of the United States."

"Why yes, I live on a ranch and ride horses and bulls, but I also have a sophisticated side to me. I play the viola in the Tulsa symphony," Billy Love retorts.

36

"Marvelous, don't you just love the opera? And to think that you play the viola. I think of all the strings - it is my favorite," Eva exclaims.

"Aunt Liz, I have a surprise for you all when Kat gets here," she continues.

I prepare the tea and pastries on a tray and bring them into the dining room as Kat arrives. She and Eva air kiss and we all sit down at the table. Petrus is at *The Garden*, working.

I watch the three young women interact with each other. They have a strong connection.

"Are you ready for my surprise?" Eva claps her hands.

"Wolf has given me six tickets to see the opera 'Sirens' at the Munich Opera house and I want you all to be my guests."

Kat and Billy Love say in unison "Who is Wolf"?

"Why, Adolf you sillies. Did you know Adolf translates as noble wolf? So, I call him that nickname."

With great effort, I try to restrain myself, not to blurt out to Eva, "You are a fool."

"Adolf and I will be in the third-floor balcony box seats. He adores Wagner."

"We have played Wagner in the symphony. It is violent, but beautiful. Epic," Billy Love exclaims.

Kat cuts in, "Eva, are you serious about Adolf Hitler? Are you having sex with him?"

Eva looks startled by the questioning. "Yes, I am serious and it is none of your business about the sex."

"Sorry," Kat apologizes. "I worry about what Hitler is doing to Germany with his Nazi party. I am scared for your safety."

Standing up abruptly, I remark, "Ladies, I think tea time is over."

****

Fritz and Petrus Braun are arguing, "Petrus, I will not take any handouts from Hitler, and I most certainly will not let my other daughters be around him. You, however, along with Liz, Kat, and Billy Love should take the opera tickets. You can spy on Eva and Adolf in their balcony. See who is surrounding Hitler, how he interacts with her."

"Fritz, we will take the tickets. I am aware you are desperate," I say, forcefully.

"Hitler never misses a Wagner opera. He adores those epic stories with the characters of Grecian gods and goddesses. Venus is the goddess in the castle in The Sirens production. I hear the costuming and the symphony accompaniment are marvelous," I continue.

"Richard Wagner hated the Jews. He wrote some spiteful letters and documents, calling the Jewish people inferior, not fit to hold occupations of status in German society," Petrus exclaims. "It is my understanding that Hitler himself is using some of those documents as direction for Nazi policy."

"So many of our performers at *The Garden* are Jewish. They are so talented—I fear for them. Hitler with his headquarters here in Munich; his presence always felt—his brownshirts everywhere. I just don't know that the Weimar government will be able to contain him and his thugs," I say woefully, grimacing.

"Let's worry about getting Eva away from him first and foremost. He is brainwashing her, lavishing her with gifts and entangling her in his inner circle. There has got to be a way out for her," Fritz shouts.

"Let me grab my opera glasses," I declare.

Chapter 9

Lola Estelle

Darmstadt and Munich, Germany
1930
Kat

"Billy Love, what did you think of the opera?" I query.

Billy Love is sitting in my dressing room, where I am preparing for the evening show.

"It was dark and mysterious, but also tremendous," Billy Love trills.

I lower my voice, "Hitler appeared menacing. He literally ignored Eva, especially when the orchestra leader acknowledged him to the crowd."

"Why, yes, they turned that big old spotlight on them. Eva actually leaned out of the light. Do you think Adolf told her to do that? To make it look like he is not attached to any women?" Billy Love questions.

"It scares me that so many bodyguards stood in doorways and in seats surrounding them. What are we going to tell Fritz about Eva and Hitler?" I implore.

"Nothing, I think we are going to keep meeting with Eva, pointing out the follies of her actions. I cannot think of anything else right now—just hope that she will tire of him. I don't want Fritz to do something that will put the rest of his family in danger."

"Billy Love, you will meet your Uncle Moody tonight. Papa is coming to my show."

A young man who appears to be around thirty, leans into Kat's dressing room. "Hello Kat, who do you have with you tonight?"

"Simon, this is my cousin Billy Love Wolf who is visiting me from Oklahoma, United States."

Billy Love assesses him. Tall, light brown slicked back hair. Distinct features, square jaw. He has on tails and a top hat, with a red bow tie.

"Simon is our master of ceremonies tonight. He also does political satire later in the show—mainly regarding the Nazis and Hitler," I explain.

"Very nice to meet you, Billy Love. Oklahoma huh? I have heard about the rodeos that go on there. Would love to see one. Not many rodeos in Germany."

"Oh, I just happen to ride bulls. I had my first ride right before we came to Germany," Billy Love says, nonchalantly.

"We?"

"My Aunt Lola Estelle accompanied me here. She will be at the show tonight," Billy Love responds, as she suddenly pictures them together as a couple.

"May I ask you something, Simon," Billy Love blurts out. "Are you seeing anyone?"

"Seeing anyone?"

"You know, going out with someone on a regular basis?"

"No, I am not."

"Good, I will see you after the show," Billy Love grins.

Liz and Lola Estelle enter the club as Simon is entertaining the crowd with his bawdy comments, mostly about women and sex. Moody is seated at the table in the front row next to the stage. The two women take the chairs next to him.

Lola Estelle is stunning in a black sequined dress with gold appliques and gold fringe flowing from the hem. She has on gold elbow length gloves and matching headband. Her kitten heeled, strapped shoes complete the look.

Simon notices. "And, who is this lovely lady?" he asks, as he bends down directly in front of her, thrusting the microphone in her face.

"Lola Estelle Ringlet, of Tulsa Oklahoma," she flippantly retorts.

"Why I just met another beauty from Oklahoma. I did not know the state could produce two exquisite beauties."

Liz waves Simon off, and he returns to the stage. "That is Simon," she whispers to Lola Estelle. "He is one of the best master of ceremonies in Munich. We shall have a drink with him after the show."

I come to the stage and perform several blues and jazz numbers, resulting in sustained applause. People are coming to *The Garden* specifically to hear and see me perform now. I am pleased.

Here is Simon and company. He is dressed as Hitler in military attire, with the skinny mustache. He parodies Adolf's mannerisms, scowling and clenching his jaw. He goosesteps around the stage, as the other men laugh and point at him.

Lola Estelle roars, as does the rest of the crowded room. The show is over.

Billy Love joins me and Papa at their table. "Billy Love, this is my papa Mood, your uncle".

"I finally get to meet the last Wolf," Billy Love declares, as she quickly shakes his hand.

"I invite you down to Darmstadt before you return to the United States. You can see where your grandparents lived and I will also take you to Merck pharmaceutical where I work as lead chemist for Morphine production. Kat, you and Billy Love can take the train down."

"Thank you so much Uncle Mood. I would love it."

"Kat, I noticed when I got to Munich today, that people were selling pills on every street corner—amphetamines, opiates—be careful, I don't want you, young people to get involved. You can get hooked and your life can be ruined."

"Yes, papa, I understand all of the issues. I did grow up with you scolding me every other day," I say, empathically.

Simon enters the main area and heads directly to Lola Estelle. He has removed all of his makeup and pulled on some trousers and a sweater.

"Lola Estelle, will you go with me next week to Berlin to the premiere of the movie 'The Blue Angel?' It will be playing at the Gloria Palast. Marlene Dietrich herself will be there."

"Oh, my goodness, how did you get invited, Simon?"

"I did some stage roles with Marlene in the early 20's - Berlin. We became friends and have written to each other over the years. I understand a director in Hollywood, America has contacted her to star in movie there. It would a great chance for you to meet her, Lola Estelle. I believe she will become a world-renowned star."

"Well, I guess I cannot pass up the opportunity, Simon," Lola Estelle blushes a bit—not like her usual confident demeanor.

"Let me walk you back to the Braun's house. We can get to know each other on the way," Simon interjects.

Simon pulls out Lola Estelle's chair, and gently helps her to her feet. They saunter from the lounge, gazing at each other.

"Whoopy!" I and Billy Love, yell in unison.

****

Kat and Billy Love are on a train headed for Darmstadt. "Tell me about Darmstadt, Kat, I know my grandparents were both born there."

"My papa tells me that the Wolf clan goes back to 1560, all of them born in the region. Isn't that crazy?"

I talk and wave my hands at the same time. I notice that Billy Love also swats me on the upper arm as she speaks. A bit annoying.

"Papa is picking us up at the station, then taking us on a tour of the Merck laboratories. It is a bit boring, but then I was around it every day growing up. Papa often brought me to work, since he was raising me alone."

I tell Billy Love that Merck is the biggest pharmaceutical company in the world, and it is headquartered in Darmstadt. Papa completed his degree in organic chemistry at the Technical University in the city.

We arrive—Papa leads Billy Love and me across the parking lot into a plain looking, red brick building. There is a guard by the front door who acknowledges us. Inside the door, Papa pulls out a key, inserts it and we are inside the morphine laboratory.

"Let me tell you about the production of morphine," Mood rambles. "It is a bitter white compound found in the opium poppy plant. In the early 1800s, a German apothecary named Friedrich Serturner, isolated morphine from dried poppy resin. He named it 'morphium' at the time, after Morpheus—the Greek god of dreams."

He goes on to describe the lengthy process of morphine extraction from the poppy plant using water, organic solvents and pH adjustments. Kat and Billy Love are catatonic, thinking instead about Simon and Lola Estelle in Berlin for the premiere of 'The Blue Angel'— and meeting Marlene Dietrich. So glamorous.

"Thank you so much for the tour, it was fascinating Uncle Mood," Billy Love exudes. I can tell she is thinking, thank God it is over.

Chapter 10

Horseback

Oklahoma and Hollywood
1931
Billy Love

It has been almost a year since Aunt Lola Estelle and I traveled to Germany to meet the rest of the Wolf family, Kat and Moody and Elisabetha. My family is remarkable—by marriage Petrus Braun, his brother Fritz and of course, Eva Braun. Not really my cousin, but she is a better sister to me than my three sisters here in Oklahoma.

Father is pleased we are back on the ranch, so to speak. He continues to rail about Adolf Hitler and his obsession with gaining power. I still have not told him about meeting with Eva. No one has—we know better.

"Billy Love, did you know the Nazis are the second largest political party in Germany? Old President von Hindenburg is doing nothing to stop him. The brownshirts are everywhere."

"Father, they are present, but we drove all over Munich and there was no trouble, even at *The Garden*."

When I returned from Germany, I auditioned for the Tulsa symphony and accepted the second chair viola position. We play all over the state of Oklahoma. Coincidentally, this year the focus is on Richard Wagner's music, specifically the operas he wrote.

Three months ago, I moved to Tulsa to live with Lola Estelle in her two-bedroom apartment. It is a relief to get away from my sisters—I am fiercely independent. On the weekends, I go out to the Howling Wolf ranch to ride my horse Lobo Love and continue to practice bull riding. Mugs gives me pointers every few weeks.

Tonight, Lola Estelle and I are fixing a small meal together in the apartment. We are standing together at the kitchen counter, chopping vegetables for a soup.

"Tell me again about the movie premiere of 'The Blue Angel' and meeting with Marlene Dietrich," I urge, even though I have heard her tell it many times before.

"Oh, Billy Love that is old news, Simon telephoned today. You know, Miss Dietrich moved to Hollywood and is making pictures for the director Josef von Sternberg. Well, my Simon was offered a part in her new movie 'Destry Rides Again.' The production company is paying his way to Hollywood next month. Isn't it grand?"

"You are surely jesting."

"No, Simon has been practicing English for the past year and he was offered a role as one of the ranchers. It's a western."

"Holy shit," I blurt out.

Simon and Lola Estelle have corresponded and telephoned for almost a year. Now, they will be able to see each other while he works on the film. I think it is a pretty serious relationship. Lola Estelle was already planning another trip to Munich before Simon got the role.

Seemingly, my aunt is independently wealthy and does not have to be bothered to work in Tulsa or anywhere else. She is free to move at any time.

"When do we leave for Hollywood?"

"We?" Lola Estelle queries.

"Yes, I plan to be a stunt rider on the set," I proclaim.

****

I informed the Tulsa Symphony conductor that I needed three months leave. He said no, so I quit. Stunt riding is more exciting than playing Wagner any old day.

My parents forbid me from moving to Hollywood—I am 18, so there is nothing they can do about it. Aunt Lola Estelle has found us an apartment to sublet on the Sunset Strip, near the movie set. Simon will arrive next week to begin reading his lines and filming. Of course, he will be staying with us.

"Lola Estelle, inform me when you and Simon have sex—I want to make sure I am out of the apartment."

"Billy Love," Lola Estelle says, indignant.

"What? I don't want to listen to all that noise. Either that, or I will get ear plugs."

****

"Do you believe there will be many reporters at the dinner, Lola Estelle?" Simon questions, as he pulls on a white jacket.

The entire cast and crew of 'Destry Rides Again' are meeting for the first time at *The Trocadero* restaurant. Lola Estelle is going as Simon's date.

I am as jealous as is humanly possible. Somehow, I need to find a way to crash that dinner—I have been unsuccessful thus far in securing an appointment with the assistants who hire stunt riders. In the movie, Marlene's character rides horses—in real life, Marlene can barely get up into the saddle. She needs a double.

Yesterday, I discovered flyers for auditions, but I need a leg up, for I am an unknown here. If I can just inform them of my talent, rodeo barrel racing and bull riding. I have pictures of me on Lobo, doing tricks. Nah, I need another plan.

Lola Estelle looks like a star herself. Her hair is combed and twisted into short ringlets; she has dark kohl lined eyes and red lipstick. Her silver, bugle beaded dress shimmers. She can compete with Marlene, that's for sure.

"Darling, you look magnificent, shall we go? We don't want to be late," Simon says, affectionately.

The minute the door slams behind them I take action. Pulling on my rodeo clothes, I run several blocks to the movie set.

"Simon, darling, come meet Mr. Jimmy Stewart, who is playing the male lead in the picture," speaks Marlene across the room. "Oh, and Lola Estelle, it is great to see you again."

"Simon Hilfman, good to meet you, Mr. Stewart," He says, stretching out his hand. He has his left arm around Lola Estelle's shoulders and pulls her in to him closely.

"Likewise. There must be a dozen gawking reporters lurking outside the restaurant. We had to push through them. It does get old," Jimmy complains.

"Everyone, come sit down. We will dine first and then go over plans for the movie," the director announces.

Marlene holds court at the table, wearing a dolman sleeved, floor length, gold beaded dress. Her blonde, curly shoulder length hair is pulled back with pearl clips. She regals the casts with tales of her youth in Germany. After dinner, she chains smokes and drinks scotch on the rocks.

Mr. von Sternburg rises to speak, then turns his head toward the door.

"What is going on in the street outside? Someone is yelling and a crowd is gathering, lightbulbs are flashing," Lola Estelle grumbles to Simon, seated on her left.

"Wow, look at that girl—she is something!" yells a young boy.

The group in the restaurant rises in unison, hurries out the door, and gapes in astonishment.

I am riding a galloping white horse down the street toward the restaurant, but not sitting in the saddle. My feet are lashed to the saddle and I am standing, facing forward, and arching my back to help balance on the horse. My right arm is held overhead and my left is perpendicular to my body. I grin and holler, as reporters furiously snap pictures.

As the horse approaches the restaurant, I plop my rump onto the saddle and stop the horse directly in front of Marlene. "Hello, I am Billy Love Wolf, and I just auditioned for your stunt double."

"Why, I have never seen anything like this," Marlene declares, with feigned indignance.

"Billy Love, how dare you disrupt our dinner," Lola Estelle admonishes. "Marlene, this is my niece. I had no idea she was planning this."

"Darling Billy Love, you are hired. I like daring people and you are one of the best. Now get that horse back to the set and come join us as we go over the script. I can see several places in the script where you can trick ride out on the ranch."

"Thanks," I grin widely at Lola Estelle and Simon. In return, I get a loud laugh from Simon and a scowl from Lola Estelle.

I lead the horse back to the set. I am ecstatic.

****

The movie wrapped three months ago— the premiere is next month, in Hollywood at the Grauman's Theater. Lola Estelle and I are back in Tulsa. Simon is staying with us until after the showing—then he will return to Germany. He has some lounge gigs lined up, and his visa is expiring.

Lola Estelle is sad about his departure. "Billy Love, shall we return to Germany next year?"

"I am thinking about applying for a position in the Bayreuth opera festival next summer. They need viola players and my stint with the Tulsa opera playing Wagner will give me an advantage. It pays pretty well and they give me lodging and meals. On the weekend, I can come down to Munich."

"Perfect, I can let Simon know. Are you excited for Kat, Moody, Petrus and Liz to arrive in Oklahoma? They are coming to the ranch first, staying in the small house where your grandparents lived," Lola Estelle explains. "You can teach them how to ride horses and bulls," she laughs.

Simon drifts into the room and rubs Lola Estelle's shoulders. "Marlene has invited us to her mansion after the showing—with all of your family too, Billy Love, even your sisters."

"Really, I know Bobbie Love will swoon, but Bitsie Love and Babe Love, do we have to invite them? I don't want to be embarrassed."

"Yes, all three sisters and your parents and German relatives," Simon is adamant.

"It will be interesting to see how my father reacts to meeting Liz and Moody, his sister and brother. I still do not know why my

49

grandparents left Liz behind to be raised by her mother's sister. Since both of my grandparents died last year, I might never know. I am pretty sure my father is aware of the circumstances, but for now he is not sharing. Liz might get something out of him," I fume.

"Let's focus on entertaining the relatives at the ranch and in Hollywood. And Billy Love and Simon, you are on the brink of becoming stars," Lola Estelle says, with confidence.

"For trick riding horses?" Why not?

Chapter 11

Germans in the United States

Oklahoma and Hollywood
Kat
1932

We just arrived at the Howling Wolf Ranch—father, Liz, and Petrus. Uncle A.R. is giving us a tour of the ranch before we get settled in at the cottage located at the western edge of the ranch. My Aunt Beulah Bell is making lunch—a barbeque with all the fixins, as Billy Love would say.

My uncle is bragging about the breadth and depth of his cattle operation. I am not thrilled about the red dust everywhere, but it is exciting to see how a working ranch operates. I take out a hanky and hold it over my mouth and nose.

"Uncle, is Billy Love here yet? I understand she is coming out to the ranch."

"Yes, she is out riding her horse, Lobo Love. She should be here soon."

Uncle A.R. is rather aloof with us. I wonder if he feels guilty for not acknowledging his German brother and sister sooner. But maybe my grandfather, Johan Wolf, failed to tell him about our existence.

I look into the distance and spy Billy Love on Lobo, galloping toward us. She has a red kerchief over her mouth and nose and a red cowgirl hat tilted down over her forehead. Riding bareback, she is crouched on her knees, waving one arm in the air, the other holding the reins. Hmm, I think, this is one of her signature trick stunts.

"My German family, welcome. What do you think of the wild, wild west?"

Lobo is pawing the ground, shaking his head back and forth, thick saliva dripping from his mouth. I step back, unsure what he might do next. Horses are alien to me.

My father, Mood, remarks, "I think Kat is scared of your horse, Billy Love." Mood is a little bit like his brother A.R., somewhat of a pessimist.

I scowl at father, "Of course not," moving forward to stroke Lobo's neck.

"Let's go on your first ride, Kat. Father lift her up behind me," Billy Love says, with enthusiasm.

Before I can protest, I am grabbed by Uncle A.R. and thrust up to straddle the horse. I am terrified.

"Now Kat, put your arms around my waist and lock your hands together. Ready?"

I squeeze my eyes shut and press my forehead into her back. What if I faint?

"We will start off with a gentle trot. Come on Lobo."

I glance over at father. He sees the terrified look on my face, but says nothing. Betrayed.

Lobo starts to trot. Not too bad, even though I am bouncing more than I would like. I dig my thighs into the side of the horse. I relax slightly.

Suddenly, Billy Love nudges the horse. He lifts his hooves in the rhythmic gallop pattern.

I feel 1 could fly off the horse with every bounce. Lobo's hooves kick up the red dust. My mouth opens in a silent scream, as the dust clogs my throat.

Finally, Billy Love pulls hard on the reins—Lobo stops the gallop, trots gently toward the family.

I am trembling and sweating from fear. A.R. helps me slide off the horse. I can barely stand; my knees tremble.

"Well done, Kat. You just experienced the wild west at its finest," Billy Love crows.

****

At the cottage, after peeling off my clothes, I collapsed into a tub of steaming hot water. I think about the horse ride. In the aftermath, I am rather proud of myself, a city girl never on a horse before, galloping. But I am also angry at Billy Love. If I had fallen off, who knows the injuries that could have been inflicted. I could have fallen onto the thorns of a mesquite tree—become impaled.

But I didn't tumble off, so I need to forget it, and get dressed. We are going to the main house for lunch.

Billy Love's three sisters will be there; I have heard so much about them, I want to form my own opinion.

As the four of us arrive at the house, we hear a radio, turned up loudly. I recognize Hitler's angry, yelling voice. He is speaking in Berlin, in the plaza. The crowd is loudly applauding. The radio voice translates in English, "Hitler proclaims Germany the strongest nation on earth." Cheering erupts.

Beulah Bell stomps over to the radio and snaps it off. "A.R., our guests don't need to listen to all that propaganda. They have enough to deal with when they are home in Germany."

Liz responds, "It is true that Hitler is rising in status and power, and we often see his henchmen in the streets of Munich, sometimes loitering outside *The Garden*, but we have not seen much violence."

Petrus chimes in, "I personally think he is posturing, but we will see when the election comes up next year. I do worry for some of our Jewish neighbors. Adolf seems to be very anti-Semitic and discriminatory, reading the essays of Richard Wagner."

I remain quiet, as I think of Eva, who continues to see Hitler. He has bought Eva and her sister a small house in Munich. He is in Berlin these days, so he doesn't see her much, but he keeps his brownshirts guarding the house. Eva still can go out and shop, but for the most part she is cloistered. I see her once a month—at age 21, she is so young to be restricted.

Fritz Braun is still determined to break ties between Eva and Adolf, but so far none of us have been able to come up with a workable plan.

A.R. breaks in, "What can we do in America to help oust him from power?"

At that moment, Babe Love and Bitsy Love burst into the room, running full speed over to me, wrapping their arms around me, and saying in unison, "Here is our beautiful cousin, Kat, the singer."

Beulah Bell motions us all to the table. She sits herself next to me, slaps my upper arm with the back of her hand, and whispers conspiratorially, "Your uncle is ridiculous with his ravings about Hitler. We just need to get on with life. The German people will not be fooled again into a war with a dictator leading them."

I nod my head slowly. Then I dig into the barbeque. Delicious, the spices exploding in my mouth.

After dinner, the whole group goes out to the porch. Seated in a rocking chair, I look out at the vast acres of ranch and feel myself relaxing. The men are offered pipes, the women cigarettes. And of course, even though it is the prohibition era, A.R. has plenty of liquor for cocktails. A whole basement-full.

The conversation turns to the movie premiere we will attend next week in Los Angeles. I can't wait. This is the America I want to see—Hollywood.

****

Uncle A.R. has rented a five-bedroom house in Los Angeles for the movie premiere of 'Destry Rides Again.' The whole extended family is going to the event—A.R., Beulah Bell, Billy Love, Bobbie Love, Bitsy Love, Babe Love, Petrus, Liz, my father, and me.

Lola Estelle and Simon are meeting us in Hollywood. They are staying with friends they met during the filming of the movie.

One thing I know about my uncle. He likes to show people his wealth.

"We are taking the Duesenberg down to L.A.," he announces. "I have taken it in the shop for polishing and it is ready to go."

I examine the automobile; it is magnificent. Cherry red, with a white topper and white wheels. He has chosen me to be his passenger on the trip. I believe I was selected because he witnessed the spectacle of my horseback ride with Billy Love. Sort of a makeup.

The rest of the family take the Ford to the event.

"Kat, what do you think of America so far? Is it what you expected?" He is smoking a cigar which I find irritating, but what can I say? We are leisurely making our journey from Enid to Los Angeles.

"Well, ranch life is more complicated than I thought it would be. You know, feeding and herding that many cattle. Then, you have to keep dogs to help keep the cattle moving. Grooming and caring for the horses takes time, too."

"To run a ranch as large as mine you need to hire extra people. I believe you met my manager Erikray yesterday?" I nod.

"He saw your wild ride with Billy Love. Said afterward, you were pretty brave. I think he has a hankering for you, Kat."

I blush. "Since I will be returning to Germany, there is no need to pursue anything with Erikray."

"Heh, heh, heh. We shall see."

Our cruising, 1930 Duesenberg enters the outskirts of L.A.

"Let's have lunch next door to the Grauman's Chinese Theater where the premiere will be held. That way, we will know where it is located. I can have the valet at the restaurant park the automobile," A.R. declares.

Uncle enters the circular drive in front of the restaurant and puts the auto in gear. A young man of about twenty-five scurries out to address us.

"Valet parking, sir?"

"Why yes. What do you think of my Duesenberg?"

"It is a looker, for sure. What is your name, so that I can return your keys to you?"

"Mr. A.R. Wolf. We are here for the movie opening 'Destry Rides Again.'"

"Are you the Jewish director?" the young man suddenly asks peevishly, scowling.

"Certainly not. Why do you ask?"

"You look like his picture I saw in the newspaper yesterday. You know, Jews run Hollywood," he gripes.

"Get on with parking the car, I don't need your nasty comments."

"Come on Kat, let's go on in. He is wasting our time."

I silently emerge from the passenger side and follow him into the restaurant. My uncle is fuming.

"Germany and Hitler are bad enough with their hatred of Jews, but here in the United States, to see such prejudice!"

"Uncle, it is just a young, uninformed young man who parks automobiles. Let's just forget about it, have a nice lunch, and then meet up with rest of the family at the rented house."

We have a meal, A.R. grabs his keys and we walk to the Duesenberg. "That man will not touch my car again."

****

The family has arrived at the rented house. We are vociferously getting ready for the evening.

"How was your trip in the Duesenberg, anointed one?" Billy Love says to me.

"Wonderful, except when we stopped to eat, the valet told your father that he looked Jewish and that Jews were taking over Hollywood. It really was a slur."

"Really? Father has railed against Hitler and his tirades against Jews for years. I wonder if other people have said something similar to him in the past?"

"I have no idea, but he was beyond upset. I hope it doesn't ruin our wonderful night. And then on to Marlene's mansion for the afterparty."

"Let's talk about something else, how are you wearing your hair, Billy Love?"

"Oh, pulled into a chignon, I want to be sophisticated tonight, something I definitely was not in the movie. I can't wait to see my name in the rolling credits."

****

Everyone is ready to depart to the theater except for the twins. At 13, you would think they could get their act together…but they are bickering with each other. Billy Love is right …they really are spoiled and obnoxious.

The uncles and father have on black tuxedos with white bow ties and gloves. The women, with the exception of Beulah Bell, have on sleeveless, drop-waisted shifts, a rainbow of colors and beading. My dress is fuchsia, with matching feather headband and kitten heels. I am carrying a small silver purse, feeling quite elegant.

I wonder what Marlene will wear. She is quite unpredictable— I have seen pictures of her in a white trouser suit and a shiny, white top hat. Outrageous, as she can be. She also plucks her eyebrows until they are so thin, they resemble an arched string.

"Bitsy Love and Babe Love, you have five minutes to get it together, or you will stay at the house," Beulah admonishes, the furrows in her brow permanently in a scowl.

"Yes, let's leave them here," Bobbie Loves says, gleefully.

"Mother, you are so unfair," Babe Love cries out, like a toddler.

"Stop this nonsense now, we are leaving," A.R. says, stomping his foot.

I am astonished that we really are leaving the twins at the house. The rest of the Wolf clan moves out the door. I look back over my shoulder and see the twins slumped, sitting on the floor back to back, both of them sobbing.

Maybe, I do feel a little sorry for the girls. But Uncle A.R. has a cruel side to him, and he just played his hand.

****

The movie reel has just finished, the credits are rolling, and the house lights brighten the room. Applause is thunderous. It really is a marvelous picture.

"Billy Love, your trick riding was phenomenal," I turn to her, and clap her on the back. "Wow."

"Thanks Kat, it was a chance of a lifetime."

"And Simon, your portrayal of the rancher, why you looked and acted like you herd cattle all day long," I tease him. Lola Estelle smiles and nods beside him, "Yes darling, I am so proud of your hard work on this film."

The director of the film is standing up to be acknowledged— Josef von Sternberg. He waves to the crowd as they congratulate him.

I whisper to Billy Love, conspiratorially, "He does look at lot like your father. I can see why the young man asked uncle if he was the director."

"Well let's keep it between us. I don't want to put father in a tailspin," Billy Love answers back.

"I, for one, cannot wait to get to the afterparty at Marlene's mansion," says Liz, as she comes up to me and Billy Love. "I overheard that Ms. Dietrich always hosts with aplomb and pizzazz."

"What did Petrus think of the movie?" Billy Love asks Liz.

"He was really proud of you and Simon, too. Oh, look, Billy Love, here come your parents. My brother is beaming for a change."

"Why, Billy Love all those riding lessons paid off. You really impressed the audience with your stunt riding. I think you will be in demand for future western pictures," A.R. declares. "It goes to show you that girls can ride just as well as boys," A.R. concedes, as he pats her on the back.

I try to stifle my laughter. Uncle A.R. is pretty much taking credit for Billy Love's extraordinary talent. Typical though.

****

Marlene's mansion is something to behold. It is a Spanish design, with a red tiled roof, walls of white stucco and large ceiling to floor windows that overlook a secluded garden and swimming pool. The garden is lush, with ivy climbing trellises, orange birds of paradise everywhere, clusters of pink roses.

Inside the house it is even ritzier, is that a word? In the formal dining area, there is a large painted mural consisting of a zebra being pursued by a black panther. This seems odd, but it fits Marlene's personality. There are two hot pink, overstuffed couches surrounding a white lacquer fireplace mantle. The curtains are a pale, slubbed, pink silk. An elaborate black wrought iron, curving staircase leads to the upstairs bedrooms. Every table in sight holds clear vases of cut flowers...roses, dahlias, orchids, hydrangeas, anemones...the smell is divine. There is original art work everywhere. Is that a Picasso hanging over the mantel?

On the patio, where the food and liquor is being served, all of the furniture consists of scrolling white patterns of wrought iron. The pool surround consists of white tile, which makes the turquoise water shimmer.

It looks like about 100 people are at the party. There is Jimmy Stewart and his wife. I will wait a bit to get my courage up to introduce myself.

Marlene herself is out on the patio, holding court, with tales of the production 'Destry Rides Again.' Cigarette in the left hand, drink in the right, she motions for Billy Love to come closer. She air kisses Billy Love, then launches into the story of how Billy Love's trick ride landed her the role in the movie.

Billy Love blushes, but I can tell she is happy to be singled out.

Marlene herself fits in perfectly with the décor. Dressed in all white, the long skirt is slit up to her thigh, the beaded top has a deep décolleté. Her breasts are pushed into a deep cleavage.

In the far corner of the patio, a string quartet is playing—two violins, a viola, and a cello. Billy Love has sauntered over to them and is having a conversation with the violist.

"Billy Love," Marlene calls out, "Did you know that I was a very accomplished violin player? When I was 20, I caught my hand in a clothes wringer and it ended my career. I was devastated, but that is when I started singing and acting, so maybe it was fate."

"Marlene, may I play a number with them? I know most of their classic pieces, and they have agreed," Billy Love replies.

"Of course. Pamela will lend you her viola for the number. Are you going to play Debussy's Clair de Lune?"

Billy Love sits down and places the viola under her chin, slowly pulling the bow across the strings. The music is haunting and beautiful, the sound pure. The crowd stops and listens, unexpectedly. When the quartet pulls their bows at the last note, everyone stands silent for several seconds, taking the music in, then they applaud heartily.

"Why A.R., Billy Love has so many talents. I bet you and Beulah Bell are so proud of her accomplishments," Marlene comments to Uncle A.R. after meeting him.

"I like to think it was in her gene pool," A.R. comments, conceitedly.

"Must be."

"Now, Marlene why did you decide to come to America from Germany?" A.R. directly ask.

"A number of reasons. For one, I am very concerned about the rise of Adolf Hitler. He is an idiot. All of his posturing and yelling about being Germany's savior, uncouth, and I think he is rising in power. What is wrong with the German people? Don't they see him for what he is, a monster?"

"I share your perception of Hitler. He is very dangerous—if he gets into power, he will discriminate against his own people, and probably put them into labor camps—especially the Jews, he hates them, and has written horrible things about them."

"Some of my best friends are Jews, singing and acting in the German cabarets like *The Garden*. I fear for them."

"Just yesterday, someone asked if I was the Jewish director of the movie, and was peevishly implying that Jews are running

Hollywood, as if that is the end of American life. So, Hitler is influencing people in the United States with his filth," A.R. comments, with wrath in his voice.

"Someone thought you were von Sternberg? He is Jewish, from Austria. He, too, is happy to have immigrated to the United States, but feels some discrimination, even in Hollywood. He is thinking about have some plastic surgery to alter his face."

"Marlene, I am contemplating having a rhinoplasty myself. It is a fairly new procedure, but I have done some reading about it and am ready to try it."

"I have had a nose job myself. The director felt my nose too wide for close-up shots, so the surgeon narrowed the ridge. I also had my back molars pulled to make my cheek bones look more prominent. The things you do to be a movie star. Anyway, I can get you the telephone number for the office of the surgeon here in Hollywood. He is well known for work on actresses."

As A.R. and Marlene continue on about the latest techniques in plastic surgery, I glance toward the pool where I discover Bitsy Love and Babe Love have taken off their shoes and are sitting on the edge, with their feet and ankles submerged; their identical dresses are spread out over their laps. At the moment, they are giggling together.

After the movie premiere, Uncle A.R. relented and swooped them out of our rented house.

"Now, I expect you girls to be on your best behavior, because if not, we will immediately depart."

"Yes father," they say, in unison.

Bobbie Love strolls over to where the twins are sitting. "Girls, it is not polite at such a grand party for you to be disruptive. Now get out of the pool and put your shoes back on."

"Why don't you make us," Bitsy says, her voice growing loud. "Yeah," says Babe Love.

I notice Bobbie Love's face is burning; her anger apparent. She runs toward the girls' backs and forcefully shoves them both into the pool, then she quickly enters the shrubbery and reenters the party, looking calm.

The twins are screaming and waving their arm, their dresses tangled around their waists. "Bobbie Love pushed us into the pool," Babe Love insists.

A.R. hears the commotion.

"I have no idea what they are talking about. I have been here with Kat enjoying the party, right Kat?" I smile and remain a silent accomplice. Those girls need a lesson.

Uncle A.R. and Aunt Beulah Bell stomp to the edge of pool, and take them out by reaching under the armpits and grabbing. The twins are bedraggled, and embarrassed by the spectacle.

"Why on earth would you jump into someone's pool at night, fully clothed?" A.R. questions, exasperated. "But father, Bobbie Love pushed us," they plead together. "Poppycock, the party's over," he replied.

With that remark, A.R. took one on each arm and escorted them through the yard to the car. They would not be allowed to leak all over Marlene's mansion.

Chapter 12

Election

Germany
1932
Elisabetha

"Tell me all about your trip to America, Petrus and Liz," Fritz says, stirring sugar into his coffee.

"Brother, you think we have a wild family, you can't even begin to describe the antics of A.R. and his entire clan," Petrus replies.

"I get tired even thinking about it. Why, they put poor Kat on a horse the first hour after arriving at the ranch. She was petrified, having never been on a horse, let alone behind Billy Love galloping at top speed," I recall.

"A.R. is still raging at Hitler every chance he gets. He is particularly angry about the Jewish situation in Germany. He insists that Adolf's rhetoric is influencing American attitude regarding Jews. He received a slur himself, as he was mistaken as the Jewish director of the film 'Destry Rides Again,'" I continue. "Now he is considering having some facial surgery, which is ridiculous—A.R. is stubborn, though, so he probably will do it."

"And the movie premiere, followed by the party at Marlene's mansion?"

"The western was great, and Billy Love as the stunt riding, trick riding double, was outstanding. Simon was also very good. Germany should be getting the picture here soon, so you can see for yourself," Petrus exclaims. "At the afterparty, A.R.'s twins jumped in the pool, so he yanked them out and they went back to the apartment early, sopping wet."

I chuckle picturing the twins. "Yes, Fritz, take Eva and her sisters with you to see the movie. It will break up the monotonous days under the pall of everything Hitler."

"Liz, I am more scared than ever about Eva and Adolf. He purchased a house in Munich and moved Eva and her sister, Gretl, in last month. Hitler is in Berlin most of the time, but he has several of his henchmen watching her every move. It is like she is in prison. Whatever are we going to do - we need a plan," Fritz wails, his hands shaking.

"Now Fritz, be assured, Liz and I want to help. Mood and Kat will too, along with Simon - let's all put our heads together. Also, Billy Love and Lola Estelle are coming over again in a few months. Perhaps we can stage an intervention, but the plan needs to be detailed and airtight. We don't want Hitler's entire army after us," Petrus, emotionally, exclaims.

"Brother, you are the best. Thank you so much," Fritz says, with tears in his eyes.

It will be nettlesome to get Eva out of her situation, especially since Adolf has her buttoned up in his house. There has got to be a way. Kat and I will make a visit to her at the house. I want to look at the layout of the rooms – also, I need to discover how often the brownshirts change shifts.

****

"Petrus, Fritz is on the telephone, I can hardly understand him. He is frantic."

Petrus grabs the base of the telephone out of my hand and jams the receiver to his ear. "Fritz, what's wrong?"

"It's Eva, she took my gun and tried to kill herself. Shot herself in the neck. We are at the hospital right now."

"Liz and I will be there as quickly as we can."

Petrus slams down the telephone and rushes to put on his coat. "Liz, Eva tried to kill herself—and all over the dictator Hitler. We are going to have to act soon."

"Did Fritz say anything about her condition?"

"No, just that she shot herself in the neck. Let's get to the hospital."

Eva is hunched over on a hospital bed, sobbing, her hands covering her eyes, as Petrus and I enter the room. She has a large gauze dressing on the left side of her neck. Gretl, her sister, and Fritz are sitting on either side of her on the bed, each of them rubbing her back.

"We got lucky, the wound is superficial. The bullet just grazed the neck. The doctor cleaned it up, and they are going to discharge her. She has been given a sedative and a shot of Morphine. I will be taking her to my home to recover," Fritz explains, calmer now that we are here and it is apparent the wound is not life threatening.

"Let's step outside and let Eva rest," Fritz motions us.

He shuts the door as we step into the hallway. In a low voice, he explains, "Gretl found her in the bedroom with the gun. Eva was startled and the gun went off, missing the target of her skull. Otherwise, she might have died on the spot. For weeks, Gretl noticed Eva moping and complaining that Adolf was ignoring her. On top of that, Hitler forbade her to leave the house unless accompanied by the goons. She felt isolated and fell into a deep depression."

"Why make herself miserable? I just can't understand why she stays with him. I guess we can't know her motives—it has been four years now, consorting with evil," Petrus complains.

"Hitler is spending most of his time in Berlin these days in preparation for the election. When he is in Munich, he governs out of his flat with a stream of political allies seeking his favor. Sometimes he will see Eva at her cottage, or summon her to his apartment. Even then, he has her wait in the back bedroom," Fritz exclaims, his voice ramping up.

"Keep your voice down. I believe Hitler has spies everywhere, especially when Eva is involved," I insist.

"Take her home, Fritz, let her recover for a week, and try to find out exactly what Eva is thinking," Petrus offers. "Once Eva returns to her cottage, Liz and Kat will pay her a visit."

****

Kat and I sit in *The Garden*, discussing our visit this afternoon to Eva's house.

"We need to carefully study all of the rooms in the house—how many accesses in and out—even from the basement. That will be your job, Kat, how many windows and doors? Also, examine the movements of the brownshirts. How often do they change shifts? Where do they set up their watch? How do they interact with Eva? I heard through gossip that President Hindenburg put restrictions on Hitler's thugs. Perhaps there will be times when no guards are around. We need to know the patterns."

"Aunt Liz, what is your role?"

"I will be assessing Eva's emotional state and talking with her to discover if there is any change in her attitude toward Hitler. The goal is to alter her perception of Hitler—get her to view him in a negative way, that she will take action to leave him. I realize, of course, that it may take more than one visit."

"Why do we need to know so much about the house itself?"

"I have a plan, but I am not ready to share it with anyone yet. Please, just do what I ask you."

We approach Eva's house. A guard is on the front porch, his feet propped up on the railing. His chin is on his chest and he appears to be sleeping. This is an important observation—they're not taking the guarding of Eva too seriously.

We see Eva peering out the window and the door bangs open, slapping against the siding.

"Come in, Kat and Liz," she trills.

The guard, suddenly startled, pulls himself upright and tries to appear attentive. You can't fool me, slacker.

The three of us enter the parlor. Every hard surface in the house is covered with bouquet after bouquet of fresh cut flowers. The smell of violets, gardenias, and roses fills the house.

"Isn't it marvelous? Adolf sent all of these flowers to little old me. See the card," Eva gushes.

To my darling Eva,
A speedy recovery.
Love, Wolf

I want to gag myself. Kat and I lock eyes, then look away, trying to hide our disgust. I am glad Fritz is not here to see all of the extravagance.

"Adolf is in Munich tonight, and has invited me to his flat. I have been bored, but now I can relax and enjoy his company—hopefully he won't have some awful meetings. When he does, I must vanish into one of the back bedrooms," Eva frowns.

Kat has disappeared into the back of the house. I hear her upstairs, then descending into the basement. Eva is paying no attention. Good.

"Eva, you are not happy. You are only 22 years old. Do you really want this life?"

"Aunt Liz, for now, yes. I know it is a cliché, but I can't live with him and I can't live without him," Eva says, dejected.

"Any time you think you could live without him, let us know. You have loved ones who care deeply."

Kat returns to the parlor with twinkling eyes. "It has been a lovely visit, Eva. Liz, shall we go?"

****

Simon, Kat and I sit in Simon's dressing room. It is early afternoon and we are the only ones around. Kat and I share our visit to Eva's house.

"So Kat, what did you discover about her house?" Simon casually questions.

"The basement has a large cellar door that locks from the inside. All of the large windows on the first floor open easily."

"The brownshirt guarding the house was sleeping when we arrived, and he was by himself. I would say security is loose. He left the house unattended about halfway through our visit," I explain.

"Ok, good information. You know Eva has that movie projector that she fiddles with, filming throughout her monotonous days. She makes Gretl film her dancing and twirling. The next time you two visit, have her give you a tour of the house and film it. Tell her she is the lovely hostess, with her home captured forever. That way the rest of us can have a permanent record of each room," Simon explains, waving his hands in the air.

"Good idea, Simon," Kat interjects.

"Eva is very conflicted about Hitler. One day he lavishes attention on her, the next he virtually ignores her. We need to keep sowing doubts about him to get her out," I continue. "If Hitler does become chancellor, the situation with Eva will become dire. Our chances will diminish with every passing day."

"Munich is becoming dangerous. Adolf's SS are everywhere, lurking in doorways and in the cabarets, drinking, and catcalling the actors known to be homosexual. Yesterday, as I was entering the synagogue for evening prayers, one stopped me and grilled me as to my intention. He grabbed the front of my shirt and pulled me up to him. I stood straight and did not respond. Eventually, he threw me away from him, and I landed on my knees. He raised his arm stiffly in a salute, then stomped down the street," Simon recounts.

"Simon, how horrible. The discrimination against Jews and gypsies is ramping up. I heard a concentration camp named Dachau is set to open in early 1933. If Hitler gains power, his political enemies will be sent there, along with other people he considers dissidents," I add, placing my hand gently on his upper arm and squeezing gently.

"Are you worried that Lola Estelle and Billy Love will be in danger this summer?" Kat inquires.

"I do think if Hitler comes to power, it will be their last visit until he is taken down. He doesn't like Americans much."

"Lola Estelle and I have a special relationship—we would like to get married, which means I would immigrate to the United States. I am sure I could get some new roles in Hollywood, working with Marlene. We will finalize plans soon. Germany will always be my home, but there is too much turmoil and darkness here."

Chapter 13

Rhinoplasty

Oklahoma
1933
Billy Love

A.R. is standing before the hall mirror, studying his nose from every angle. He is scowling, stretching the skin across his face with his index finger, pinching the nostrils together. I am watching him with some amusement—he is so vain.

He has summoned me to the ranch to discuss my upcoming trip to Germany, where I will play in the orchestra pit at the Wagner opera festival.

"Billy Love, Hitler has now become chancellor of Germany: there are swastika flags everywhere, and the country is on the verge of going to hell. The people are desolate and desperate, with little food or money. It is no place for young women, either you or Lola Estelle."

"Father, no matter how you beg us, we are going. Simon, Uncle Mood and Uncle Petrus will look out for us. I promise it will be my last trip to Germany while Adolf Hitler is in power."

"I will hold you to that promise, but I am still very unhappy with you, Billy Love. Where did you get that stubborn streak?"

Father knows darn well that I inherited his determined nature. I smile and stare him down.

Last month, he traveled to Hollywood with Beulah Bell. There, Dr. Feinstein surgically altered his nose to make it smaller and straighten the nasal tip. Now, he has decided it was botched.

"I trusted Marlene and her stupid plastic surgeon to get it right," father exclaims. "He did not take out enough of the bone and cartilage to my satisfaction."

"Oh, father it looks fine to me; actually, you did not need to have surgery in the first place."

"You are wrong. I will have another revision next week in Tulsa. There is a renowned plastic surgeon pioneer there. I had the consultation with Dr. Walker last month. Since Beulah Bell almost passed out when she saw all of the swelling and bruising, could you drive me for the procedure?"

Beulah Bell enters the room and joins the conversation. "Billy Love, I so appreciate you driving your father. I can't go through this again. Plus, I have to get the twins to school."

"Mother, why does father want to cut up his face? I can't believe you put up with him—he wants to be a peacock, strutting and showing off."

"Billy Love, when your father decides something, you can't change his mind. I learned that before we were even married."

"Heh, heh, heh, Beulah Bell, you still married me, did you not?" he chuckles.

"I will pick you up next week, father. Can I drive the Duesenberg?"

****

Prior to taking father for his nose reshaping surgery, I completed research about the procedure. He is having a closed process, where the bone and cartilage are redefined completely inside the nose. That way, there will be no noticeable scarring. The sutures are invisible. I freak out when I look at the pictures of the surgery in its various stages. The surgeon uses a small hammer and chisel to literally break the bones, prior to reducing their size. Who would voluntarily agree to this?

Father is stoic and he does know what to expect, having had a previous rhinoplasty. I hope he is satisfied this time.

I sit in the waiting room outside the operating room. The time is creeping by—over two hours now. Why is it taking so long?

Finally, the door opens and father is wheeled out on a gurney. A splint holds the nose in place, with layers of gauze taped over its top. I can see dark bruises starting to circle his eyes, his face is puffy, almost non-recognizable. He is moaning.

"The surgery went well," Dr. Walker addresses me. "I will have Nurse Jones get him a shot of morphine. He will be in recovery for a few hours, then we will let you take him home. He can come back in a week to get the stitches out and the splint removed."

The smell of ether wafts through the waiting area. Yuck, it makes me want to puke. Nurses scurry in and out, carrying syringes on trays. Their long white, starched dresses rustle, their caps secured at the back of their heads. Nurses are the eyes and ears of hospitals, I think to myself. The epitome of a professional— but not for me.

I start to doze off, when someone screams, "Call Dr. Walker. Get him back to the operating room." It is Nurse Jones, and she is rapidly pushing the gurney through the waiting area.

I gasp. Father is covered in bright red blood, his gown seeping. The nurse's white uniform is splattered, too. I sniff the metal smell of the gushing fluid, becoming nauseated, and lightheaded.

"Dr. Walker, A.R.'s blood pressure is 80 over 40. It is bottoming out from the blood loss."

"Take him to OR number 8, and give him some blood. I will scrub in; get the cautery tools out," Dr. Walker hollers to the nurses.

The OR doors close, and father disappears from sight. I stand up and pace, sweating and shaking. Why did father insist on having this done? What if he dies?

After another hour, Dr. Walker emerges. He is disheveled, his mask hanging loosely around his neck.

"Your father is going to be okay. We burned the small vessels so that they stopped bleeding, then we repacked his nose, which puts pressure on the inside walls of the nose. We gave him blood and his blood pressure has climbed to 100 over 60, which is stable. We will need to admit him for a couple of days to make sure bleeding does not reoccur. Since your father had a previous nose job, it made him more susceptible for this complication."

"Thank you, Dr. Walker." What am I going to tell mother?

****

"Today we will see the results of my revision," father declares. We are on our way to see Dr. Walker two weeks after the surgery. This time, I insist that mother come along.

"Father, remember, there will still be swelling—you won't know the final shape of your nose for a couple of months."

"I am aware of that possibility," he says, impatiently.

"A.R., I am not going in that tiny exam room while you get the packing pulled out and the stitches removed. Why, I might faint dead away," Beulah Bell retorts.

"Me neither," I chime in.

Father's skin around his eyes has turned ugly - greenish yellow. His nose looks extremely prominent with the extra layers of bandages. I hope for the best outcome—I can never go through another surgery with him.

Mother and I have coffee while we wait.

"Why does father have such an obsession with having his nose rebuilt?"

"He always has complained about it, even when we first met. I am as clueless as you. Maybe he is just a vain man; I do know that about him."

"Oh, look here he comes," Beulah Bell says, motioning toward the hallway.

"Billy Love, Beulah Bell, what do you think?" father demands, tilting his head to one side so that we can see his profile.

Praise Jesus!

Chapter 14

Bayreuth Festival

Germany
1933
Billy Love

It is June—a lovely day in the rolling hills of Bayreuth, Germany. I am giddy. It seems impossible for a woman born and raised in Oklahoma to be selected to play in the festival orchestra. Why, there are only 200 people selected from around the world for this honor. And only 30 of us are women.

Rehearsals for the opera Tristan and Isolde start tomorrow. Of course, I know the viola part well, having played the scores with the Tulsa orchestra, but playing with a whole new group will be challenging. The festival opens the middle of July, which means we will have about a month before the opening.

The orchestra members, stage hands, makeup artists, costumers and singers all stay in dormitory facilities a mile from the opera house itself. The quarters are small—most of us have roommates, but we have free room and board, plus a stipend.

Festival House, where all Wagner operas are performed, is magnificent. Richard Wagner, himself, designed it with unique features to enhance the aesthetics of the audience experience. It has an ancient Greek feel to it, with no boxes or galleries, just tiered rows encircling the stage. The walls are wood, floor to ceiling, which enhances the sound. To avoid having the audience distracted by shiny instruments, a cave-like structure exists under the stage. The structure is tiered, with the violas assigned to the second top tier.

Wagner's operas all have a magical dream aura to them. There are two large arches around the stage which makes the stage appear further away, which adds to the mystique of the show.

"Billy Love Wolf, come and meet your roommate." Apparently, I have a housemother who oversees check in, meals, and who knows what other rules by which I will have to abide. Really? I am twenty-one now. I bet the men are free to roam about as they wish.

"I am Bessie." The housemother stretches out her hand and takes mine in hers.

"This is Valentina Steinman, she hails from Paris, and she also plays the viola." I step forward to acknowledge Valentina, or Tina as she likes to be called. "Nice to meet you," I begin.

Tina looks to be around my age. Her dark brown, curly hair cascades to her shoulders. Her hazel/green speckled eyes look at me shyly, with not much eye contact. She takes a step back.

This won't do. I will need to get Tina loosened up. Maybe the Parisians are just snooty—wouldn't know, have never been there. All I know is that I am not going to spend my summer playing the viola by day and getting locked into my dorm room by night with a prude for a roommate. For heaven's sake, festival runs for two months, and there will be days off for adventure. I plan to travel to Munich and Darmstadt to see my relatives, and party at *The Garden.*

"Hi," Tina peeps.

"Bessie, show us our room. We need to get settled in, then grab us some grub," I express myself loudly.

Tina's eyes widen, but she follows Bessie and me down the hallway to a cramped room.

"Now Tina, I may be a high brow violist player, but I also am a decorated rodeo star from Oklahoma United States. We are not going to be cowed by some hovering old bat. Lucky for us, we are on the ground floor of the dormitory. Let's check out the window."

I stride over to the window and thrust up the sash. "This should be adequate for us to squeeze through."

Tina is standing erect, red faced, and frowning. "What are you doing? What if they kick us out of the orchestra?" she wails.

"SHHH," I admonish. "I know how to steer clear of trouble. We will complete a practice run tonight after lights out. I met some cute men from London during check in. We can meet them down by the lake."

"But," Tina stammers.

"No buts, let's go find the guys in the mess hall."

****

Valentina refused to go with me tonight, but I will loosen her up eventually. She doesn't know what she is missing. I have two guys to myself instead—William and Harry. Very funny, I love their British accents. I regale them about riding bulls; they in turn, tell me stories about the royal family and attending boarding school.

William plays the cymbals and Harry, the Wagner tuba. We discuss the plot of the opera Tristan and Isolde, which is quite dark. Isolde is voyaging to marry the king, who she rejects. She wants to marry Tristan, a soldier who is accompanying her to the king. Somehow, Tristan and Isolde are given a love potion and they fall madly in love. Isolde is forced to marry the king—she has an affair with Tristan anyway and they both are killed by the king. The guys and I ruminate that Wagner's wife probably cheated on him, and that fact gave him the plot for the opera.

William and Harry urge me to skinny dip with them—I tell them to go ahead, maybe next time. They strip off their shirts and pants and dive into the pond. Not bad. William is sinewy, with sandy blonde hair. A firm rump. Harry is a redhead, covered with freckles. These two new friends are keepers. Once I tell Valentina about them, I am quite certain she will give in.

"Bye guys, I need to sneak back into the dorms before the hag catches me. See you at practice tomorrow."

****

We practice every morning for four hours, then have the afternoons off. The first week consists of solely playing the opera score. The singers are added gradually until the opera is enacted in its entirely.

Once the show is opened to the audiences, our practices are cut to two hours daily, from ten to noon. The opera starts at four pm. After two hours of theater, everyone breaks for dinner on the lawn, then the opera continues for another two hours, ending around ten pm.

****

We are preparing for our fifth performance of the opera Tristan and Isolde. So far, so good. I am resining my bow, the orchestra conductor has the pitch pipe in his mouth, ready for us to tune our instruments. Valentina is concentrating on arranging her sheet music, squinting a bit.

I wave to Harry and William. They smile and nod back. Middle C is tweeted by the conductor—we all tune for several minutes.

Just as the opera is about to start, with the theater dark, there is a commotion. Adolf Hitler strides in and sits in reserved seats, surrounded by twenty body guards. He is in full military attire, a red sash encircling his torso. He stands while the audience lavishes applause upon him. He gives a tight smile and nods his head.

Ascending to Chancellor the previous January, we all know that Hitler is consolidating his power. The newspapers report on arrests of those who oppose him. Dachau, the labor camp, opened, with political enemies sentenced to hard time there.

"Billy Love," Tina whispers to me, "Whatever shall we do? I am so afraid of him."

"Act like it is just another performance," I say. "Hitler loves opera, especially Wagner. He comes to the festival every year. He won't pull anything political today."

The conductor signals with his tiny baton, and the overture begins.

Two hours later, intermission occurs. Tina and I make our way through the crowd, where a plate of delicious German food awaits us - potato dumplings, shepherd pie, cabbage and coleslaw, flaky buns with butter and strawberry jam, apple pie. Food is a big perk for those of us hired to play in the orchestra. Because of the depression, many Germans are experiencing rationing, with food and gasoline among the many restrictions.

I feel a little guilty, but still, can't help shoveling the food into my mouth as fast as possible.

"Yum," I say with my mouth full. "Harry, William, over here," I wave.

The four of us walk from the groaning tables of food--we move toward a shady grove of trees—intending to sit on the ground to finish our meal.

Suddenly, I feel a hand clamp down firmly on my shoulder. "Hello, little lady."

Spinning around, I am face to face with a brownshirt. I am nervous, shaking inside, but determined not to show it. "What do you want with me?" I give my plate to Tina and smooth down my navy-blue orchestra uniform, trying to get my sweaty palms to dry.

"The Fuhrer would like to meet you. He is pleased with the Wagner performance, and the orchestra in particular."

"Just me? Why?"

The brownshirt points to Tina. "And her."

"Come on Tina. He is the leader of Germany now. We should be gracious." I say, rather unconvincingly.

"Follow me." Valentina walks beside me, looking like a scared rabbit.

What would father say if he knew I had been summoned to meet Hitler? I can never, ever tell him.

The Fuhrer is seated at a picnic table, smoking a pipe and commenting on the opera house. "Is it not magnificent?" he exclaims to no one in particular. "Ah, here are two young ladies I wished to meet."

Tina and I are standing inches in front of Hitler. I observe his greasy, stringy hair-- his breath smells oniony. He has that teeny, tiny mustache patch in the middle of his lip. What does Eva Braun see in him?

I bravely address him. "Hello, my name is Billy Love."

"You are American, by your accent?" Adolf asks.

"Yes, I auditioned for the orchestra and was selected for the Festival this summer. It has been a great honor to play in such a renowned place."

I nudge Tina. She quietly speaks "I am Valentina, from Paris."

"So, we have two foreigners. I want to thank you both for a splendid performance. I look forward to the next two hours."

Hitler turns away and seems to dismiss us. I take a deep breath, to calm myself, then Tina and I swiftly walk toward the orchestra pit.

Harry and William climb up to our section to discuss our encounter with Hitler. "Blimey, what did he say to you?" William demands.

"It was a strange encounter. He wanted us to know that he is enjoying the orchestra. And then he commented on us being foreigners. I hope I never meet him again. He really is quite horrid," I say.

"Better keep that last comment to yourself. You don't want to get shipped off to Dachau," Harry laughs.

I do not return his mirth. Indeed, I tell myself, maybe father is right about Adolf Hitler. Germany is headed for trouble. I pick up my viola, and jam it under my chin, ready for the next two hours of opera. Hitler be damned.

****

"Valentina, we have the weekend off. Would you like to take the train down to Munich with me to visit my Aunt Liz and cousin Kat? Kat sings at *The Garden*, a cabaret my aunt and uncle own."

Chapter 15

Roller Skates

Munich
1933
Kat

I am at the train station, waiting to pick up Billy Love and her roommate, Valentina. They should be here shortly. My mind wanders. It has been five months since Hitler rose to power—how turbulent, in such a short time. Eva has not seen much of Wolf, as she calls him. He spends much of his time in Berlin these days. Most of the time, Eva is melancholy, depressed and surly.

Billy Love, her roommate and I, are taking Eva roller skating tomorrow at the Munich Incrediroll Rink. After Hitler grabbed power, he created the German League of the Reich for Physical Exercise. It is a source of propaganda and message to the rest of the world—to promote sports to harden German spirits, meaning a strong, unified Germany. One of the designated sports is roller skating—it has its own department, with oversight in dozens of districts throughout Germany.

Billy Love and I can roller skate. We can both do crossovers around corners and flip backwards. Neither one of us skate with a high level of skill. Eva is a dancer, but has only been on skates a couple of times. We hope getting her out of her house will do her some good and actually improve her mood, give her an activity with friends. Afterwards, we can go for a drink at *The Garden*, if we can ditch the goon who hangs around her house.

"Billy Love, how is the festival going?" I say, as we are driving to Aunt Liz's house from the train station.

"The festival itself is going well, but Tina and I were summoned to meet Hitler at an intermission. He was quite rude to us and we were relieved to get away, disappear back into the orchestra pit." Tina shakes her head in agreement.

"Let's talk about something else," I exclaim. "What do we need for tomorrow's skate date with Eva?"

"I have my own skates with me - Tina and Eva can rent skates at the rink. We need to purchase black skirts at the department store," Billy Love explains.

"The twins are fantastic roller skaters. They go to competitions all over the United States. Really, it keeps them busy. They are fifteen now, and are finally growing up, although they still argue and fuss with each other at meets. Bitsy Love specializes in figures and dance. Babe Love does artistic freestyle," Billy Love continues.

"What is the difference between the three types of roller skating?" Tina asks Billy Love.

"With figures, there are interconnecting circles drawn on the floor. The skater has to trace the line perfectly, on one foot, sometime going forward and sometimes, flipping around backwards. It takes perfect balance and concentration. It looks easy, but it is incredibly difficult."

"Bitsy Love has a male partner in dance. They skate to music and have complicated steps that they must do in perfect unison. They compete in different categories, like the waltz and tango."

"In artistic freestyle skating, the skater has more liberty to have unique routines. Babe Love skates to music, but she gets higher points if she does certain jumps, spins and footwork passages. Some of the jumps are called the salchow, the toe loop, the lutz, and the axel. Most of the jumps take off going forward, but the axel, which is the hardest jump, takes off backwards. You have to get the jumps all the way around, 360 degrees to get the full points and if you fall, you get no points. I could go on, but again, roller skating is not for the fearful. It's right up there with bull riding."

"No, I find it all very interesting. I would love to see your sisters skate," Tina declares.

"Well, you need to make a trip to the U.S. next year, Tina. Maybe you can come for Lola Estelle and Simon's wedding. By the way, Kat, what has Lola Estelle been doing the past couple of months?"

"She and Aunt Liz visit Eva often. She comes to *The Garden* almost every night to see Simon. They are planning their wedding."

"You heard that Simon was pushed to the ground as he was going to synagogue? Marlene Dietrich is working on getting him a passport to the United States as soon as possible. Once he is married, he will become a United States citizen," I continue.

"Aunt Liz, this is my roommate and friend, Valentina," Billy Love says. "She hails from Paris and is a fellow viola player."

"Welcome, welcome," Liz says as she warmly grabs Tina's hands in hers.

****

Eva, Billy Love, Tina and I are sitting on long benches, lacing up our skates. Up on a platform sits the organ player, his feet and hands working feverishly together, producing loud music. Fernando's Hideaway is the current selection. We have to shout to each other in order to be heard.

"Eva, you look nice in your skating skirt. This will be fun," I yell.

"I am a little scared. This is only my second time on skates," Eva replies.

"I will give you a lesson and Billy Love will help Tina," I assert.

"Come over to the bar and hold on with your right hand, Eva. Now, practice while standing still—turn both of your feet inward, this is called the inside edge. Good. Now, turn both feet in the opposite direction, this is the outside edge. You will use both of these movements in skating—they help you to keep your balance as you roll. Start to roll forward, slowly, still holding onto the bar. Now, turn toward outside edge, then inside. See how it gives you momentum?"

"How am I doing?" Eva asks me, laughing.

"Great. Now practice along the bar ten times, then I will lock arms with you and we will skate together."

Looking around, I see Billy Love already skating with Tina. Tina seems to have caught on quite quickly. The rink is crowded. A few are falling and pulling down others with them. I see two men in uniform watching Eva. Damn, can she ever get away from them?

Eva and I giggle and skate together. "It is time to try it solo, Eva."

"Do you think I am ready?"

"Yes, of course."

I watch as Eva starts into the crowd, uncertain, but determined. She is starting to get the rhythm down, when someone bumps into her, hard. Down she goes, landing with a thump on her behind.

A tall young man immediately comes to her side to assist her.

"Are you ok?" Eva nods her head. "Let me help you up." He reaches down and pulls her to standing. She is face to face with him. He locks arms with her and they skate together over to the bar."

"What are you doing with her?" the uniformed goon demands.

"Why, nothing, I just helped her up," the young man replies.

"This young man was being a gentleman by assisting me after I fell," Eva says furiously to the guard. "I am just roller skating and trying to have fun. You and your buddy need to leave. Kat will take me home later. I will not be treated like a prisoner."

"Yes, Miss Eva, but we will need to inform Adolf."

"Go ahead," Eva shouts. The brownshirts slink out of the rink. The young man who helped her up looks puzzled. "Adolf? Hitler?" he queries.

"Unfortunately," I comment.

Eva scowls at me. I think to myself, the handsome young man would be a much better mate for Eva than that nasty old man Hitler.

Chapter 16

Dream

Munich
1933
Elisabetha

"Petrus, I had a horrible dream last night," I say, as I pull on my robe and grab a cup of coffee.

"Do tell, dear."

"I think my subconscious thoughts—fear is coming into my sleep. It seemed so real."

"In my vivid dream, Adolf decided to marry Eva in a state ceremony. He invited heads of countries from all over the world. Fritz was forced to walk her down the aisle. He was sobbing, grief stricken. Eva was smiling in her flowing, beaded white gown."

"The chancellor was dressed in full military mode, with 20 brownshirts serving as groomsmen. When Fritz got close, Hitler's face turned into a mask, his eyes black holes, and his teeth were rotted. Blood ran down his cheeks."

"Eva's mother Debra, sitting in the front row, started to scream and Hitler ordered his goons to arrest Debra and take her to Dachau. Then Fritz, trying to stop them, was shot point blank in the chest. He dropped over, dead."

Petrus is listening, intently.

"Eva realized her mistake and tried to run. Two brownshirts grabbed her on either side and dragged her up to Hitler. The Lutheran minister put his hand on the bible and forced Eva to take the vow of marriage. He pronounced them man and wife."

"Eva feel to her knees, terrified and shaking. Then Hitler addressed those in attendance and asked those who were Jewish to stand up. He screeched at the body guards to arrest them all, including Simon Hilfman."

"Before they could get to him, Simon pulled out a pistol and shot Adolf in the head. Hitler fell on top of Eva, pinning her to the floor, his blood spurting onto her pure white dress."

"Simon shot several more henchmen before he was shot dead. The patrons were in a frenzy, running and shouting. Eva crawled out from under Hitler, stood up and fainted. The Lutheran minister grinned evilly."

"My goodness, Liz, such dark thoughts you have these days. Do you really think Hitler will establish policies that discriminate against Jews to that extent? To jail them for being Jewish?"

"Yes, Petrus, I think he is determined. I fear for Simon. The sooner he can get a visa for the United States, the better. Because of his cabaret act satirizing Hitler, I believe he could be an early target. Even now, some of the cabarets with Jewish performers are being shut down."

"Liz, *The Garden* may be at risk soon. Business is starting to slow, nightly the brownshirts come into the cabaret, and they menace our patrons and performers."

I sip my chicory, steaming coffee—I hope my dream is not a prophecy. Then, I shiver.

****

I am standing in the kitchen, surrounded by mountains of fresh produce, fruit, cheese and meats. Billy Love is chopping vegetables, and I am making bratwurst sandwiches. The aroma of baking bread wafts through the house. Empty baskets sit on the floor, waiting to be filled. Several bottles of cabernet wine line up on the counter top.

"Billy Love, your father called yesterday. He is insistent that you come home immediately," I continue. "He also wants Lola Estelle out of Germany."

"The festival ends next week, and I want to travel for a few days throughout Germany. There is a horse ranch near Darmstadt. I can stay with Uncle Mood and ride horses out into the country.

Also, I have never been to Berlin. I hear there are some wild cabarets with topless women and homosexual men dancing about."

"Well, I am just telling you that your father is getting frantic. He might come over here and drag you home."

"He and Marlene are working together to get Simon a visa. It will be completed in the late fall—then Mr. Hilfman can travel to Tulsa."

Lola Estelle enters my kitchen and sits down at the table. "Thanks for the information, Liz. I can't wait to let Simon know. I am so anxious about his safety. He has been very outspoken regarding the Nazi regime--the SS is watching him closely. Just the other day, one of his friends, who was handing out flyers denigrating Hitler, was charged with a crime against the government and sent to Dachau. Imagine—two years of hard labor for protesting."

"Let's change the subject. I am so tired of everyone yapping about Hitler," Billy Love declares. "Now, who all will be at the picnic in Munich square later today?"

"Well, the entire Braun family, Fritz, Debra, Eva, Gretl, Petrus and me. Then, you, Kat, Mood and Valentina, along with Lola Estelle and Simon. That makes twelve of us. I hope we have enough food," I say, as I line the picnic baskets with a checkered cloth.

"It is such a beautiful summer day. If the picnic tables are full of people, we can spread blankets out on the ground. I believe a small band will be playing German folk tunes," I say.

I wonder about Eva. Kat and Billy Love regaled me about their roller skating adventure. It alarms me that the two thugs intervened when Eva fell, and that she admonished them in public. Who knows what they told Hitler about her? Today will be the first time I will have seen Eva in about a month. Fritz continues to worry about her: He and Debra stop by her house every other day.

"Petrus, come help me pack the baskets and then carry them out to the car. Lola Estelle, you get the dishes and utensils ready. Billy Love, you are in charge of the wine and glasses. Oh, and also call upstairs to see if Valentina is ready. We don't want to be late," I order.

I see myself as quite the organizer. After years of running *The Garden*, I know how to make things hum along, in a timely manner. If only the rest of the family would take on this characteristic.

****

We are seated in groups, on three large blankets, under towering oak trees; Eva, Gretl, Fritz, and Debra—Lola Estelle, Simon, Petrus and Valentina—Mood, Kat, Billy Love and me. There is a slight breeze flicking over us; the shade from the trees cools us on a hot day.

The food is devoured and we are all seated, lolling on our elbows, curled up next to each other, finishing the wine.

"How are things at Merck Pharmaceutical?" I ask Mood.

Mood lowers his voice so that I am the only one who can hear him. "I had a visit from a Dr. Morrell last week. He brashly entered my department and asked to meet with me. It seems he is Adolf Hitler's personal physician—he showed me official documents—and then he demanded large amounts of injectable and powdered amphetamines and cocaine."

"What? Those are pretty powerful drugs. Why would he want to treat Hitler with those?"

"He said they keep him focused and increase his ability to stay awake for long periods. He said they also give him energy to give his long, fiery, oratory speeches. However, the amounts he asked for are quite obscene. All chemists know that patients can become addicted to amphetamines and cocaine easily, needing increasing amounts over a short period of time."

"Dr. Morrell is an obese man with fetid breath, I about gagged when he got close to me. Can't imagine him as a personal physician," Mood continues.

I start to raise my voice in alarm. "So, the leader of our country is already consuming large amounts of drugs that can cause him to be impetuous and irrational? Lord help us."

"Quiet, I don't want Eva to hear us. I fear for her being around him. What if he has the doctor start injecting her too?" Mood questions.

"I will try to ask Eva about it. Somehow, subtly." I add.

"There is something else I am concerned about. The doctor asked me to step up production of methamphetamines for the SS troops. It seems they need for the brownshirts to be alert with less rest—for example, to drive trucks across Germany for trips that may last over twenty-four hours." Mood explains.

"Methamphetamines are also highly addictive. I told Dr. Morell that he needed an official order from the military arm of Germany to get the drugs for the troops. He argued with me, but I held my ground. I also referred him to my boss who runs Merck. I was certainly not going to be the only one involved in this scheme."

"Mood, should we let Fritz know about this development?"

"For now, no. He is too wrapped up in Eva's situation with Hitler. When you are a parent, the focus is on your child. I would worry that he might endanger himself, get himself arrested by Hitler's thugs."

"Yes, let's keep it between us for now and monitor the situation," I agree.

Chapter 17

Bier Garden

Germany
1933
Kat

It is October, perfect, with crystal clear blue skies, 50 degrees, and time for a weekend celebration. Billy Love, Valentina, and I are meeting William and Harry at Schiller Park. The leaves on the trees are still intact—a riot of vibrant reds and golds.

As the three of us enter the park, we see a bald-headed man lustily playing the accordion, deftly weaving the instrument in and out, with the right hand manipulating the keyboard. He is playing a polka—surrounding him, couples dance. To his left, a giant olive-green tent claims the ground. Barrels of dark beer sit on long tables. People crowd and line up respectfully, in good moods, carefree, beer tickets in hand.

The women wear dirndls in multiple, bright colors. My silk dress is turquoise, with a wide, long skirt. Under the dress, I wear a white blouse—over the dress, tied around my waist is a gold apron.

Billy Love's dress is fuchsia, with a lime green apron—Tina's is emerald green, the apron royal purple. All three of us have braided our hair into two long plaits, tied at the ends with multiple ribbons.

I spy William and Harry coming toward us, gleefully skipping and hollering our names. They each have on gray knickers with patterned lederhosen pulled up to the knee. William has on a rusty red vest—Harry a deep orange. They both have on small, brown hats adorned with feathers.

William grabs me and twirls me around, off my feet. "My darling Kat, so good to meet you. Billy Love's description of you does not do you justice. A stunning beauty, really." I blush, and smooth my apron as he puts me down on the ground. "And you are William or Harry?"

"Why William Butler, my dear. And this is Harry Zeller. We both played in the orchestra with Tina and Billy Love this summer. Those two know how to have a good time when off duty. Why, the skinny dipping was marvelous," he says, winking at Tina and Billy Love.

"William, I did not skinny dip with you and Harry," Tina says indignantly.

Billy Love is looking down, not making eye contact with me. My cousin is quite guilty, I think. That girl finds trouble everywhere she goes. Oh, well, she is unique and fun, so who am I to be prudish about skinny dipping. I smile and clap her on the shoulder - "Well done, cousin."

Billy Love grins broadly. "Let's get some beer and brats, then we can dance and party the rest of the day."

The thick, brown beer, with the inches deep heads of foam, slides down our throats. We clink our steins together and devour the brats. What a glorious day. I look up to view the Brandenburg Gate and the Hotel Adlon: Nazi flags hang on poles, fluttering the length of the building.

I become sober at the sight, but I think to myself, Adolf Hitler and his henchmen will not ruin my day.

****

"Billy Love, what time are you racing today?" I ask. It is the second day of the beer festival.

"High noon, Kat. I need to change into riding apparel, the get-up Mugs sewed for me."

"William and Harry, have you placed your bets on me yet? They are selling tickets alongside the beer tent. Because I am the only woman, they have me at 20:1 odds of winning. Those silly German men running the show are sexist ... they have no idea I am a rodeo champion in both barrel racing and bull riding."

"Why, Billy Love, I am betting $100 on you," William declares, his mouth twitching into a grin, his eyes slightly crinkling at the corners.

"Me, too," Harry chimes in.

Tina, Harry, and William lock arms together and run to place their bets.

"Are you racing the black steed over there? I say to Billy Love, pointing in the distance.

"Yes, I rented him from the Stallion Ranch near Berlin. He is a beauty and responds well to my commands. He is one of the finest quarter horses in Germany."

"There are ten of us racing. My number is 35 ... look for me. Did you bring the binoculars?"

"Of course."

The race track is on the east end of Shiller Park. Horse racing is a tradition at Oktoberfest, a staple of the party atmosphere. I have no idea how Billy Love was able to wrangle her way into the race. That woman has more finesse and guts than anyone I know. She does not take no for an answer. She is tough, but can be charming to get her way. I need more of her nerviness, is that a word?

Billy Love is at the gate. The quarter horses are pawing the ground and whinnying. Because Billy Love's odds are 20:1, she is in the far outside position. Seated on the horse next to her is a young man in uniform, the costume of the SS.

We are seated closely together on the top row of the stands. I pull out my binoculars to spy Billy Love. She is talking to the young man next to her, no, yelling at him. I quickly train my binoculars on him—he appears livid, spittle dripping from his mouth, deeply scowling, his eyes narrowed.

Suddenly, the SS officer throws his right arm stiffly at Billy Love and screams, "Heil Hitler." Billy Love looks straight ahead, with no response to his gesture. The start gun barks.

I observe Billy Love digging her spurs into the stocky stallion, raising her whip to his rump, clutching the reins tightly. For a quarter of a mile, she goes flat out, there is no pacing.

The crowd is standing, waving, and screaming. Billy Love is leading, but the young man next to her is pulling even, glaring at her. Billy Love lunges forward in the saddle and urges the stallion onward. She crosses the finish line and twists her head to the side...she wins by a nose. Elated, she throws both hands in the air, then trots the horse around for a victory lap.

The SS officer pulls his horse close to her. I am certain he said something nasty to her. She ignores him—jumping off the horse and leading him briskly back to the stables, stone faced. She never looks back at him.

William and Harry celebrate. "We just won $2000," they scream in unison. They rush to the betting office to collect their monetary rewards.

Tina and I wait for Billy Love to change into a dirndl...then, we journey with her to collect her purse of $10,000.

Billy Love strides toward us. "What did that awful man say to you?" I query.

"He told me Americans are not welcome in Germany, especially snooty women. The idiot said he would be following me during my stay. I must admit he scares me a little...that is why I walked away and did not respond, at least verbally. Papa is right, it is time for me to be back in America."

"Do you go home next week?" I ask.

"Yes, Tina and I both go home. Also, William and Harry return to London."

"Papa and I, along with Petrus and Liz, look forward to next spring, when we will come for Lola Estelle and Simon's wedding."

"I can't wait...I am so happy for them," Billy Love announces.

I think to myself—now that Hitler is in full power, I am relieved that Simon and Lola Estelle are ensconced in Tulsa. And once they marry, Simon will become an American citizen. Even though this beer festival was raucous and celebratory, I fear times will become darker for Germany.

"The center of a wolf's universe is its pack, and howling is the glue that keeps the pack together. The pack that howls together, stays together."

~Nova on-line

Chapter 18

Wedding

Tulsa and the Howling Wolf Ranch
1934
Billy Love

Papa, Uncle Mood, and Aunt Liz are together again, the Wolf clan reunited. They relish and cherish each other, as they were thrust apart from each other when my grandparents immigrated to Oklahoma. Aunt Liz is the most resentful, as she was left in Germany, to be raised by her mother's sister, with no real explanation, even now.

Papa knows something more about the situation, I can tell. A shadow comes across his face, and he grimaces every time Uncle Mood or Aunt Liz questions him about my grandparents. He grunts short answers, fails to look them in the eye, and outright refuses to answer some pointed queries. Somehow, he is protecting my grandparents from a secret that may be quite dark, I just don't know.

Lola Estelle and Simon will be married at our ranch, The Howling Wolf. It will be a small affair, as none of Simon's family was able to obtain visas to enter America. Even now, Hitler is restricting Jews in many ways, the travel bans among them.

Marlene Dietrich and her entourage plan to attend. And of course, Lola Estelle's parents, Theodor Karl and Hildie Mae Ringlet—also Kat and Petrus Braun. Aunt Liz and I tried to convince Eva to come to the wedding, as she has become good friends with Lola Estelle—Eva refused, insisting she needed to be at the Fuhrer's side for a big political convention. Ridiculous.

"A.R., you look different to me, but I can't put my finger on it," Mood comments. "Have you lost weight? Your face looks thinner."

"Heh, heh, I had a little work done, do you think I look younger?"

"Uncle Mood, he had two nose surgeries—the second one he almost bled to death," I remark, shaking my head back and forth.

"A.R., what were you thinking? There was absolutely nothing wrong with your nose in the first place," Liz exclaims.

"We all tried to tell him that," mother chimes in. "But he was determined."

"Well, I am pleased with the final results and would do it again if needed," father proclaims. "People were using slurs about my looks and I couldn't have it."

"Father, you should have just ignored those idiots," I retort.

"It is done now, and I don't wait to discuss it further. Let's talk about the wedding," he says, to change the subject.

****

It is Lola Estelle and Simon's wedding day. The barn is festooned with garlands of flowers wrapped around wooden beams—baskets of pink roses sit on every table, low lit candles shimmer. A chuppah, the canopy covered by a massive riot of hydrangeas, roses, and dahlias—dominates the corner of the barn where they will be officially married. A glass, covered with a cloth, sits under the chuppah, awaiting the ceremony.

There are two officiants, our Lutheran minister and a rabbi from Tulsa. Lola Estelle and Simon will each keep their faiths, which father considers a bit scandalous.

I am Lola Estelle's lone attendant, so I intend to be on my best behavior. I will make sure her dress and veil are smoothed and in place…gather her bouquet and generally make her day seamless.

My dress is a floor length pastel satin, cowl neck, long sleeve beauty, with a short train. I am ready early.

"Lola Estelle, let's get you into your gown," I say. "The ceremony starts in thirty minutes. Are you nervous?"

"Not at all, I have been waiting to marry my love for over a year. I am so glad Simon is out of Germany and will become an American citizen. I'm worried about his family, though, especially his brother Leon, who has been knocked around by the SS."

"Let's not worry about the German situation today. We are focusing everything on you and Simon and your love for one another," I advise.

"You are right. Help me into my gorgeous gown. Mother imported it from Paris—Coco Chanelle."

I hold the gown gingerly, and Lola Estelle steps into it. Pulling the dress gently up her body, I place her arms into the long-fluted sleeves—then I deftly button up the shimmering pearl buttons, lining the back of the gown.

"Let me look at you, so beautiful," I observe, as I turn her toward the full-length mirror.

Lola Estelle stands radiant in her white satin gown with the tapering train. Her white veil trails down her back and meets the edge of the train. Her satin kitten heeled, strapped shoes match her dress. I place a bouquet of calla lilies in her arms.

Hildie May enters the room and bursts into tears. "My darling, the most beautiful bride in the world."

"Oh Mother, I am so happy. Let's find Father. It is time for you to walk me down the aisle to meet my husband."

I pick up her train, and descend the stairs out of the house, toward the barn. The sky is crystal blue—there is no wind on this spring day, unusual for Oklahoma. The setting is akin to a postcard; picture perfect.

The rabbi and the minister are gathered in the back of the chuppah. Simon is waiting, in a black suit—the skull cap on his head. He is smiling widely.

Lola Estelle's parents are on either side of her, walking slowly to the quartet music—up the aisle toward Simon. Her mother and father both cry silently, but not Lola Estelle—she is striding confidently toward Simon.

The rabbi and the Lutheran minister greet the guests and conduct the ceremony together. The rabbi reads passages from the

Old Testament of the Bible, and the minister reads scripture from the New Testament. "We pronounce you husband and wife," they say together.

"I love you," Simon says, as he gently tilts Lola Estelle backwards and passionately kisses her.

Under the canopy, between the couple, is the white cloth covering a glass. Simon picks up his leg sharply and brings it down on top of the glass…nothing. The audience laughs, and so does Lola Estelle and Simon. "Try it again," Marlene shouts, in a high-pitched timber.

Grinning, with a bit of a blush creeping up his neck, he stomps even harder—the glass shatters and there is applause and happy shouts of "Mazel tov."

Mother baked a three-tiered angel food cake—it is her specialty, decorating it with pink sugar flowers. Lola Estelle and Simon pick up the knife together and slice into the cake, then they cross arms and feed it to each other. We applaud. I am eager to get my own piece—to taste the sugary confection.

Uncle Theodor gives a toast to the couple. "To my only child, Lola Estelle and her new husband Simon Hilfman; may your life together be joyful, passionate and blessed."

Marlene suddenly stands up, "I also have a toast. May I?"

"Of course," Lola Estelle says.

"Simon, you got the girl, so you better be heavenly good to her or I will come and take care of YOU," Marlene playfully says.

"On another, more serious note, I want to express my concern that your family, Simon, was unable to get visas to come to the wedding. Germany is under siege, with Hitler adding more and more restrictions on those who practice the Jewish faith," Marlene says, getting worked up.

"My vow to you, Lola Estelle and Simon, is to help you monetarily or in any other way, to get your family to America," Marlene says, in her deep sultry voice.

"Here, here, count me in also," cries father, from the back of the barn.

"Marlene and Uncle A.R., Simon and I are so grateful for everything you have done for us," Lola Estelle says, as she rushes first to Marlene and then to my father, hugging them each tightly.

"It's the least we can do," father responds. "Now, let's get the reception party started. We have a lot to celebrate."

I am seated to the left of Marlene. As others at our table have frivolous conversations, Marlene wants to find out about last summer and fall, when I was in Germany.

"What is the general mood there?" Marlene questions me.

"Generally, the German people are not paying a lot of attention," I tell her, "but I keep close tabs on Eva Braun, and through her, I know that Hitler has a hatred for the Jews. Simon was followed by Hitler's henchmen to synagogue and pushed to the ground outside the door."

"Damn him," Marlene says with force, scowling. "His propaganda minions actually had the nerve to ask me to come back to Germany and make moving pictures there. I will not step foot in Germany until Hitler is gone, one way or another."

"At the opera intermission, he asked to meet me and Valentina. Once he found out I was American and Tina was French, he dismissed us, with his haughty voice. He just turned away and acted like we were not even there," I angrily exclaim.

"Bastard," Marlene erupts.

"Let's talk about something more pleasant, Billy Love. I understand you are good at quarter horse racing," Marlene says. Apparently, she knows more about my trip to Germany then she previously revealed. I grin.

"Of course, I was the only woman in the race and I won, so, yes, I am proficient in horse racing, much to the chagrin of the other competitors."

✶✶✶✶✶✶✶✶✶✶✶✶✶✶

It is the day after the wedding. Simon and Lola Estelle left this morning with Marlene and her entourage. Marlene offered them a wing in her Hollywood mansion for their honeymoon.

Kat and I are in the kitchen, sitting leisurely, having coffee and cinnamon rolls—courtesy of mother.

I smack my lips and swab a napkin across my face. "Kat, let's take a stroll around the ranch, stretch our legs a bit, get away from the rest of the family."

"Ok, Billie Love, give me a second to pull on a shirt, pants and a pair of your cowboy boots."

"My parents are pleased you are staying for a month, even though Mood, Liz and Petrus must return to Germany next week."

"I know. It will be fun to spend some time sightseeing—and Marlene invited us to Palm Springs. She just purchased a house there. I understand the city is the new playground for movie stars. Gosh, maybe we could meet some, or better yet, party with them."

There is a rumbling sound as Babe Love literally skates into the kitchen, twirling in circles interrupting our conversation. "What are you doing Babe Love? Mother will have a fit if you damage the oak floors with your skates," I say, agitated.

Babe Love ignores me, digs in her rubber toe pick and completes a flip, throwing her arms out, and turning 360 degrees— landing with a loud thud. "Practice makes perfect Billy Love, and regionals are coming up next week. Why, I am a sure bet to be Oklahoma's champion."

"Nevertheless, you should go to the skating rink instead of practicing in the house," I admonish her.

"It is cousin Kat I came to see--not you," Babe Love proclaims, stopping short of skating into Kat.

"What is it?" Kat asks.

"I was out at the barn this morning and Erikray asked about you. I think he is sweet on you—and he is cute. Big old dimple in his left cheek when he grins. Tight butt, too," Babe Love exclaims.

"Babe Love, stay out of this, NOW," I declare.

"Make me, Billy Love. And Bitsy Love was with me, too, so both of us know he is interested in cousin Kat, here. We are matchmakers now."

Chapter 19

Oklahoma Weather

Enid
1934
Kat

I daydream as I climb unto the first rung of the fence near the horse barn at Howling Wolf Ranch. Hanging my arms through the fence opening, I call for Lobo Love, Billy Love's horse. He comes up close and nuzzles my hand. I hold out a golden apple. He bears his teeth and chomps down, as I run my hands through his thick mane.

"Good boy." I continue to pet his neck, talking softly to the horse as he nickers. It is early six AM; most of the relatives are still asleep. I crept out of the house for some solitude.

My thoughts drift to Erikray Black. Somehow, the last time I was at the ranch, he seemed sinister, not at all appealing to me—but yesterday, I caught a glimpse of him in the field and wow, what was I thinking at the time?

Today I spot him again, coming out of the bull pen; all dark brown clothes, cowboy hat, boots and skin, not quite leathery, sexy. The stupid cliché ruggedly handsome applies to him. He spies me and tips his hat slightly—revealing his jet black hair, which is a little longish, covering one eye. His years in the sun have created tiny wrinkles at the corners of his mouth and eyes.

Erikray's leather chaps hug his thighs in all the right ways, his boots caress his feet—embossed with turquoise inlays. A red bandana encases his neck. He is gesturing and coming closer. Suddenly, he jumps up on the fence rung beside me.

"Top of the morning to you, Kat."

He is so close, I feel faint. My pheromones kick in, as I breathe his scent—soapy, yet masculine. My pulse picks up and my pupils dilate. Never before have any of the German boys interested me like Erikray. Compared to Erikray, those German boys are children, still learning how to take two steps in front of each other.

"Kat, you look beautiful today."

This morning, I meticulously pinned my dark chestnut hair into a chignon, and applied a little rogue and bright lipstick. I threw on a long, navy blue, slightly tight dress that brings out my blue eyes; I pulled on black cowboy boots to complete the look. Now, my attention to my appearance is paying off.

"Thank you, Erikray. You are up early. Everyone else is sleeping in."

"This is the time when I can get things done. Sometimes, the more people who are around, the harder it becomes—everyone thinks they are the boss, you know."

He continues. "As the ranch manager, early rising lets me get perspective on the day, get a feel for the weather."

"And what is your prediction for this spring day?"

"The cattle and the horses are restless, moving together and then apart, jostling each other. The horses are rearing up, their nostrils flaring, whinnying constantly. And the wolves are howling in the distance. You can see their packs; they are biting each-others' necks. I tell you, there will be a sharp change in the weather by this afternoon."

"Really, Erikray, I am a bit worried."

"Kat, the sky is already darkening, see there in the west? There could be heavy rain. I am going to check the storm cellar and make sure we have supplies. I will also need to get all of the horses into the barn, and into their stalls—then we need to lock everything down."

"Now you are frightening me."

"We just need to be prepared. This is typical of Oklahoma spring weather. I am going up to the house now and wake A.R. We may need to call in some extra ranch hands to protect the ranch from the elements. But first—"

Erikray puts his arms around me and pulls me to his chest. Then, before I can protest, he hauls me off the fence, tips me back and eagerly, but firmly, kisses me thoroughly. I can hardly breathe. "Been wanting to taste you for some time now. You didn't disappoint me, Kat."

I pull away and look into his dark eyes. "And what did I taste like, Erikray?"

"Fresh, like a sprig of mint. Exactly what I imagined. I am very perceptive, you know," he says, slowly, drawing out his words for full effect.

"Well you now have your own set of red lips, courtesy of me," I say, laughing, as Erikray grabs the handkerchief from around his neck and scrapes it across his face.

"Come on, let's get up to the house. There is no time to dawdle," Erikray says.

He grabs my hand and we run toward the house. I feel giddy, like a schoolgirl.

****

Mood, Liz, and Petrus gather in the living room of the small ranch house. They are peering at the sky—it is ominous, black clouds swirling, hanging low toward the ground. The wind is picking up; rain is starting to spurt.

I sprint to their porch, and urgently open the door. "Erikray and Uncle A.R. have locked down the animals. We need to all go to the storm cellar—now. Erikray thinks conditions are ripe for a tornado. Enid is in the tornado corridor of Oklahoma, you know."

"No, I was unaware," Mood mutters. "What about the rest of the family?"

"They are already in the shelter—with the exception of Bobbie Love who is in town. Come now," I say urgently.

I grab papa, and Liz and Petrus hold hands. We fling ourselves off the front porch and start running. The rain and wind pick up; I slash the rain out of my eyes—I can hardly see ahead. The shelter is three hundred feet away.

I see it in the distance, a spinning black top coming toward us, touching the ground and then lifting up, picking up everything in its path. The surrounding sky is a sickly yellow and the wind has stilled. "Twister," I yell. The tornado is upon us.

Erikray is standing by the shelter, straining to lift the heavy door. "Hurry," he says.

We reach Erikray—the door gapes open, and we tumble down the stairs: as Erikray is the last one in—he slams the door behind him and pulls the latch. We are safe—for now.

I dry off with a stack of towels and try to catch my breath. I feel my heart hammering and I shiver with fear.

Above us, we hear a furious sound, a scraping across the ground. Loud bangs assault our ears. Leaning into Erikray's neck, I seek out his warmth and reassurance. He folds me into him. I smell his musky scent. It is pitch black in the shelter, the howling wind seems to go on and on.

The power is out. Uncle A.R. strikes a match and calmly lights several candles. Faces appear eerily above the candlelight.

"My God, is this a typical storm?" Mood demands.

"Well, I would say it is more severe than usual, but this is why we all have storm cellars. I am more worried about the damage to the ranch right now. And the safety of the animals." Uncle A.R. replies.

There is a sudden stillness. "Is it over?" I inquire. "No, this is the eye of the storm, the vortex. It is directly above us now," Erikray says.

I sit up straight, gulp, then plunge back to Erikray's side. He chuckles and puts his arm around me to pull me close. "It will be over soon; we Oklahomans know how to handle tornados. It is the cleanup that will be a pain."

The banging resumes for two minutes, then nothing is heard but the pounding of the rain. Slowly, I pull away from Erikray's grasp and try to act brave.

"It went through—we will stay put for another hour. Then, Erikray and I will go out first and assess the safety of the area.

106

There may be some power lines down—and we want to check on the animals," A.R. shouts to us.

****

Erikray and A.R. exit the shelter as the rest of us stay put, waiting for the all clear from them. Papa, Liz and Petrus still seem on edge, but the rest of the family takes the weather in stride. The twins play cards, while Beulah Bell watches.

Billy Love is grinning stupidly at me. She scoots over to my side and whispers rather loudly, "Why Kat, it appears you have a new admirer and you admire him back."

"Shhhhhh, we are getting to know each other. Tomorrow he is taking me into town, for dinner at the Scat Diner and then some dancing at the Gas Lamp Bar. Do you think you can teach me some steps?

Billy Love says, "Cousin, I am turning you into a bonafide cowgirl."

"I am liking the wild west lifestyle and the real-life cowboy. Maybe this storm was meant to be." I giggle, as Erikray pulls open the heavy shelter door. The sun sends beams of light into the shelter. Erikray clambers down the stairs, pulls me to my feet and lifts me off the ground in a bear hug.

"All clear. Unfortunately, there is a lot of damage to the barns and fencing. But the animals are all safe."

"We will all pitch in. It is the least we can do," Liz and Petrus say—in unison.

"This is a vacation I won't forget anytime soon. We Wolfs are lucky to have each other," Mood states, to no one in particular.

Chapter 20

Palm Springs Visit

California
1934
Billy Love

It has been a week since the tornado struck the ranch. The family is lucky that no one was hurt. However, father needed to hire three extra men to help repair the damage. Even now, I hear them shouting to each other, as they repair the fences. "Ralph, come hold this end while I nail the rung back in place."

Our entrance sign to the Howling Wolf Ranch is hanging by one chain, looking forlorn, as it twists in the wind—and the front porch at the main house is a disaster, with missing planks, as if the tornado selected boards for random removal.

"The ranch will be humming along, back to normal in another week or so," father declares, as he surveys the ranch. I am riding along with him in the old black pickup truck. Every once in a while, he stops the truck and throws some debris in the back.

We talk as we ride. "I see my boy Erikray and my niece have a thing going."

"It is pretty obvious, right? I mean, you saw them, father, all lovey dovey in the shelter…And every night since they have gone to town for dinner and country dancing. Kat is talking about extending her visa while she can. She wants to have more time with Erikray and generally explore singing at a lounge in Tulsa."

"She should extend the visa now. Hitler is tightening things up for all the Germans, not just Jews and gypsies. Plus, *The Garden's* business is under scrutiny… the reality of the depression is that people don't have extra money to spend in the clubs over there."

"I will talk to Kat when we get back to the ranch. I can take her to the immigration office in Tulsa tomorrow," I say, as we approach the main house.

Pulling the truck to a stop, father puts the gear in position and turns to me. "Liz called your mother. She, Petrus and Mood are back in Germany. When they arrived at the Munich airport, Viktor Lutze was there, ordering passengers into lines, looking at passports in customs."

"Who is Viktor Lutze?"

"None other than the commander of the Storm Detachment or as they call it in Germany…the SA. It is the military wing of the Nazi party," father says in an agitated voice. "Liz said that one of the soldiers yelled at an old woman and dragged her off to a room where you could hear them interrogating her about her passport. She was crying and asking for her son." He continues, "Lutze is a son of a bitch—every bit as bad as Hitler."

"Father, calm down."

"I will not—and I do not understand why President Roosevelt is being so passive in regards to our relationship with Germany. Why is he not putting sanctions on Germany? And what the hell is Ambassador Dodd doing to be tough on the Nazis? I heard a rumor that he is anti-Semitic."

Scowling, father tugs his cowboy hat low over his brow, and slams the pickup door hard as he exits.

✶✶✶✶✶✶✶✶✶✶✶✶✶✶✶

I seem to be unlucky when it comes to love…twenty-one now and still a virgin. Ridiculous—me, accomplished in the viola, traveled the world, bull rider, barrel champion, etc. etc. Men must be intimidated by me—Harry Zeller and William Butler, my English boys, were not, but I have no romantic connections with them; they are friends only.

My sisters all have steady boyfriends. Bobbie Love is dating college boy Lance Leland Anderson, the star football player at Tulsa University. She brought him out to the ranch—pretty boy, with his slicked back dark brown hair, broad shoulders and narrow waist. Classic athlete—dumber than a post, too. I doubt he will graduate and amount to anything.

The twins are dating the Walker twins. Can you believe it? Identical twin girls dating identical twin boys. Bitsy Love is attached to Judd John (JJ) and Babe Love goes out with Phillip James (PJ). All four of them are blonde and blue-eyed. My sisters are sixteen now—JJ and PJ are seventeen. There are rumors at the high school that they mix up their pairings all the time to prank their classmates. Why even my own family has trouble telling Bitsy Love and Babe Love apart. When they were little, I noticed that Babe Love has a small mole beside her left nostril that helped me distinguish her from her twin. I pay attention to small details.

Now my cousin Kat is paired up with Erikray...my last single friend, unsingled. Is that a word? I will probably hear all about the sex on the way to Marlene Dietrich's winter home in Palm Springs California. We are taking the Duesenberg down tomorrow.

Let's hope the parties Marlene throws will have some handsome, single men. I need to get off the ranch, buy new clothes, including a swimsuit, and have some fun.

Palm Springs here we come.

****

"Kat, it's too bad Erikray had to stay at the ranch, but I have you all to myself," I say, as we travel the highway toward Palm Springs. It will take us two full days to reach Marlene's abode.

"Yes, I will miss Erikray, but I also like girl time with you."

"Tell me about the sex. I can see your lazy sated look every morning when you come to breakfast. Are you on top or bottom?"

"Billy Love, why would I tell you about that? It's personal, between Erikray and me."

"Oh, come on, don't be such a ninny. It is 1934 you know."

"Well, I will tell you Erikray was not my first. There was a performer at *The Garden*. We did it in the dressing room after the show—the first time it hurts and you fumble around a lot. So, with

111

Erikray it is all slow and fast burn. He knows how to make me come every time."

"I never would have guessed you had sex with some random guy at *The Garden*. You seem like such a prude," I say giggling.

"Looks can deceive. Of course, I would never tell Papa—he would have a fit."

"Yes, Uncle Mood would be in a BAD mood, huh?"

"Billy Love, I just saw a sign-- Welcome to Palm Springs. Do you have the directions to Marlene's cottage?"

"Yes," I reply, as we drive into the valley.

The mountains ring the valley, a few of them, snowcapped— deep gray rocks jut up into a brilliant blue sky. I crank the driver's side window all the way down. The 85-degree temperature hits my face as I tilt it toward the sun. "Aaaaah," escapes my lips.

As we continue toward Marlene's, I look at the small cottages with the tile roofs, settled neatly in rows, their yards manicured with cacti garden. Yellow blooms are everywhere. Palm trees, neatly trimmed, reach into the sky. Magenta bougainvillea fall like capes over entry walls.

"Kat, this is a magical place. I can understand why the Hollywood crowd would want to escape the city. Marlene told me studio contracts stipulate stars must be no further away than two hours in case the movie directors need to reshoot a scene—Palm Springs is exactly two hours from Los Angeles."

"My goodness, I want to move here. Oh, I see Mary Pickford out in her yard, honk Billie Love."

I press my palm on the horn. Miss Pickford turns toward us and we wave and smile. "We love you," we shout. She smiles and waves back.

"Billie Love, turn left at the next intersection," Kat instructs, as she reads from the written directions.

I turn left and there it is, Marlene's little brown cottage, surrounded by lush, six-foot hedges. I pull the Duesenberg into the graveled driveway. "Why, it is so cute, a bit different from her mansion in Hollywood," I declare.

I observe the pool shimmering out the back of the house. The sun is starting to set, making the cottage seem mystical against the mountain boulders. I honk the horn, and we quickly jump out of the car, grabbing our bags from the back seat.

"My beauties, you are here," Marlene shouts as she emerges from the front door. "We are going to have a gay old time, nothing but swimming, sunning and partying." Kat and I both get air kisses, then we are led into the bungalow.

I look around. The house has German roots in the décor—cabbage pink rose fabric covers two arm chairs. The couch is a subtle green, soft and luxurious…you could sink into it and never get up. The curtains are creamy silks covering the floor to ceiling windows. "Marlene, your house is darling, did you furnish it yourself?"

"Yes, Billy Love, I did, but Greta Garbo helped me. She has great taste."

"By the way, Greta will be at the party tomorrow night. She is staying just down the block."

"We saw Mary Pickford and she waved at us," Kat says.

"Let's just say I am surprised she acknowledged you—she can be quite the nasty woman," Marlene huffs, scowling. "Now let me show you to your room."

Kat and I wink at each other as we follow behind her. Marlene is wearing the fashion of the moment…dark blue knitted beret tilted at a precise angle over her blonde bobbed curls—a nautical striped navy and white top and blue velvet knickers. Her feet are bare as she pads across the living room, revealing brilliant red toenail polish…which happens to match her lipstick.

"Here you are. Now relax a bit, then we shall have a late dinner and cocktails by the pool. You girls can have a late swim."

I close the bedroom door and squeal to Kat. "We are going to have the time of our lives. And my goodness, the added bonus of Greta Garbo. I wonder how many other movie stars we shall see. Wasn't Marlene funny about Mary Pickford?"

"Marlene is so opinionated." Kat declares. "You know, I heard a rumor about Greta Garbo and Marlene."

"What did you hear?"

"Let's just say they are very comfortable with each other."

"Well, I for one don't believe it. She is married, you know."

"We will just have to keep our eyes open, see for ourselves at the party," Kat whispers conspiratorially.

"Let's get ready for pool time." I reply.

I throw my suitcase on the twin bed and click it open. "Wait till you see my new swim suit." Reaching between the tissue layers, I pull out my prize—a gleaming solid white suit which ties in a bow around the neck—the lower half of the suit features tiny shorts.

"Oh, Billy Love, I am so jealous. Father made me wear my suit from last year—an old rag."

"Now Kat, it is precious, in that baby blue color. It makes your eyes stand out."

"You are just being nice, cousin."

"No, I mean it. Come, let's get our suits on."

Quickly, we strip out of our sundresses—tugging and pulling the suits up over our hips and breasts. Kat ties my suit in a bow around my neck. We pull our dark tresses into ponytails and look at each other in the full-length mirror.

Almost identical in height at five-foot six, we have hourglass, yet fine-boned frames. Kat has the fuller bust, I have thinner hips. Anyone can tell we are cousins—we have been mistaken for sisters many times.

We throw our sundresses back on over our swim suits, lock arms and march in lockstep to the back of the house, emerging onto the patio.

Marlene is sitting at a glass table smoking a cigarette in a black holder and sipping a dirty martini. "Come sit with me," she motions us over to the table. "Henrietta has prepared a marvelous meal, dumplings and German pot pie, my favorites."

"Thank you so much, we are famished—we skipped lunch so that we could save time on the road," Kat explains.

We quickly polish off the meal, accompanied by martinis--- then dig into a strudel for dessert. The apple strudel is warm, sweet, and crunchy, with the tangy juicy apples popping with flavor.

"Marlene, this strudel is the best I have ever eaten. Give Henrietta my thanks," Kat says.

"Kat, look across the pool, the sky is pink against the mountains."

"So beautiful, Billy Love."

"Ladies, time for a dip in the pool," Marlene suggests.

Kat and I hug each other, then we strip off our sundresses, revealing the swim suits underneath. Holding hands, we jump feet first into the deep end of the pool. The water cascades up onto the patio, barely missing Marlene.

Our heads pop out of the water...we dog paddle and gasp at the frigid pool temperature...immediate goose bumps pop up on our arms and legs.

Marlene laughs, "I forgot to tell you, the pool is not heated."

****

It is a glorious day in the desert; endless palm trees stretch across the view—backdropped by a cloudless turquoise sky. Various types of cacti dot the foot of the mountains. Marlene has a garden of round cacti in her courtyard...just starting to sprout bright yellow flowers. The heat and the fragrance of the desert combine to make me feel tranquil and languid.

I am still lolling in bed—the window is thrown open, so that at night, when the temperature drops, chilled air sails into the room. The overhead fan whirs above me. Turning to my side, I snuggle under a blanket.

Kat is already out of bed, in the kitchen, having coffee with Marlene. In solitude, I think about the party Marlene is hosting tonight. It is sure to be raucous; Marlene's crowd is not timid in any way. There will be a lot of new people—Greta Garbo, my goodness, and I understand Loretta Young and Clark Gable, who recently became the "it" Hollywood couple, might show up.

Last night, Marlene informed me that she wants to introduce me to a movie producer named Bart Jackson. Apparently, he is single, around 30, and wealthy. I am leery of such set ups, but since Marlene seems to like and respect him, I will spend some time getting to know him at the party tonight. What do I have to lose?

"Billy Love, come join Kat and me for coffee. We are still in our robes, talking about the party tonight."

I throw off the blankets, gather my robe and saunter into the kitchen.

"I was telling Kat about Bart Jackson. He has a reputation as a bit of a scoundrel, but Billy Love, I believe you—if anyone, can tame him," Marlene asserts.

"Oh, great, should I dig out my horse whip?"

"Now Billy Love, Bart also owns and rides horses on his personal ranch—so you two will have a lot in common."

"Alright, one drink and small talk with him. If he is pompous, boring or condescending in any way, I will give him the old heave ho. In this day and age, I should not have to put up with controlling men. I would much rather be independent...like you, Marlene."

"Billy Love, why do you think we get along so well? We both do and say whatever we want."

"Amen to that," Kat chimes in.

"Let's talk about the party tonight. I am going to greet my guests in the front courtyard. There will be photographers there, so I will give them something to photograph. I am wearing a black tuxedo with tails—and a black top hat that I will lift and tip to each of the guests as they emerge from their limousines."

"Oooooh, how decadent. Your picture will be on the cover of all the gossip rags," Kat coos.

"Exactly. I know how to throw a party like no one else. You have to keep the surprises coming. Billy Love what do you think?"

"You are brilliant."

"The caterers will be here soon to set up. Why don't you two get in some pool and sun time. After all, you are on a Palm Springs vacation.

****

Kat and I are glamorized, ready for the party. Marlene lent us her dressing table, which holds every imaginable lotion, powder, makeup, lipstick and eyeliners. It almost feels like we are playing dress up as little girls—but—we are grown women, of course.

I think about meeting Bart Jackson. Marlene showed me pictures of him in the Hollywood Reporter. Not bad looking, although he seems to be snarling in one picture…certainly there are no photos of him smiling. The pictures are in black and white— his hair appears to be light brown, curly. In another photo, he tilts his head toward the woman at his side, she is smiling up at him. He has his arm around her, possessively. HMM—Marlene claims he is single. I will get to the bottom of this, if I have to interrogate Mr. Jackson. From what I know about men connected to Hollywood, most of them are cheaters.

People think since I hail from Oklahoma, I am naïve about the world of glamour. Ha, I went to Germany twice and spent a lot of time in Aunt Liz's cabaret. I know the secrets and the seediness that can be found not so far below the surface of the glitzy world.

"Kat, I wish Erikray could have come down to Palm Springs for the party."

"Yes, I do too, but the clean- up continues on the ranch. Your father is so dependent on him."

"Erikray has always looked after me. I sort of view him as my bodyguard who could protect me from Mr. Bart Jackson."

"Billy Love, really. Marlene and I will be right here at the house. We all have each other's backs, right?"

"I know you do, thanks cousin. By the way, you look marvelous tonight, in your long satin gown. Let's grab some

117

martinis. I need a little buzz before I am introduced to Bart the producer."

We make our way poolside and flirt with the bartender. "Hank, Kat and I are very thirsty. We hear you make the best drinks in all of Palm Springs."

"Why for you, little ladies, only the best. You both look lovely tonight."

Hank quickly mixes and shakes our drinks—he then pours them into martini glasses and hands them to us—we saunter across the lawn and sit down together poolside. I drain my glass in big gulps, then chew on the olives in the bottom.

"Billie Love, slow down."

"I feel better already, Kat, just what I needed—for now, I am done."

Marlene is coming toward us with a guest. I shield my eyes and squint to make out the figure. Oh my, I can tell it is Bart Jackson. He looks exactly like the photographs Marlene showed me.

"Billy Love, this is Bart Jackson, my friend from Hollywood," Marlene says to me.

I jump up and extend my arm to shake his hand, but instead he grabs my hand and bends to kiss it...instead of shaking it. How brazen, I think.

"Why, Miss Billy Love Wolf, you are even more beautiful than Marlene described. And you are a knockout in your blue satin dress that hugs all of the right places, if you get my drift," he says, winking at Marlene, his voice growly and slightly slurred.

It is clear to me that Bart Jackson had several drinks prior to arriving at Marlene's party. I panic a little—it is going to be a long night.

"Just let me grab us some drinks and then we can get to know each other," Bart declares, striding to the bar. "Hank, two martinis, make mine a double."

I turn to Kat and roll my eyes at her. "Be sure to keep an eye on me. He is already drunk."

"I will, but I need to help Marlene put out the food in the dining room."

Bart is suddenly back, glued to my side, putting his arm around my shoulders and handing me the martini.

He pulls me onto his lap and laughs loudly. "Billy Love, where did you get your name? Your parents must have had fun coming up with it. It has a nice ring to it…maybe I will name a character after you in the next movie I produce."

I squirm, push my hand against his chest forcefully and stand up. "I don't sit on men's laps five minutes after meeting them."

Bart is roaring now—and chugging his martini with gusto. The other guests have moved into the house for dinner. "You will do more than sit on my lap, Billy Love, oh yes you will. I have a lot of power in Hollywood. Women flock to me."

"Never."

Bart angrily grabs my arm and starts dragging me toward the thicket of trees at the back of the property. I try to scream, but he slaps me and clamps his big hand over my mouth. I claw at him and scratch his neck. "Damn you, Billie Love." We are in the clump of trees, he is tearing off my dress, and unbuttoning his pants. I am terrified, but unable to get away from him.

"Marlene, come quick, Bart is forcing himself on Billy Love," Kats screams to Marlene, as she runs toward them.

"That asshole. I will be right there," Marlene says, running into her bedroom, where she forcefully opens a bedside drawer.

Kat is a banshee. She jumps on Bart's back and pounds him. He turns around long enough to back hand her hard across the face, sending her scuttling to the ground. I find my voice and scream.

Suddenly I hear a loud crack and watch as Bart's eyes roll back - he crumples. The back of his head bleeds profusely.

Marlene is straddling him, a gun in hand. "Billy Love, always keep a gun handy for pistol whipping when necessary. I was wrong about Mr. Bart Jackson."

"Hank, put Mr. Bart Jackson in the truck. When he comes around, take him to the police station. The party is over for him."

I watch as the unconscious Bart is carted away by Hank. Marlene saunters and sways her way back into the bungalow, pointing her gun toward the ground; I hear her alto voice call out, "There you are Greta, darling. You are late as usual—you missed all the action. Our friend Bart Jackson misbehaved and had to be taught a lesson."

Greta air kisses Marlene as I stare, my mouth open. Greta has on a rhinestone turban—her eyebrows are plucked so thin, so arched, they seem as if they might take flight. Her lips are painted bright red, her cheeks rouged. She and Marlene make a statement together—Marlene in her tuxedo and tails—Greta in her white satin floor length gown and rhinestone turban.

All the guests now surround them, clapping their approval. I fix my dress, find Kat, and join the circle.

"Cousin, this has been one heck of a vacation."

Chapter 21

Eva versus Hitler

Munich
Elisabetha
1934

It is late autumn in Germany. Snow is predicted for the next few days and the wind is picking up—howling really. The mood in Germany is grim these days, as food is being rationed, along with gasoline. The glory days of the 1920s are long gone. Petrus and I decided to shutter *The Garden* four days a week, as we cannot afford to pay our staff—and some of our best performers, Simon Hilfman and Kat to be specific, are in America.

"Petrus, I understand from my brother, A.R., that Kat's visa got extended for a year. She is performing in a nightclub in Tulsa now; living with Billy Love there."

"Liz, didn't you also say Kat is coupled up with Erikray, the Howling Wolf ranch manager? I like that guy—I wonder what Mood thinks of the relationship?"

"I phoned Mood last night. You know how protective he is of Kat. So far, though, he is being cautiously optimistic."

"With everything going on in Germany, Mood is relieved that Kat is safe in the United States and has extended her visa for a full year," I continue.

"I also got a letter from Billy Love. I will read it to you."

Dear Aunt Liz and Uncle Petrus,

I hope you are well. The news coming out of Germany these day is grim. Why, I don't know if you will even get this letter, as it might be confiscated. Father is obsessed with Hitler and his grim regime. It is all he talks about really—he drives mother batty with his rants and responses to radio reports. Petrus, father is especially concerned about Eva, and her mental and physical health. He feels she is being abused by Hitler. Anyway, Kat has moved in with me. We went to see Marlene's new bungalow in Palm Springs California. It was a doozy of a trip. One night she had a party and all of the Hollywood stars showed up including Greta Garbo. Unfortunately, a big time producer (I won't reveal his name) tried to force himself on me, but Marlene pistol whipped him and had his sorry ass hauled off to jail. She is one tough broad. Do not tell father, as he will forbid me from ever associating again with Marlene and her Hollywood crowd. But really, I am almost 22, so what can he really do? Kat is worried about Uncle Mood, too. It is rumored that Hitler's army generals are buying large amounts of drugs from him to give to soldiers. He is under a lot of pressure, but you probably know that. Sorry if this letter is rambling. Love to you both. The Wolf clan cannot be separated now that we have all found each other again.

Fondly,

Billy Love

"We should remind Billy Love not to talk about Hitler and, especially Eva. There are spies everywhere. If Hitler finds out, all of us left in Germany could be in danger of some kind of punishment," Petrus says, scowling.

"Did you remember that we are due at Fritz and Debra's house in an hour?" I ask.

"Yes, we can no longer meet in public places; Hitler has his people in every shop and café—listening and reporting. Then a week later someone disappears. I heard last week that the Jewish shopkeeper Amos was drug out of his home, his business shuttered, and he was sent to Dachau for hard labor. And for what? Being Jewish?"

"Certainly, we all have read Mein Kempt. Hitler's rantings about the Jews is horrendous. Things are only going to get worse for them particularly."

"Fritz has some recent news to share about Eva. I don't know how things could possibly get worse; we need to be as supportive of him and Debra as possible," Petrus says, raising his voice to me.

****

Petrus and I are walking to Fritz's house. It is only a few blocks away and with gasoline rationed, we need to conserve. I pull on my woolen stockings and smooth down my ankle length gray woolen skirt. My cream-colored sweater is a heavy knit—my overcoat is thick—I am fully padded, ready for the elements.

Pulling on my fur lined boots I call to Petrus, "Are you ready? It is time to depart."

Petrus nods and pulls open the heavy front door. The wind sweeps into the house and we hurriedly slam it shut behind us. I lower my head in the wind and grab Petrus's arm. Big fat snowflakes are coming down now, forming a curtain all around us. "Hurry," I say, as we start to run past guards at every corner. A rancid, sewer smell drifts into the street. We cover our mouths and noses with scarves, trying to block the smell.

A guard steps in front of us, blocking our route. "Where are you going?" he shouts at us, threatening us with his gun.

"To a friend's house for coffee," I reply.

123

"Well, you can't go beyond this barrier. Fuhrer Hitler is at his Munich apartment for a meeting with Nazi party officials. Take a different route."

"Heil Hitler," the soldier shouts, as he straightens his arm in the Nazi tribute.

We do not respond. Slowly, we turn around to leave. Out of the corner of my eye, I see the soldier rapidly approaching us. I see him raise the butt of his weapon and swiftly bring it down on Petrus' spine, making a cracking noise.

Petrus is on the ground, moaning and curled in a ball. "That will teach you—it is not good to disrespect the Fuhrer." He strides away and takes his place back at his post.

"Petrus," I scream, as I drop to the frozen ground beside him. "Please, can you move your legs?" I beg.

"Yes, I will be ok," he said, with a catch in his voice. "Help me up. I will have one hell of a bruise on my tailbone."

I help Petrus to a stand and throw my arm across his shoulders, supporting his weight. He winces and leans into me as he limps the two blocks to Fritz and Debra's house. I bang on the door—Fritz pulls it open and stares at Petrus' slumped body, pain clearly written on his face.

"Debra, get the ice bag," he calls. "Petrus is injured." Fritz takes over from me, pulling Petrus onto the couch, lying him down.

"Let me look at your back," Fritz says with a sympathetic voice, pulling off Petrus' coat and hiking up his shirt. "You have quite a knot on your spine and it is looking dark purple, but there is no break in the skin or bleeding."

"One of Hitler's thugs did this to Petrus when he wouldn't pledge his allegiance with that ridiculous salute," I say, with contempt.

Debra enters the living room, skidding to a stop, ice bag in hand. "Nasty," she remarks, as she views the injured back. Placing the cold pack snuggly over the injury, she retreats to the kitchen to make hot tea for all.

"Petrus, you stay on the couch and rest," Fritz declares, throwing a thick blanket over him. "Liz, Debra and I will sit in the dining room and discuss Eva and Hitler's recent situation. Liz will share information with you later."

Debra brings the tea and I sip slowly, trying to warm up and calm down from our misfortune. It was a close call –I could have been attacked too, then where would we be? Lying together on the frozen tundra, freezing to death—or worse yet, thrown into the back of a truck and hauled away to God knows where?

Fritz throws thick pine logs into the fireplace, making the whole house cozy and fragrant. He sits back and begins his latest tale of Eva and Hitler.

"We went to see Eva last week, and boy—is she a mess." Debra nods her head in agreement, furrowing her brow, her lips turned down.

"From the minute, she opened the door to let us in, she screamed, cried and paced relentlessly…we could not get her to calm down enough to tell us what was wrong," Fritz continues.

"Finally, I grabbed her and put her in a bear hug for several minutes to stop her shaking," Debra recounts, "Then I wrestled her onto the couch, got some blankets over her, and had Fritz sit with her while I heated up some chicken noodle soup."

"I spoon-fed her the soup, which she ate to my surprise. Debra and I sat on either side of her on the couch, rubbing her back— after about an hour of this comfort therapy, Eva finally was calm, but in a scary way. She was so flat, you know, just staring, not making eye contact. When she did speak, it was monotone and so soft we had to ask her to repeat her words."

"Oh, my goodness, it seems Eva is worse than ever."

"It seems that whenever Adolf is staying in his Munich apartment, he sends for her. Right now, he is holding meetings at the apartment, planning and plotting for who knows what," Fritz says.

"During the meetings, Hitler tells Eva to stay in the back bedroom. Apparently, they have had many rows about this arrangement, ending with Hitler threatening her, slamming the door in anger," Debra explains.

"Good lord, so he is mentally abusing her—does he hit her?" I ask.

"Eva claims not, but I saw a large yellowish-brown bruise on her upper arm. It looked nasty," Fritz adds.

"There are other issues. The obese, personal physician is constantly giving Hitler medications, both pills and injections. One of those medications is methamphetamine, which Mood says will make you hopped up and sleep deprived. Then the doc gives him antidepressants when he comes down from a manic episode."

"Eva overhead the doctor telling one of his cabinet officers that the Fuhrer has early Parkinson's disease. Eva has noticed that his left-hand shakes. To cover it up, he holds his hand firmly at his side or puts it in a pocket in his uniform.

"Because Parkinson's disease is a neurological condition, it can alter one's mood and decision-making capabilities. Eva does not know from one minute to the next how he will relate to her— she is panicked and starting to doubt her future," Debra says.

"Fritz and Debra, maybe we are coming to a breaking point for Eva—an opportunity for us to release her from the beast's grasp. I will telephone Mood and have him take the train up to Munich. Mood knows every drug known to mankind and every side effect. He also knows what happens when you mix drugs together. He has knowledge of diseases, which will be helpful."

"What are you plotting, Liz?" Fritz questions.

"At this point it just some vague thoughts. Right now, help me bundle up Petrus and take him home to recover."

****

"Mood, Eva is starting to come to her senses. She is seeing Hitler for the evilness and debauchery he spills," I start the conversation.

"If we can get her to agree to leave him, it will make it much easier for us to initiate the plan. We must make a move in the next few months. Germany is starting to isolate itself from the rest of the world," Mood says grimly.

"Only the three of us, you, A.R., and I will know of the plot to smuggle Eva out of Germany. There are too many spies trying to get information to Hitler. I don't think Petrus and Fritz should know either, as they will surely be interrogated."

"Yes, I agree, we might have to enlist Simon, as he has contacts here in Germany with the resistance, but he doesn't need to know the whole plan."

"Mood, once we draw up the plan, I will smuggle a letter out of Germany to A.R. He will be a crucial link, do you agree?"

"Absolutely."

"You complete a proposal and I will do the same--then we can get together and see what works best. Think through the drugs; which ones work best for our task at hand."

"Yes, I will have my idea ready by next month. Why don't you come down to Darmstadt?"

Mood departs and I think to myself—if we can pull this off, it will be the coup of the century. Suddenly, I am terrified.

Chapter 22

A.R.

Oklahoma
Billy Love
1935

I am restless. Life is standing still for me…I need adventure, change and yes, even chaos, to motivate me in new endeavors…to become fulfilled. After our stay with Marlene, which I admit was raucous, considering I was almost raped by a scumbag, I am treading water, bored. Kat is gone every night, singing at the club in Tulsa; or spending time out at the ranch with Erikray.

I don't begrudge Kat, she found her soul partner—but I, on the other hand, have no serious relationships at 22.

Bull riding is in my past, left to my youth (after breaking my wrist, dismaying my parents at the thought of me never playing the viola again, I acquiesced).

Father always encouraged me to be a strong, independent woman—unfortunately, many men want their little ladies to be at their beck and call. That's not going to happen with me. So, if there is someone out there for me, maybe I will find him. I am not going to sweat it. In the mean-time, I am playing part-time in the Tulsa orchestra, and looking for other ways to fill my days and nights.

I go to the Howling Wolf Ranch once a week to help with the bookkeeping. Father is teaching me and giving me more responsibility. I signed up for and started a bookkeeping class in Tulsa. Never any good with numbers in high school, I now see why reading a balance sheet is important when running a business. When something is practical, it becomes meaningful to me.

Today, I am in father's study, hunched over, examining the maze of numbers in the ranch ledger. I can hear my parents murmuring to each other in the kitchen, but can make out no words.

Squinting, I double down, trying to do my job. Father's voice suddenly rings out, "Beulah Bell, did you check the mail?"

"Yes, A.R., there is a letter from Liz addressed to you. No post mark, I don't know how it got here, mysterious," she says, handing it to him. I stand up and peer around the corner. I see the envelope is thick with papers. Father quickly strides out the door onto the porch. I watch him pace back and forth as he reads the letter, scowling, eyebrows knitted together. He lights a pipe and puffs smoke into the cold air. He rereads the letter, then drops wearily onto a rocking chair.

"Father, what is it?" I ask, as I hurl myself onto the porch. Father looks up at me, but does not make eye contact. "Billy Love, this doesn't concern you. It is between Liz and me. Why, I can't even disclose its contents to Beulah Bell."

"But father, does it have something to do with Adolf Hitler? Your mood scares me."

"I need to protect you. I will say nothing further."

"Father, I am not a child, please..."

"Nothing you say will change my mind. Now, go back to keeping the books."

I pout and return to the study. What could that letter contain? I ponder.

****

It has been a month since father received the letter from Aunt Liz. He has not mentioned it once, not once. I am so curious—I even talked to Kat about it—she has no clue as to its contents either. I tried to look for the letter, thinking he stored it in his desk, but no such luck. I even searched Erikray's office, to no avail.

I surmise the letter has something to do with Hitler's reign in Germany. Father is so obsessed with everything going on. Simon told us that many of his Jewish friends are being allowed to immigrate to other countries...only if they first hand over all of their worldly possessions to the German government. I think of the discrimination going on—breathtaking, terrible.

Here in Oklahoma, nobody talks much about the Nazis. The people here are ignorant. They don't want to understand what is systematically happening to the Jewish people, and others, like the gypsies—all sent to concentration camps for small infractions.

I need to find that letter; for now, though, I need to work on the ranch's finances. Entering father's office, I plop down onto his large chair and slam open the ledger—sigh.

Forcing myself to examine the detailed columns of numbers (I am a forest person rather than tree person, by nature), I pursue the past month's earnings and expenses. The ranch is turning a comfortable profit, which is expected. What is unexpected - the number of extra expenses.

Drawing a ruler from father's desk, I isolate the expenses. There is a large payment to an unidentified person—the payment is not linked to the ranch, it seems. Then, there are some unusual items: padlocks and bars; furniture, beds and sofas; train tickets. Train tickets? Are my parents taking a trip?

Talking to myself, I grab a pen and scribble down every one of the mysterious items, then jam the paper deep into my pocket. I slam the ledger shut just before father comes into the study.

"Father, the ranch is doing well, turning a healthy profit," I say, as I greet him, tying to smile. He is in one of his moods, running his hands through his thick, slicked back black mane—scowling, daydreaming, not really listening to me.

I will keep my discovery to myself for now. Playing detective suits me. I am determined to find out father's secret.

"Billy Love, how are you coming on the bookkeeping?" he says, offhand.

"Father, I am learning so much. Thank you for sending me to classes. I believe I am getting better at reading the ledger."

"Well done, then. I know some of the bookkeeping is tedious, since you don't like to focus on detail."

I think to myself, today I focused on detail—jackpot.

****

It has been a few days since I discovered the discrepancies in the ranch ledger. Since then, nothing new has turned up. To clear my head and think, earlier today I saddled up Lobo Love, my beloved horse, and rode at a swift gallop across the great expanse of our ranch. The wind, coming from the north, ruffled through my flowing shoulder length hair; the sky crystal blue, cloudless.

"Lobo Love, you always put me in a good mood," I say to him as I dismount and enter the barn, leading him to his stall. I pull off his bit and saddle, rub his downy nose, and pull an apple out of my flannel lined jeans.

"Here, my darling," I murmur to him, bringing the apple to his mouth. I laugh, as Lobo Love whinnies and chomps the apple, nickering and pawing the ground. "See you soon. I won't stay away so long the next time." I give him one final pat before locking the stall, and head up to the main house.

I climb up the three steps to the veranda—through the glass door I see father in the hallway, his back to me, talking on the telephone, which is situated in the alcove. He is waving his arms about, pulling the black phone cord tautly. The window is open— I can hear his animated voice.

I slow my feet, then tiptoe to the side of the window… I can make out his side of the conversation.

"Simon, I need your help—I need you to contact your brother, Leon, in Munich. There is a pause as Simon responds. "I understand it is getting more and more difficult but it is now or never—the window is closing." More silence.

"The passport and identification needs to read…" father is mumbling now. I strain to hear, but the name is out of reach. Why is father talking to Simon about obtaining a passport for someone in Germany—changing someone's identity?

"The passport destination needs to read New York City. How soon can your brother get the paperwork drawn up?"

"Yes, I know it is a big risk for Leon, but it is of utmost importance." Lowering his voice again to almost a whisper, father directs Simon as to where the passport should be delivered. Darn, I cannot make it out.

Abruptly, father slams down the telephone. I cringe into the porch wall. He strides down the hall, into the kitchen, calling for mother. "Beulah Bell, where is Billy Love? We need to examine the ledger."

"She went for a ride on Lobo Love—she should be back soon. Why don't you have a smoke and a cup of tea? Relax, A.R. You seem so on edge lately."

"There is no time for relaxing—these are chaotic times. I am worried about Mood and Liz in Germany. Thank goodness Kat is here on a year-long visa and Simon is now a United States citizen. Hitler is sending more and more people to concentration camps for small infractions of his imposed laws."

I quietly open the door and slip into father's study. I pick up the ranch ledger and stride into the kitchen, where my parents seem to be squaring off with each other, staring each other down.

"Here I am, ready to work," I grin.

"It's about time," father grumbles.

My mind is wrapped around the new pieces of information I just gleaned. What does it mean and how does it relate to the expenses I discovered?

****

Kat and I are home together in our apartment tonight—indeed, a rare event. We ordered Chinese chicken with broccoli carryout from the China Palace. We are digging into the cardboard boxes with our chopsticks…chatting with our mouths full. Finally, full, I turn to Kat with a serious expression.

"I have made some discoveries at the ranch that have something to do with the letter Liz sent to father, you know, the one I told you about."

133

"Billy Love, really, should we be meddling into something that your father wants to keep confidential?" Kat says, as she leans back onto the couch and stretches her legs up on the coffee table.

"Absolutely we should. I know it has something to do with Aunt Liz. She and others might be in danger. I am sure it has to do with the Nazis and if we can help in any way, we should. Too many Americans are turning their backs on ordinary people in Germany. Why, don't you remember how Uncle Petrus was struck in the back by the Nazi goon—for not returning the Heil Hitler salute, for God's sake."

"I supposed you are right," Kat says, wearily, "tell me what you found out, Sherlock Holmes."

"I made two big discoveries. One, when reviewing the Howling Wolf ranch's ledger, there were some odd, extra expenses."

"Like what?"

"Oh, furniture items, a bed, two chairs, a kitchen table. And padlocks and bars—weird don't you think?"

"Certainly, the main house is crammed with furniture. There is no need for anything new. Wait, right after we stayed at the guest house for Simon and Lola Estelle's wedding, wasn't there a small fire in the kitchen?"

"Yes, the smoke ruined the furniture. Father threw it all out and had the house fumigated. But why is he ordering all of this now? It has been many months; it seems to come out of the blue," I say, with suspicion.

"Another big expense I found--two train tickets purchased for travel from New York to Tulsa. I have looked for them in father's study, but so far, no luck. I have no idea who they are for or the dates of the travel."

"Wow, that is interesting."

"The second piece of evidence—I eavesdropped a conversation father had with Simon. Of course, I could only hear father's end."

"Billy Love, you eavesdropped, really," Kat exclaims.

"Listen, this is important information. Father asked Simon to contact his brother in Germany and get a passport and identification papers for someone. He lowered his voice and I was unable to make out the name."

"This is real now. I finally see how you would be concerned about your father's involvement."

"Kat, I think your father is involved in all of this secrecy, too; there is a plot and somehow, my father, Aunt Liz and your father are all working together." My voice is wavering a little, shaking. I continue, "Will you call your papa in Darmstadt and question him?"

"Papa is quite good at keeping secrets as you are aware, but I will try to phone him tomorrow."

"Thanks, Kat." I grin slightly. My life just got filled with a new adventure—a humdinger of an adventure.

****

"Billy Love, I just got off the telly with papa. He was tight as a drum--acted all evasive, pretended life was boring in good old Germany."

"Did you get anything at all?"

"I only got him to confess that Aunt Liz came to visit him last month; claims it was a social visit, to catch up on the family, ha; I don't believe him for one minute."

"Let's summarize what we have so far. The small unoccupied house on the ranch is being outfitted for someone who will stay there; someone who is currently living in Germany. The padlocks and bars presumably will be installed at the small house, either to keep this person in, or others out."

"You have me so far, Billy Love, that seems to be a plausible story."

"Hear me out. The person in Germany presumably will be smuggled out of the country because Simon's brother Leon has access to passport information—he will change the name to an alias. I think the train tickets from New York to Oklahoma means the German will travel by rail to our ranch."

"But, missing from the puzzle is *who, when,* and *how*," Kat exclaims.

"Yes, who is this person? When will the intervention happen? And how will they get the person to New York City? We have more detective work ahead," I say, as I jump up from the couch, knocking over the leftover Chinese food; chopsticks flying across the room.

I clap my hands together, then reach over and thump Kat on the back of her arm several times.

"Damn you, Billy Love, I hate you."

"Brush it off, Kat, you can take a little pat on the arm. Now, which one of us is going to call Simon? We need to have a ruse for calling him, as father swore him to secrecy regarding the alias on the passport."

"Simon and I are close; we talk regularly about what is happening in Germany to the Jews, including his brother, Leon. The situation will be dangerous for everyone involved in Germany," Kat says. "I can handle Simon."

"Sooner rather than later, Kat."

"I am going to bed—more bookkeeping at the ranch tomorrow—and hopefully, more clues."

Chapter 23

Plan A and Plan B

Darmstadt Germany
Elisabetha
1935

I am late for the train which will carry me from Munich to Darmstadt. I scurry down the stairs toward the tracks—people are boarding now, I need to hurry. I clutch my black pocketbook tightly to my side as I full on run toward the open door, leaping into the car and stumbling into an empty seat.

Gasping hard, I can feel my heart beating heavily in my chest. The doors slam shut, the train whistles—we are on our way to Darmstadt—to see my brother and to discuss plans to get Eva Braun out of Germany.

Now that my breathing and heart rate are steadied, I carefully look around the car. It is mostly empty—a couple of college students sit together in the back, kissing and stroking each other. There are no soldiers in my compartment—good. I pull off my drab brown headscarf and heavy olive green wool coat. The car is steamy.

Settling in my seat, I picture the contents in my pocketbook— I secure my purse across my lap; in the false bottom rests the lynchpin of our objective to get Eva Braun safely out of Germany- -a passport embossed with a new name.

I was late for the train, because I was meeting with Leon Hilfman, Simon's brother, in a shadowy alley near the train station. We did not speak to each other—he tipped his brown fedora at me, and I slid the papers into my olive coat.

Then I had hurriedly entered a restroom, locked the door behind me, and opened up the false bottom of my purse to hide the passport.

Now, sitting on the rumbling train, I silently review my plans to share with Mood. My palms sweat as I think of the dangers involved for all, including Leon—he puts himself in danger every day, as part of the resistance. And because he is Jewish…he is under intense scrutiny.

Petrus is angry with me because I refuse to share my ideas. I told him over and over again—it was for his safety. No one can know, not even Eva.

"Miss, may I see your ticket?"

I jump, and sit up straight. "Of course." I unclasp my purse and pull the ticket out. The attendant stamps it and makes small talk.

"I see you are going to Darmstadt."

"Why yes," I say quietly, "My brother lives there. I am visiting with him."

"Have a nice time. I understand the Merck pharmaceutical factory is humming down there, supplying medications for our soldiers."

"Yes, that is what I hear," I respond meekly.

Please go away. I sit back, and daydream about the name on the passport: Giselle Gregor—lovely.

****

"Mood, I almost missed the train," I tell him, as we sit together in the kitchen of his cramped, one-bedroom apartment. He looks pale, his round wire rim glasses are dirty; and his scruffy beard reveals he has not shaved for several days.

"The meeting with Leon was harrowing, in the back alley, but we were able to pull off the handoff without anyone noticing."

"Liz, thank you for getting the passport; it is crucial to getting Eva out of the country," Mood states, warily. "I haven't been sleeping well, thinking about this whole operation, making lists, crossing off schemes as unworkable—trying to understand every angle."

"As you know, I brought the film footage of Eva's cottage. We filmed every room including the basement, so we know locations of all the doors and windows. We also know where the guards are

138

stationed and the times of their shift change. Getting Eva out of the house will be the most difficult part of the whole thing."

"Good, I will carefully go through the footage." He jumps up, entering the small bedroom—then re-emerges with a large black leather satchel.

"Liz, I think it best that Eva has no idea what we are going to do… or when it will occur."

"I agree, she is too high strung and she might give something away, become emotional. I don't think she should even know the name on the passport until she is away from the cottage."

"What is in the bag?" I wonder.

My brother carefully unlocks the satchel, and lifts the lid. My eyes widen as I peer into the bag—there are multiple bottles and hypodermic glass syringes filled with clear liquids—they are all labeled. In addition, there are tubes of pills, along with handkerchiefs.

"As head chemist for Merck, I have access to all pharmaceuticals. I have been collecting them for months—morphine, amphetamines, chloroform, sedatives, ether, and others."

"My plan involves using chloroform and ether to drug the guard or guards, then inject large doses of morphine to knock them out for several hours. Following that procedure, we enter the house, and give Eva enough sedatives to keep her calm and let her sleep. We take nothing from the house but Eva—too dangerous."

"Mood, if we get caught, you know we will be sent to Dachau, right?"

"I am well aware—that's why you, me and A.R. are the only ones who know about our efforts to get Eva to the United States. A.R. doesn't even know about the pharmaceuticals. I am willing to risk it, my hatred for Hitler runs deep."

"I will purchase a black wig, and new clothes for Eva. We need to get her out by the end of 1935. Germany is closing its borders, making it harder and harder to leave the country.

"Our brother purchased train tickets from New York to Oklahoma, so we know our window of time," I say with certainty.

"So, what do you propose after departing the cottage with her? And what do you think of Eva's new identity—Giselle Gregor? Isn't it marvelous?" I giggle nervously, to lighten the solemn mood.

****

After lunch at a small café, Mood and I take a long, leisurely walk along the boulevard on Main Street, trying to clear our minds—contemplating how best to get Eva safely to Oklahoma. We are in agreement as to how to get her out of the cottage in the cloak of darkness. I am reassured that Mood will handle the thugs guarding her—using drugs to render them unconscious.

The street is deserted. We are alone. I share my thoughts. "Mood, I think we should drive over the border to Rotterdam, in Holland, which is a major seaport. I will drive and you can sit in the backseat with Eva and attend to her. At the check point into Holland, Eva will be sedated and calm, perhaps even sleeping.

"It is a seven-and-a-half-hour drive from Munich to Rotterdam, and the sun will be up. If we can make it past the first checkpoint, I feel fairly confident we can pull this off."

"Yes, Liz, good thoughts. I agree; in addition, I know a plastic surgeon from Rotterdam…who is also in the Hitler resistance. I met him last year when he came to Darmstadt—he placed a large order of drugs and we had a brief private conversation—about Hitler—before he left to return home."

"I have his telephone number. When we get into Holland, I will call him. He can perform some minor facial surgery on Eva—so that no one will recognize her. We have to be extra cautious. Following a couple of days recovery, the new *Giselle* can board a passenger ship for New York." Mood explains, pulling the phone number of Dr. Klein out of the leather satchel, squinting at it.

140

"Mood, you need to accompany Eva to Oklahoma; tell people you are her uncle, or make up a scenario. Eva is too unstable to travel alone by ship—she could panic and reveal herself—then get shipped right back to Germany and into Adolf's clutches."

"Okay, I will contact Leon to get new identification papers and a passport. I can't use my real name."

"Certainly not. The Nazis might make the connection that you disappeared with a cache of drugs around the same time that Eva went missing."

Mood and I pick up the pace as we walk into a brisk wind. The clouds hang low in the sky; spitting rain is starting to coat the sidewalks. I tug my coat around me and tighten the belt.

"Let's get back to the apartment. We can finish talking there," I say.

As we enter the apartment, I reflect on our plan so far—this is really going to happen. We are smuggling Eva out of Germany and into America. God help us, so many things can go wrong.

Chapter 24

Secret

Oklahoma
1935
Kat

I am sitting with Erikray—the lounge is closed, the patrons departed. The crowd tonight was sparse; people have no money for entertainment and drinks; a night out is not much of a possibility anymore.

Erikray and I hold hands. He kisses me gently. Tears are slick on my cheeks.

"Kat, what is wrong?"

It is hard for me to speak. I finally utter, "I miss Papa, and I am so worried about him. I tried to call him several times but couldn't get through. The phone lines are either jammed or Hitler has cut off Germany from the rest of the world."

"Did you call Simon? He seems to be able to communicate with his brother, Leon." He takes his handkerchief—gently, wipes my eyes.

"Yes, I called him. But even he says it is too dangerous to call now. Phones are being tapped all over Germany, especially the Jewish people. Leon is running a scary game and it is getting worse every day," I explain, as my voice becomes stronger.

"Erikray, something is going on with Uncle A.R." I blurt out. "A while back, Billy Love overheard him talking on the phone to Simon—asking him to call Leon and get a passport for someone in Germany—also, there are some suspicious expenses at the ranch. You know Billy Love is helping with the bookkeeping there now, right?"

"Are you sure you aren't being paranoid?"

"I am sure. When I called Simon to ask about trying to call papa, I also questioned him about contacts in Germany, how to get

143

a passport. He absolutely refused to discuss it with me—shut down the conversation and hung up shortly after."

"All of this started with a secret letter from Aunt Liz to Uncle A.R. I would not be at all surprised if papa was involved in the situation," I say, adamantly.

"So, what you are saying is someone, you don't know who, is being smuggled out of Germany. And A.R., Liz, and your father are somehow planning for it."

"And it appears the small house at the ranch is being renovated; whoever is coming to Oklahoma, will be staying there—at least for a while."

****

Billy Love, A.R., Beulah Bell and I are seated around the fireplace, in the front sitting room. It is a Sunday afternoon: a quiet day at the Oklahoma ranch. Erikray is tending to the cattle—my cousins are with their respective boyfriends—tooling around in Enid—probably fooling around too, if I know them.

A.R. tamps the tobacco into his prized German pipe, lights it, then sucks it into his mouth. You can smell the smoke the minute you come up on the front porch. Its odor is like heated cherries. I cough a little as he exhales and blows it out into the room.

"A.R., when are you giving up the pipes?" Beulah Bell says, crabbily. "You are making us all sick—see there, Kat is coughing."

"A little smoke never hurt anyone. I enjoy smoking my pipes—one of the few pleasures I have these days." A.R. is frowning at us. I sit back—deep into the red velvet cushions—I am a bit intimidated by my uncle. He never laughs much these days.

I contemplate the first time I met him. He would act shocked (an act) at some outrageous statement Billy Love or I would make—raise his eyebrows, make a silly face, and say, "Oh my!"

Billy Love told me about how he played this crazy game with her and her sisters. He would lift his right leg over his left, forming what he called the 'rabbit hole'. Then, they played the rabbit from

Alice in Wonderland, diving head first on their way to a most marvelous adventure. Billy Love remembers it as a magical time—the giggling and the laughing, the "Oh My."

But these days, Uncle is solemn, angry and grouchy. Billy Love sees it too.

As the fireplace crackles, Uncle A.R. spreads the Tulsa newspaper out on the ottoman—he flips through it, stopping at page four.

"The bad news never stops coming from Germany—and what does the Tulsa paper do? Bury it in a small article. I don't understand why we are becoming an isolationist country, not caring about what is happening in Europe."

"What are you taking about, Uncle?"

"Yes, father, what is it now?" Billy Love chimes in.

"Hitler and his Nazis have enacted the Nuremberg laws," A.R. scowls menacingly, as he waves his hands in agitation.

"What are they?"

"Let me quote the article. 'These laws exclude Jews from Reich citizenship and prohibits them from marrying or having sexual relations with persons of German or related blood'. My God, basically they have created laws that declare Jews are not German. This is unhuman," A.R. says, as he throws off his glasses and rubs at his eyes.

Uncle balls up the paper and throws it into the fireplace; as it is consumed by flames, I feel my face and neck redden.

Billy Love is right, I think to myself. A.R., Aunt Liz and my papa must be wrapped up in a colossal plot. It has to involve Hitler and his grip on Germany—and somehow, Jewish people are part of the story.

I pull a blanket over me and shiver. "Uncle, how do they determine who is Jewish?"

"The original laws used the term Jew, but did not give a definition. The more radical Nazis wanted to include 'quarter-Jews, a person with one Jewish grandparent. Mark my words,

Hitler will use these laws to revoke citizenship, deny decent jobs, and send Jews to labor camps for perceived infractions."

"I worry about Simon's brother, Leon." And wonder whose name is on the passport. There are still more questions than answers.

Erikray wipes his boots on the porch rug and slams the screen front door. He confidently strides across the room, cowboy hat in hand—he leans down and kisses me passionately. He smells of cattle. I do not respond.

"Kat?" he says frowning, as he looks around the room.

We are quiet and somber. And we are all, now, entangled in something that will change our lives forever.

Chapter 25

The Search

Howling Wolf Ranch
Billy Love
1935

It is high noon…I am finished with the bookkeeping for the day. My mind wanders to last Sunday afternoon. Father was, once again, so jumpy and angry about all the evil in Germany. There has to be something else going on—and it all stems from the letter Aunt Liz sent to him a couple months ago. That is when his mood went from dark to black.

Kat and I talked when we got back to the apartment that night. We decided I would search the ranch for the letter. Oh, I know father will be in a rage if I find it, so I must be clandestine, outright sneaky. I have a hunch it might be hidden in the small house; but, of course, father has it sealed up tight as a drum.

"Mother, I am going out on a walk. I will be back in about an hour," I yell to her upstairs.

"Be sure to pull on your boots and take your earmuffs," she replies.

I mutter, "Ok, I am 23 now. I can dress myself."

I slam the front door and head toward the barn. I peek into Erikray's office. Good, he is nowhere to be found. I think he planned to mend fences today. Father drove into Enid to buy supplies about an hour ago—I have some time.

There is a keyring in the desk drawer. I pull it out and examine it. There are ten keys…I will have to experiment. Sliding the keys into my coat pocket, I run out the door. I can hear the keys colliding in my pocket. I arrive at the small house, out of breath—going to the back door, I pull out the key ring.

The second key I try fits—I am in. Looking around, I observe the cottage has been scrubbed from top to bottom. It glistens—no furniture yet, but I know it is ordered. Someone is going to be living here—someone from Germany.

There are three small bedrooms, a sitting room, bathroom and a kitchen. I search each one, opening drawers and closets. I am thorough, tapping on the bricks surrounding the fireplace, trying to see if one is loose. Nothing so far.

The last room is the bathroom. It contains a pedestal sink, a small medicine cabinet and a claw foot tub. I open the cabinet—empty. Then, I notice the claw foot tub's bubbled side butts against the wall under the window, creating a ledge.

I get into the tub and reach my hand onto the ledge. I feel papers rustling under my fingers. Gasping, I pull it out and clutch it to my chest.

Climbing quickly out of the tub, I almost lose my balance. I plop onto the floor and open the letter - It is from Aunt Liz.

It seems surreal as I start to read; for indeed, there is someone who will be smuggled out of Germany and into Oklahoma. I stare and reread the sentence—that person is Eva Braun—and father, Aunt Liz, and Uncle Mood are going to pull it off.

Holy Mother of Jesus. Wait until I tell Kat.

I quickly refold the letter and return it to the tub's edge. Then I rapidly exit the house and return the keyring to the barn.

There is only one question on my mind. What does Eva Braun have to do with the Jews? She is Catholic?

✳✳✳✳✳✳✳✳✳✳✳✳✳✳

"Billy Love, I can't believe it. Are you sure it is Eva? I can't imagine what Adolf Hitler would do to my father and Aunt Liz if this escapade is discovered before they can pull it off," Kat says, pacing back and forth in the apartment. She is still in her pink robe and matching slippers, even though it is already late morning.

"Yes - I am sure. I reread the letter three times. Now I understand why father wanted to keep everything top secret. It feels like our family is working an undercover operation. Aunt Liz didn't even tell father how she and uncle would get her out of Germany."

"And you said Aunt Liz didn't even tell Petrus?"

"That is correct. There are only five people, including you and me now, who know the whole plan. Simon was only involved in getting a fake passport and identity papers. He doesn't know it is for Eva Braun."

"Really, Kat, we must protect each other. I want to find a way to help."

"I am so worried about papa. You know I have not been able to contact him lately."

"In the letter, Aunt Liz indicated that she and your papa were fine—just being very careful."

"That reassures me somewhat," Kat says, sighing.

"Kat, it just occurred to me that there are two tickets purchased for the train. That must mean that either your papa or Aunt Liz is accompanying Eva."

"Oh, I hope it is papa. It makes sense for it to be him. The Nazis would be suspicious if Liz Braun disappeared at the same time as Eva."

"Aunt Liz also indicated in the letter they would act before the end of the year—something about Hitler building a château in the mountains near Berlin—moving Eva from Munich once it is completed. Eva would literally become Adolf's prisoner if she was installed there.

"Okay, my next task is to find those train tickets and get the dates of departure from New York to Tulsa," I say.

"Why?"

"Because I am going to New York to accompany *Giselle Gregor* and, presumably your father, back to the ranch."

"*Giselle Gregor?*"

"Yes, we will call her Gigi. Never again will we mention Eva Braun."

"Got it. One more thing, Billy Love. What does Gigi have to do with the Jews in Germany?"

149

"Kat, I am convinced there is another missing piece of the puzzle. We will find it together, right?"

"Yes, the wolfpack sticks together."

****

The search for Aunt Liz's letter is complete; now, Kat and I are on the hunt for the train tickets. We need to find the date of the train's departure from New York. Based on the letter, *Giselle* and company will be whisked out of Germany by the end of 1935.

Kat is engaging father, distracting him by telling him stories about The Garden, the cabaret in Munich. I can hear them, and the creaking of the rocking chairs, as they converse with each other on the porch. Father is even laughing—a rarity these days.

I lock the door behind me as I start to search father's office—I try to imagine where father would hide them. Yesterday I searched every drawer in the desk, with no luck. Now I examine the rest of the office. The bookcase is too obvious…under the lamp? No.

I glance up at the deer antlers hung above the door. They command the room-- each antler is attached to the side of a large oak medallion. HMMM. I drag a chair over to the door and climb up. Now I am eye level with the medallion. My fingers explore behind each of the thick antlers.

There is a flap of paper-- I am sure of it. I poke my thumb and forefinger further behind the right antler until I can extract the paper from its hiding place.

Bingo. One train ticket. New York to Tulsa, Oklahoma. December 2, 1935. *Giselle Gregor.*

I memorize the date and replace the ticket behind the antler.

Eagerly, I claw behind the left antler and pull out the second ticket.

New York to Tulsa Oklahoma. December 2, 1935. *Glen Garfield.*

Glen Garfield must be Uncle Mood's alias. The second ticket eliminates Aunt Liz accompanying Gigi to Oklahoma.

150

Scrambling now, I hear Kat and father's footsteps tromping across the porch. I drag the chair back to its original position, unlock the door and step out into the hallway.

Smoothing my hands over suede skirt, I hide my glee with a poker face.

"Billy Love, I was just telling your father some tales from *The Garden*. I am sure you have some good memories of your own."

"Why yes, Simon was always putting on a great show."

"Kat actually had me laughing."

"Well, father you could use some lighthearted conversation," I say, as I make significant eye contact with Kat. I am sure my eyes are twinkling, giving me away.

"Where is your mother, Billy Love?"

"In the kitchen, where else?"

Father turns and I wink at Kat.

"Kat, I want to show you something in my old bedroom. Let's go upstairs."

We try not to race upstairs. Our steps are measured.

"I found the tickets behind the antlers—two names, *Giselle Gregor, Glen Garfield,*" I whisper.

"And, the date?"

"December 2, 1935. Soon."

"Glen Garfield has to be papa, right?"

"I would bet a million bucks on it."

"How do you think father is sending the train tickets to New York?"

"Hmm, he has to have a contact there. Someone else is involved. Either that, or he has a post office box where papa, I mean Glen, can collect them when he and Gigi arrive in the city."

"I think there is someone else. A New York City contact. One more secret to unravel, right Kat? Father should be mailing the tickets in the next couple of days."

"Billy Love, I am going to park myself outside the post office for the next couple of days. I know the postmistress well—Ida May Jones—I will chat her up and steal a look at the name and address."

****

Yesterday, I purchased my train ticket to New York City...no one but Kat knows that I am going. I depart on Thanksgiving Day.

My parents think I am visiting Marlene Dietrich in Los Angeles, gathering with Simon and Lola Estelle to celebrate the holiday together.

Of course, nothing could be further from the truth. Something in me changed in the last several years; I have matured—still a risk taker, but I am now more thoughtful. I understand life is not black and white...but gray, with many nuances.

Getting Gigi away from Hitler and out of Germany will literally save her life—I do not see a future for the Nazis in the world.

I see my role in Gigi's life—protector, friend, and confident.

Hitler must never find out where she is located. It would mean the end of our family.

It is the one secret that can never be unveiled.

Chapter 26

The Escape

Munich and Rotterdam
Elisabetha
Late 1935

I am prepared. The suitcase lies open on the bed—in it, three long woolen skirts—black, navy and brown. A black, mannish looking wool jacket sits beside two sweaters, one pink with pearl buttons, and one light blue.

Included in the suitcase are three pairs of underwear and three braziers—nothing fancy, basics. Two long flannel nightgowns and a robe, along with two pairs of sturdy shoes, round out the wardrobe.

Everything is new. There can be no chance of recognition. Even the packed toiletries are completely different from what *Giselle* usually uses. A dark brown, wavy wig sits on top of the heap.

Mood arrives in about an hour. Petrus is at *The Garden*—I told him I was going to visit a friend in northern Germany.

Our selection of the date to move *Giselle* out of Germany is no coincidence, for tomorrow is Repentance Day, a unique German holiday. The Nazis hold big celebrations in Berlin; many of the brownshirts stationed in Munich are pulled to Berlin…for crowd control. Hitler is the center of attention. The situation works to our great advantage—everyone will be distracted. A perfect time to implement our plan.

Mood and I understand that *Giselle* will be at her cottage alone; her sister is in Berlin. And there will be only one person standing guard; likely sleeping, at one A.M.

I click the suitcase shut and haul it down the stairs, where a picnic basket stuffed with food and drink awaits. Then, I grab the passports and identification papers for *Giselle* and *Glen*, along with their passenger tickets for the ocean liner the SS Lily.

****

"Liz, let's go over the situation again. We can't make any mistakes," Mood says, as he lifts the suitcase into the trunk of the car. His satchel of drugs sits on the front seat.

"I'll drive and park about a block away. You go first - render the guard unconscious, then I will enter through the back door, get Eva disguised, and give her—her new identity. *Giselle Gregor.* You will give her a sedative as we depart for Rotterdam," I explain.

"I need to knock the guard out for at least seven hours… so that we cross the border into Amsterdam before he wakes up and discovers she is gone."

"*Giselle* will be surprised at our intrusion, but hopefully I will call out to her and calm her as I enter the cottage. She knows something is going to happen, just not the semantics and the timing of it," I say.

"The trip to Rotterdam takes about seven-and-a-half hours. That puts our arrival at Dr. Klein's office around eight-thirty. He will perform the surgery there. Then, we check into the hotel for 3 days, apply heavy makeup over the bruising and dye her hair chestnut brown," I continue.

"We have an airtight plan. Let's hope it works," Mood declares.

****

The night sky is inky, with low lying clouds blocking the moonlight. I park the car and quietly turn to Mood.

"Ready?"

Mood grabs his satchel and a flashlight. "Give me 10 minutes. I will knock the guard out with chloroform, then administer a large dose of Morphine."

I watch as he exits the car and stealthily makes his way down the street. When he disappears, I quickly check my package holding clothing and the wig. Saying a silent prayer, I pick my way toward the cottage. I hear no sign of a struggle. Good or bad news?

154

The cottage is just ahead. I can see a figure lying on the porch, with another standing over him—Mood. My heart thumps. I run to the side of the porch, my face questioning, my brow furrowed. Mood is reaching into his satchel, pulling out the syringe of morphine. The strong smell of chloroform reeks from the handkerchief, which rests on the guard's chest.

"Thank goodness, Mood." I say, as I watch him swiftly inject the syringe into the guard's upper arm.

"Go ahead and enter the house. I will be there shortly," he says curtly.

My boots crunch on the gravel as I creep to the back door. Every movement seems amplified, although it is all in my mind.

I call out as I turn the key in the lock. "Eva, it is Aunt Liz."

"Aunt Liz, what are you doing here, in the middle of the night?" she says, her voice quivering. She is standing in the hallway, leaning against her bedroom door, looking disheveled and confused.

"Mood and I are taking you out of Germany tonight."

"Tonight?" Tears start to leak slowly down her cheeks.

"Yes," I say as I hug her to me. "We must act swiftly. Come, put on this skirt and sweater."

Eva is wooden, standing still, trying to process what is happening to her. I peel off her nightgown and dress her in the new clothes…then I pull the wig into place and smooth out the curls.

"Aunt Liz where are we going?"

"It is still a secret for you. As of right now, you are no longer Eva Braun. Your passport and identification papers name you *Giselle Gregor*."

"*Giselle Gregor?*"

"That's right."

There is a sudden commotion in the front hallway. I run toward it…Mood is dragging the drugged guard inside.

"Can't leave him outside so that others see him when the sun comes up." He grabs the guard's gun and stuffs it into the leather satchel. Then he straightens, and turns toward us. "This gun might come in handy."

"Hello Giselle, I am Glen Garfield and I am taking a trip with you. I am your uncle."

"Mood?"

"Nope, from now on, *Glen*."

"Oookay," she says, stammering.

"Here is a sedative. Take it. I want you to sleep as much as possible on our journey."

****

Giselle dozes in the back seat of the sedan, snoring gently, her head thrown back. I drive as *Glen* stretches his legs in the passenger seat. Our plot is working so far, but the journey is far from over. We will reach the Germany/Netherlands border in an hour—the Nazi soldiers will ask for our passports at the checkpoint. It is imperative we all remain calm.

"Madam, may I see your passport?" the young, tow headed soldier says, as he leans into the window.

He can't be more than seventeen. I observe the red arm band embossed with the swastika.

"Why certainly, and here are the other two passports. We are traveling to Rotterdam—our extended family lives there."

The soldier barely glances at the passports, but he does peer into the back seat. "*Miss Giselle,* you are right pretty. I would love to take you out sometime."

Giselle stares back at him and replies coyly, in a mysterious voice, "Why, thank you soldier, but I am already taken by another soldier."

"Is that right? What a shame. All right, now, you have a good trip to Rotterdam." He waves us through the checkpoint.

We are out of Germany. Relieved, we stop at a park to eat some cheese and freshly baked bread.

Giselle is more alert now, and asking questions.

"Why are we going to Rotterdam?"

"We are taking you to see Dr. Klein, a plastic surgeon," I say.

"What are you talking about?" She says, alarm ringing in her voice.

"It has to be done. Once Hitler finds you are gone, he will search for you. You no longer exist. It is the only way."

****

It is morning in Rotterdam—people are in the streets, rushing to work, or sitting leisurely at small cafes throughout the city, enjoying coffee and pastries. I pull the car behind Dr. Klein's office.

"Giselle, put on this head scarf and these sunglasses. Dr. Klein is expecting us…you are the only patient today," I say.

Glen (Yes, Glen, not Mood) gave her another sedative a couple of hours ago. She is docile now, but solemn and pale. I put my arm around her shoulders and usher her up the stairs to the second-floor office. Glen follows behind us, clutching his satchel full of medications.

Dr. Klein is waiting at the top of the stairs. He is wearing a white lab coat; a stethoscope hangs around his neck. He says kindly, "Hello Giselle, I am Dr. Klein, please come into my office where we can talk."

She is shaky, her legs buckle a bit. Dr. Klein and I each take an arm and escort her to an overstuffed chair, where she collapses. Only now is she realizing the enormity of her life-changing situation.

Dr. Klein gently takes Giselle's hand and talks softly to her. "I am going to do facial contouring surgery to change your appearance. It will involve reshaping your nose, making the bridge thinner. I also will complete cheek and chin implants which will make your face longer, not as round."

Giselle listens silently—grimacing.

"Do you trust me? Once the surgery is complete, I have arranged for you to stay at the Rotterdam Hotel for a few days. I will visit every day and check on you."

Wide eyed, Giselle nods.

"I brought the ether, Dr. Klein. I will administer it prior and during the surgery. I also have pain medications with me, and of course, sedatives," Glen interjects.

I volunteer to stay in the waiting room—as Giselle is helped into the surgical suite by Glen and Dr. Klein, I lean back and shut my eyes. It has been a very long twenty-four hours.

****

I must have dozed off—I awake to the sound of Glen's voice.

"The surgery is complete—it went well. Giselle is sleeping for a few hours. At nightfall, we will go to the hotel. Dr. Klein has arranged for us to enter through the back entrance."

Entering the recovery area, I observe Giselle's bandaged face. She is sleeping, her breathing even and shallow.

"Thank you so much, Dr. Klein. I know the risk you took to help us."

"Hitler must be stopped—and if this is one small way to contribute to the resistance… it is worth the risk."

"Here is a payment for the surgery," I say, as I reach into my purse and pull out a roll of money.

"Absolutely not. This one is on the house," he says adamantly. "Now, let's get Giselle to the hotel."

Chapter 27

The Professor

Oklahoma
Kat
Late 1935

I am sitting in the truck, waiting for Uncle A.R. to emerge from the Enid post office. Billy Love telephoned me this morning—warning me that he was headed to the post office with the letter containing the train tickets…one ticket for Giselle Gregor, the other for Glen Garfield.

Here comes uncle. I duck under the window of the truck and wait for him to start the Duesenberg. Then, I peel out of the cab, pulling my wool coat snugly around me. It is a bleak day. A major snow storm is predicted. I need to complete my task and report my findings to Billy Love. She leaves tomorrow for New York City.

I take the steps up into the small brick post office—I burst into the center of the room and look around. Ida May is behind the counter waiting on a customer. I stride over to the basket of outgoing mail and glance inside.

"Kat, I will be with you in a minute," she calls out to me.

"No problem, I just need to buy some stamps."

I pretend to be looking at the criminal "wanted" posters, concentrating on each one—but furtively and repeatedly, I look into the mail basket… Ida May is gossiping with Mrs. Jones, not paying attention to me.

There it is—I recognize uncle's handwriting. I am not sure what I expected, but I never would have imagined the person for whom it is addressed.

Dr. Parker O'Rourke
Economics Professor
Columbia University
New York, New York

An economics professor at a university? I am more confused than ever. What would be the connection to Uncle A.R., Liz and Mood....and especially Eva Braun?

I snap out of my daydream, memorizing the name and place listed on the envelope.

"Now, Kat, let's get you some stamps. How many do you need?" Ida May asks.

****

Billy Love is in the bedroom at our Tulsa Apartment, packing for the train trip.

"Why would your father contact an economics professor and trust him with the train tickets?"

"I have no idea, but I will find am going to see him the minute I get into New York."

"But... what if he is dangerous in some way?"

"Father trusts this person--and thinks he is crucial to Giselle's resettlement at the ranch here in Oklahoma."

"Just be careful—I don't want to lose my best friend."

"I will - I have a feeling that Dr. Parker O'Rourke is involved beyond handing train tickets over to Giselle and Glen. My gut feeling is that he will be on the train, escorting them to Oklahoma, making sure they arrive safely."

"Kat, the furniture arrived for the cottage today. Father was all secretive again, telling us that the guest house is functional again. I almost laughed out loud, but I suppressed it—he is so crabby these days."

"Yes, Billy Love, I try to avoid your father, too."

"We got what we needed from him, so I am done thinking about father and his temper. I am packed and ready to go. New York City - here I come."

Chapter 28

Negotiation

New York City
Late 1935
Billy Love

I step onto the tree-lined Columbia campus, headed toward the office of Dr. Parker O'Rourke. Students walk in bunches, laughing together on their way to class, carrying stacks of books. The girls wear plaid mid-calf skirts, topped with sweaters. The boys wear dark slacks with gray blazers. They jostle each other and call out—"Hey, how's it going?"

It is my first visit to New York City...I am a bit nervous, but at the same time, excited to be here. I took extra time getting ready this morning at the hotel, pulling my dark locks into a snugly pinned chignon. With my black and white lace trimmed dress and kitten heeled shoes, I look sophisticated, unlike the giggling young students wandering around the campus. In fact, I feel much older than the immature students, even though I am still in my early twenties. Maybe it's because I have a sense of mission—a sobering mission, one that disconnects me from the carefree students.

As I walk, I focus on the information Kat and I have gathered so far. Father, Uncle Mood and Aunt Liz are all involved in bringing *Giselle Gregor* to Oklahoma—to live on the Howling Wolf Ranch: to get her away from Adolf Hitler. And somehow, Dr. O'Rourke is involved. He has no idea I am coming to his office. Really, I am not sure what I will even say to him.

Arriving at the large four-story, red brick building, I enter and climb the stairs to the second floor. My mouth is dry—I can feel my heart thumping. Pull yourself together, I think, as I stop at the receptionist's desk.

I clear my throat. "Hello, I am here to see Dr. O'Rourke."

"Do you have an appointment?"

"No, I stopped by on the chance he was in."

"Go on in if you must. He is prepping for a class." She is viewing me with suspicion. I ignore her, and her pettiness.

I push the door open and stride into his office. He is sitting, reading a book. I stare. Oh, my.

"Hello, sir." He looks up at me, his brilliant blue eyes studying me. I notice the sandy, curly, somewhat shaggy hair that brushes his collar - and the broad shoulders and small waist. He has on an argyle green and gray sweater, with gray wool slacks.

He stands, and takes off his wire rimmed glasses. He is tall, over six feet. "Yes, do I know you?" he frowns slightly, as he takes a step toward me.

I plunge right in. "My name is Billy Love, and I am here to discover what you have to do with Giselle Gregor!" I finish, out of breath.

"What the hell are you talking about?" he says, menacingly, as he storms across the office and slams the door shut. He is inches from me now. I step back, alarmed.

He grabs me by the shoulders and shakes me. I tremble. "Tell me now!" he says, his tone somber.

I want to scream - but know I can't attract attention. "Let go, let go of me, and I will tell you."

He responds to my tone. Checking himself, he releases me and gestures toward the table and chairs in the middle of the room. "Sit."

I compose myself and sit rigidly—I force myself to make eye contact with him. He glares back at me, waiting for my response.

"My full name is Billy Love Wolf—A.R. Wolf is my father."

His nostrils flare…I see recognition in his steely blue eyes. He pauses—I can tell he is uncertain how to proceed with the conversation.

"And how do you know about me?" he demands.

"Look, you have important information, and so do I. Our mission is the same—to get Giselle Gregor safely to Oklahoma," I say with force.

162

"How do I know to trust you? You are an attractive woman—you could be a spy," he says, angrily.

"So, could you," I retort. "Ask me about the Howling Wolf Ranch in Enid Oklahoma, where I grew up."

"Ok, talk."

"I rode horses and bulls in rodeos. I still ride today. I am at the ranch a lot—I also do bookkeeping. Father and I are close…we also butt heads a lot. For the last year, father has been evasive and angry, mainly about Hitler and what has been going on in Germany."

"What does any of that have to do with me here in New York?"

"Look, I know that father mailed the train tickets to you. The names on the two tickets are Giselle Gregor and Glen Garfield. I want to know your connection to the whole situation. We need to negotiate, if I am to help."

"Who asked you to help? You are a young woman—too young to be mixed up in this."

"This is life and death for my family. I have relatives still in Germany who are in grave danger—and I can keep secrets as long as needed."

"For now, I cannot tell you the nature of my connection to your father. Does he know you are in New York?"

"No, he has been cross as hell. He forbade me to read the letter from my Aunt Liz in Germany."

"You obviously read that letter, Miss Wolf," he says sternly, as he leans back in his chair.

I blush a little, but don't admit anything. I need to keep a few secrets to myself.

"Well, I will be on the train with Giselle and Glen tomorrow, headed to Tulsa," Parker declares, calmer now.

"So will I, only in a different passenger car. I don't want them to know yet—I am relieved that you will accompany the two of them. Giselle's English is not the best—you can translate for her, right, as you have been to Germany several times, giving economic lectures?"

"How did you know that about me?" he stammers, a little unnerved.

"Let's just say I did my homework. Now, how can I help you with the mission, Dr. O'Rourke?"

"Call me Parker, and from now on, we don't use the term "mission".

I notice that he is grinning slightly. A dimple emerges in his left check. He looks boyish, but I guess he is close to thirty.

"Call me Billy Love, and yes, I know, who names a girl Billy Love?"

"It is certainly unique, but it fits your personality," he says, eyes twinkling.

I think to myself—why, Parker O'Rourke is flirting with me.

****

Parker, I mean Dr. O'Rourke, and I are at the train station, waiting for Giselle and Glen to arrive. The SS Lily docked this morning—and the train leaves for Oklahoma this afternoon. Yesterday, we hatched our plan. I am to be observant of any aberrant passenger behavior in my car; he will do the same in his car…sitting with Giselle and Glen. Hours into our journey, Parker will enter my car and sit beside me. If either of us has seen anything or anyone suspicious, we will indicate so by blinking rapidly three times.

If there is an indication that someone is following Giselle and Glen—when the train stops in Kansas City, I will make a commotion—not sure yet what that will be…this will allow Parker, Giselle and Glen to exit the train quickly, without being noticed. Parker knows an economics professor at the University of Kansas who has access to a car. They can drive the rest of the way to the ranch.

There is only one problem—when father sees me emerge from the train he will be livid. However, I am the important connection. He thinks Parker, Giselle and Glen will be on the train. And if they aren't, I hold the key to the mystery. I just pray that father accepts my role. He really has no choice.

I am in a lookout position in the bowels of the train station, hiding in the shadows. Parker is waiting at the bottom of the stairs…train tickets in hand. I study him intently; in profile, his chiseled chin and nose are in perfect proportion on his face. He seems steady, not nervous, leaning back against a pole; occasionally checking his watch. I honestly don't think I have ever met a man so beautiful—and that includes many Hollywood stars. Maybe, Cary Grant could compete.

I think about our conversation in his office. He is still somewhat guarded with me. And, I still have not figured out the relationship he has with my father…but I will.

"Giselle, Glen, so glad to see you," Parker calls out, as two people descend the stairs.

One of them is clearly Uncle Mood (Glen I mean), but the woman is unrecognizable in appearance. She could be a Slavic model—high cheekbones, a pointed chin, an oval face, and a small thin nose. Her hair is raven. She has on a black wool skirt and pink sweater—she is tiny, a waif really. Nothing about her is familiar now - whoever worked on her…fabulous job.

Giselle and Glen shake hands with Parker. Glen clutches a large black satchel as Giselle speaks, but her voice is too soft for me to hear her from my vantage point. Glen looks a bit haggard. Kat will need to attend to her father when they get to the ranch. It is so good to know that he is safe along with Giselle. They made it out of Germany onto United States soil.

The final leg of their journey is about to begin. Parker hands them their tickets, and they board their passenger car, Parker bringing up the rear. He tips his hat toward me as he enters. I come out of the shadows, climb aboard, and take my seat next to the window in my passenger car.

I stare at all the people boarding the train…and I wonder about Adolf Hitler's response to Eva's disappearance—rage, concern, or something else? You just don't know when a person is so evil and demented. What I do know - he and his goons are looking for her.

****

The conductor collects our tickets, as the train slowly pulls away from the station, blowing its whistle in short bursts. I look around the interior of the train, a sleek, art deco design, newly minted earlier this year—it's plush red velvet interior is sumptuous, with indirect lighting casting subtle shadows. The train is powered by diesel and electricity, so the ride is quiet—no clickety clack sounds as the train glides along the rails.

I lean back into the velvet upholstery and try to relax…I take some deep breathes and close my eyes for a few seconds.

"Miss," I hear someone speaking to me.

I startle and open my eyes. A man about father's age is seated across the aisle—apparently, he is speaking directly to me. I become wary. "Yes?"

"Are you traveling alone? Is it your first time on a train? Where are you going?" Endless, pointed questions, he staccatos them out-- all without waiting for me to respond.

I decide to lie vigorously. "I'm a senior student at Columbia University. We just finished final exams, so I am going home to see my parents in Albuquerque, New Mexico."

"Well, now isn't that lovely. What is your major? How do you like living in the big, bad, city? What do your parents do in New Mexico?"

Now I am getting very annoyed. "Economics, New York is great, and my father is a pimp and my mother is a prostitute," I reply, my voice strangled.

"Well, I never. You don't have to get smart with me," he grumbles. My expression is stony as he snaps his newspaper open and pretends to read.

I hope my retort will shut him up for the rest of the trip— however, I am not counting on it. I look around the car itself—it is

166

only half full. There is a sleek table at the back of the car—two young men play cards, probably poker.

One of them continuously eggs on the other. "Hah, got you, Lou. You haven't won a hand yet. Guess you can't read my poker face."

The two seem out of place—too boisterous, as the other passengers relax and read books and newspapers: They act like they are putting on a play. I have a hunch about them. There is reason for me to doubt them and their intentions.

Lou folds his cards and stands up. "I am going into the other car to find another card player, someone who doesn't cheat." He strides down the aisle and enters the car where Parker, Giselle and Glen sit together.

I become alert. I observe the man remaining seated at the table. He takes out a pad of paper and starts to scribble on it. What could he be doing? Describing everyone in our car or something more sinister?

Lou comes back and says loudly, "No takers on poker." He flounces down and immediately lowers his voice, almost to a whisper. I can't make out what they are discussing, but I am almost certain that Lou was casing the other passenger car.

It is two hours into journey. Parker enters my cabin, greets me and sits down beside me. The snoopy man across the aisle raises his eyebrows at me. I will have to tell him another lie when Parker returns to his seat.

"How is your ride going so far?" Parker says, banally.

"Lovely really, for the most part."

"Me too. What beautiful décor, so soothing."

I turn toward Parker. The minute the old man looks away, I blink rapidly three times. Parker looks at me knowingly. The three of them need to exit the train in Kansas City. They are being followed, I am certain of it.

Parker returns to his seat, as I concoct my distraction. I might actually enjoy this, I giggle to myself, ignoring the old man for the time being.

"Kansas City, next stop," the conductor blares.

I feel the train lurch to a stop. Turning to the irritating man, I yell out in a booming voice, "You insult me and my parents! I won't have it." Raising my hand, I jump across the aisle--and swiftly slap him across the cheek with my open palm.

"Now listen here, girly," he screams in pain. He grabs me around the waist and lifts me up, starts to shake me.

"Help me!" I yell. Passengers respond and move toward us, including the two card players. They pull the man off me and push him into his seat. He rubs his cheek, glaring at me.

"Are you okay?" someone asks. "I am fine now, but I want to move to another car…away from that awful man."

The train is moving again; I glance out the window. Giselle, Parker and Glen head out of the Kansas City train station—arms locked.

Phew. Time to sleep. And to think about how to deal with father when I arrive home alone.

****

"Tulsa, next stop."

The train pulls into the station. Looking out the window, I see father far back in the crowd, searching each passenger's face as they step down from the train.

Father is starting to scowl—he sees no familiar faces.

Pulling on a head scarf, I am the last passenger to emerge. I keep my head down, keeping to the edge of the crowd, away from father, hoping he doesn't spot me.

It is snowing—almost a white out—visibility is only ten feet. The weather is in my favor. I put my collar up and run toward the parking lot, where I know Kat will be waiting to pick me up.

I yank the door open and slide into the front seat. Taking deep, gulping breathes, "Kat, wait until you hear the whole story. You won't believe everything that has happened on my short trip. Drive

168

directly to the ranch—I want you to be there when I tell father why Giselle and your father were not on that train."

"Billy Love, don't keep me in suspense."

"It is a long tale, but I need you there with me. I don't want to be alone with father right now. He will be unhinged at first. I will have to convince him I was vital to the "mission", although I can't use the word."

"Huh?

"I will tell you that Dr. Parker O'Rourke is a hunk of a man— he is escorting Giselle and your papa to the ranch."

"OOOh, I can't wait to hear more about the hunk. Where are they now?"

"In route. I will tell you everything when we get to the ranch."

Kat skids into the ranch lane and puts the truck in gear. Father is not back yet—I get out and head directly toward the main house, with Kat trailing behind.

The telephone is ringing persistently. "Hello," I say.

"Billy Love, it's Parker. Tell your father we will be at the ranch by tomorrow night—all is well and we are safe."

"I will, if I am still alive after my confession to father."

"Well, you don't have to tell him every detail, right?"

"Right. Good point. See you tomorrow."

I slam down the receiver. Father is stomping toward the house—and he looks menacing—his face gray and his eyes foggy.

"Billy Love, come into my office. I have something to tell you," he says, as he tugs off his heavy coat and boots. "Kat, this is between Billy Love and me."

"Yes, father, I have to share something with you, also."

"I went to Tulsa today to pick up our house guests but they were not on the train, and I am quite worried about them."

Hhhm, maybe I don't have to reveal my espionage yet. The phone call will buy me time.

"Oh, father, that is what I wanted to share with you. A Dr. Parker O'Rourke called just now—He said a Giselle Gregor and

Kat's papa Uncle Mood, will arrive at the ranch by car…tomorrow night…and that they are safe."

Father looks relieved. He slumps into an overstuffed chair and puts his hands behind his head. "Thank goodness."

I play coy. "Who is Giselle Gregor and why is Uncle Mood with her?"

"Mood traveled on a visa as Glen Garfield. He needed to have a false identity to get out of Germany unnoticed."

"He accompanied our other guest, Giselle Gregor, out of the country, across the ocean and into New York City. They were both supposed to arrive in Tulsa by train. I don't understand why they are traveling by car."

"Father," I blurt out, unable to stop myself. "I know who the other guest is—Kat and I both know, and we will keep the secret—always."

"What? How? Get Kat in here," he says.

I poke my head out the door, only to find Kat trying to eavesdrop on my conversation. I nod and motion for her to come into the office, lifting my eyebrows, trying to give her a heads up.

"Now, you both might think you are playing detectives, but this is deadly serious, life-threatening reality," father mutters.

"Yes, Father, in fact I was on the train and staged an intervention that allowed Giselle and uncle to get off the train in Kansas City."

"Huh? I thought you were at Marlene's. I don't understand," he says, frowning and knitting his bushy eyebrows together.

"To be frank, I lied to you—and I read Aunt Liz's letter. The situation in Germany was untenable for Giselle, or Gigi, as Kat and I call her."

"I took the train out to New York," I continue, "and met with Parker O'Rourke."

"I had forbidden you to get involved," father roars.

I look over at Kat, who is cowering in the corner of the office. I punch back at father.

"If I had not been on the train, it is likely they would have been discovered. Parker and I are fairly certain that two men were following them. They were ready to make a move when they arrived in Tulsa."

"And what was your role?"

"I slapped an old man and caused a commotion."

Kat tries to suppress a giggle, but fails. "When the old guy tried to pick me up and shake me, the other passengers rushed to help. My cover allowed Gigi and Uncle Mood to slip out of the train."

"Uncle, try to understand why Billy Love wanted to help. We care very much about Gigi and her safe passage out of Germany. And with papa involved, well, once again, we are in it together."

"Billy Love, get me my pipe, I need a smoke."

"It is important that no one else, and I mean no one, not even your mother, knows about Giselle. Hitler is escalating his bitter language and implementing all kinds of brutal laws," father says, between puffs on the pipe. "He most likely has some spies within the United States feeding him information, possibly looking for Giselle."

"We understand," Kat and I say in unison.

"And we are concerned about Aunt Liz left in Germany, too," Kat says.

"Yes, Liz took quite a risk. We will need to monitor her situation closely."

"Billy Love, why don't you and Kat stay at the cottage tonight—help get it ready for our visitors who arrive tomorrow."

"Good idea, father."

"And Billy Love, even though you can be a willful daughter who drives me crazy...thank you," he trails off.

I make eye contact with Kat, and sigh with relief. Slumber party with her tonight. I can't wait to talk about the hunky Parker O'Rourke.

Chapter 29

Escalation

Munich
1936
Elisabetha

"Liz, Fritz called. He sounded panicked—apparently, Hitler has summoned him to Berlin…to grill him about the whereabouts of Eva," Petrus informs me.

"Does Fritz know something about her disappearance?"

"No, he is as bewildered as everyone else."

"Then, he can just be truthful."

"He is fearful; I can hear it in his voice."

"Why don't you drive him to Berlin? You can be a witness, give him a pep talk."

"Good idea."

In the weeks since our mission to usher Eva out of Germany, I am calm and steady—certain that Eva and Mood made it to Oklahoma, although it is too dangerous to communicate in any way with A.R. right now.

Through the underground resistance, I learned that Paul Goebbels has Hitler's ear now…guiding him and preparing for the summer Olympics in Berlin, where the whole world will witness the Nazi regime putting on a show.

It is rumored that the propaganda minister, Goebbels, is dismissive of women and their role in Nazi Germany; he considers their place to be raising sons into manhood.

When Hitler became distraught and unhinged after Eva went missing…raging for days, Goebbels allegedly talked him down, telling him over and over again—Eva was creating problems for him…being too emotional, suicidal, demanding of his time.

Goebbels informed Adolf he could have his pick of a million different women; that it will help his image to be seen as the single alpha male leader of the mightiest country on earth. Hitler, the narcissist, listened to the flattery, but he is still paranoid about Eva, who vanished one day. Hence, his call to Fritz and his summoning to Berlin.

I am pleased that Fritz and Petrus know nothing about the disappearance of Eva. Hitler can grill Fritz all he wants; nothing will come of it.

My thoughts turn to my Jewish neighbors—I sigh. The Nazis are increasingly imposing rigid laws and restrictions on them— taking away jobs, forbidding their children from attending public schools, declaring that they are not citizens.

There is a new law, a new definition of the word Jew, designed to protect the pure Aryan race. If only one of your four grandparents if Jewish, you are considered a Jew. Conversion to another religion is not valid—it is a truly evil law, designed to promote blue eyed blonde people, the alleged superior race. Of course, Hitler himself is rumored to have a Jewish grandparent…never mind the hypocrisy.

****

Fritz is back from Berlin, where he received a brow beating from Hitler as to the whereabouts of his daughter.

"Liz, he stomped and screamed, trying to intimidate me, but in the end, Goebbels dismissed me. Hitler clicked his boots together…and strode out of the room, turning his back to me. Then Goebbels ushered me out, with a stern warning to immediately inform him if I had any new information."

"I am worried about Eva. How is someone just gone one day? She could be anywhere, or dead," Petrus chimes in, darting his eyes from Fritz to me.

I keep my face expressionless and say quietly, "You two— keep the faith and stop being negative. There is a good chance she is somewhere safe. I feel it, intuition."

"Well, my wife is distraught. She can't decide which is worse…Eva under Hitler's control, or Eva being kept prisoner somewhere," Fritz proclaims. "It has been weeks now, with no news."

"Let's have tea and scones," I say, as a distraction. I put the kettle on the stove and wait for the water to boil: I contemplate the enormity of getting Eva out of Munich and into the United States.

In the last year, Mood and I have been part of the resistance to the Nazis—joining the Red Orchestra group. Mood grew up in Darmstadt where Dr. Arvid Harnack, the leader of the group, also lived. As one of Germany's economic ministers, he has access to intelligence regarding Nazi plots and policy proposals. Mood initially contacted him, met him for coffee, reconnected with an old friend—and quietly joined.

There is a small group of us undercover now, although our ranks are growing. Only Dr. Harnack and his wife Mildred are aware that Giselle was smuggled out of the country—and I told them about it after the fact. Ultimately, the goal is for Giselle to disclose additional information about Hitler and his top aides that can thwart the evils he is inflicting on Germany.

We are meeting in a barn outside of Munich tonight. With Mood hidden in Oklahoma, I am left to influence the group. Many of the Jews original to the Red Orchestra fled Germany with their families, including Simon…there was no future for them here.

So, the Gentiles are managing the resistance. There are women and mostly older men—all of the young men have been in scripted into the army.

* * * * * * * * * * * * * * * * * * *

We sit in a circle, on hay bales, murmuring quietly with each other. Dr. Harnack and his wife Mildred are here, along with four older men and three young women. I am the only middle-aged woman—probably, I look the least likely to be in the resistance…the kind, grandmotherly figure.

Arvid is a slight man, with a receding hairline. His lips are thin, his nose sharp, his ears big. Mildred sits beside him: attractive, dark hair pulled back, pinned in a bun. Her long face is composed in a serene look.

Mildred was born in the United States; she has the additional skill of translating English into German and vice-versa—very important to the resistance—along with translator, she can break codes.

The preparations for the Berlin Olympics this summer come up for discussion.

"I have been in touch with some U.S. agents who will pose as coaches. Some of you will serve as German reporters and meet with them. The whole world will be watching Germany. It is Hitler's chance to show off—he will be distracted," Dr. Harnack explains.

"Who is your intelligence contact in the United States?" I ask.

"I must keep him under wraps for now."

He continues, "America has an isolationist political position in the world. Many of its citizens, and even President Roosevelt, want nothing to do with Hitler and the Nazis. The U.S. does, however, have a fledgling communications intelligence agency within the army; I am relying on them to gather information that will help us sabotage Nazi operations here in Germany."

Still feeling smug about my covert operation with Giselle, I volunteer to masquerade as a reporter. One of the older men also raises his hand.

"Thanks, Liz and Fredrich. One of the assistant rowing coaches is our American contact; he will be with the team at all events. Mildred and I will give him your description, Liz—you will be his personal reporter for the duration of the games. Do not write anything down related to intelligence. Keep it all up here," he says as he points to the side of his head.

"I guess I better bone up on the sport—really, I know nothing about it except that Hitler and his buddies love rowing, and that they expect Germany to win a boatload of metals, no pun intended," I smile.

"Yes, indeed, the Nazis will be at the event, hoping to sing that dreadful anthem The Horst-Wessel-Lied—it translates to The Flag on High—at the gold medal ceremonies," Mildred explains, frowning. "That song is guttural."

"It is rumored that Goebbels will be scrubbing Berlin this spring, taking down all of the signs barring Jews from establishments...and the Nazi storm troopers have been ordered to refrain from any violent actions against them. Any deemed undesirable people will be sent to a concentration camp. Of course, all of this is done to create a false impression. Part of your role, Liz and Fredrich, is to give the "coaches" information as to what is really going on in Germany, including the number of prisoners sent to concentration camps," Dr. Harnack says, with animation.

I glance at my watch. It has been two hours...Petrus will question me if I stay much longer.

"Group, I best be going."

I scurry out of the barn and climb the car, thinking as I pull away...keeping confidences is hard. I wish I could call Mood and A.R. tonight to hear their voices and ideas. Impossible, at least for now.

Tomorrow I will go to the library and check out a book on how to row. Or maybe, better yet, I will attend some of the German crew practices and learn first-hand. Yes, that is exactly what I am going to do.

Chapter 30

Giselle

Howling Wolf Ranch
1936
Kat

It has been an interesting month at the ranch. Giselle and papa are settled in at the cottage—Billy Love and I made sure they felt welcome…stocking the cupboards with groceries, placing freshly ironed linens and quilts on the beds, fluffing pillows. Every room was filled with fresh cut flowers. We even decorated a Christmas tree, and stuffed it with brightly colored lights and glass blown balls.

Uncle A.R. is clearly relieved that papa and Giselle made it to the ranch. He is relaxed, even jovial at times. I have not seen him happy like this for a year; he comes by the cottage daily to check on Giselle.

Aunt Beulah Bell is behaving peculiarly, avoiding Giselle. She doesn't understand why papa is staying on at the ranch. And she has no idea the real identity of Giselle, or really why she is here in Oklahoma, seemingly out of the blue.

When Papa arrived at the ranch, I carefully hugged him, but once we were in the cottage, I clung to him. We both sobbed…I, so relieved he was safe.

And what can I say about the stunning Giselle? Even with dark circles under her eyes, and a face expressing wariness, the transformation is remarkable. No one would recognize my friend. When Uncle A.R. helped her from the car that fateful day, I stood and stared, dumbstruck.

Now, a month later, Giselle is even more beautiful. Sleep has restored her complexion to a youthful radiance, and she is comfortable with the routine on the ranch. Today, she is sitting at the kitchen table, with bright light streaming through the window, her raven hair clipped back to one side. She knows Billy Love and I are keeping her secret.

Giselle cries most days, but those jags are tapering off. Yesterday, she even smiled and laughed a bit, when A.R.'s Corgi puppy, Pepper, jumped into her lap. "Why you adorable little thing," she commented, as she stroked the puppy's head.

"Gigi, would you like to tour the ranch today?" I ask, stirring oatmeal, then dishing it up to her. I sit down across from her. We sip tea together as we linger at the kitchen table—Giselle in her pink negligee and matching plush robe.

"Yes, I would like that," she says in broken English. We practice English every day—it is improving, but there is a long way to go before she will be fluent.

The first weeks at the ranch, conversations have consisted of banal small talk...what she misses about Germany, especially her family. Uncle A.R. bought her a new movie camera; she has been filming around the ranch.

"Get out of your robe and pull on those corduroy pants and a flannel shirt. The wind is brisk today. Oh, and the cowboy boots with the turquoise inlays."

"I love my new boots, Kat," she says, with a heavy German accent.

"They are pretty awesome. One of these days, Billy Love will get you on a horse—those boots will come in handy."

Today, I am ready to find out more about Eva's life with Hitler and his aides. What are they planning and plotting for Germany?

Billy Love and Parker are riding horses this morning so I will have Gigi to myself—one on one. Phew, Parker, I will think about him later, but "oh, my," Billy Love is smitten with him. I have no idea where it will lead as he needs to go back to Columbia University next week for the start of the spring term. For now, they are inseparable.

Giselle and I pull on our heavy, ankle length woolen coats, don earmuffs and mittens - then head out to the ranch. Uncle has asked Billy Love and me to talk with Giselle. I am not sure what he will do with that information, but I know that I must be discreet and confidential. It is crucial that there be no link to Giselle's true identity.

Billy Love and I are still unclear as to the relationship between papa, Dr. O'Rourke and Uncle A.R.....at this point, we are content to gather information.

"Gigi, my nightclub in Tulsa is cutting back my hours. I guess the depression has affected the nightlife here—no money for entertainment. Anyway, A.R. invited me to stay at the ranch and help you with your English. Parker is going to stay at the main house and I will take the third bedroom in the cottage." I start the conversation with a light topic.

"Oh, good, it is nice to have girl talk. It makes me remember the times with my sisters. I do miss them, although we fought constantly growing up."

As we stroll, I point out the horses in the field and wave to Erikray, who is moving and stacking hay bales inside the barn door. We catch a glimpse of Parker and Billy Love in the distance—galloping their horses, probably racing each other, if I know Billy Love.

"Tell me what it was like to spend time with Hitler in his Munich apartment," I say quietly, as I lock arms with Giselle and stride toward the cattle pastures.

"No one has really asked me about this before—the first couple of years, he was very attentive, fawning over my every wish, with romantic dinners and flowers for every occasion. But once he became the Fuhrer, everything changed. The old fat doctor started pumping him full of drugs. Every morning after breakfast, the doc would give Adolf injections—along with a cup of pills."

"Adolf could be mellow one minute and fly into a rage the next—and he started ignoring me. If I wanted to cuddle, he pushed me away."

"What, from your perspective, made him change?"

"Why, the influence of his aides, always pushing him. Goebbels and Himmler, especially. When they visited him at his apartment, he relegated me to the back bedroom, but I could hear them, did they think I was deaf?"

"Can you give me an example?"

"Goebbels pressured him to make the Summer Olympics the biggest show on earth—to showcase the Aryan race. Adolf really could care less about athletics, but Goebbels kept insisting, and he caved. After Goebbels left the apartment one night, Adolf paced, in a foul mood. He really did not want to spend money on an event of this magnitude. He was intent on building up the military, instead."

She continues, speaking rapidly in German now. "He insisted I immediately go back to my house. As I left, escorted by his henchman, he was speaking angrily on the telephone, yelling. I am not sure who he was berating. The doctor rushed in the door, panting heavily, as I was leaving, probably summoned by Goebbels—to give him a sedative injection—to calm him down."

"Kat, I was scared."

"Gosh, Gigi, I would have been, too. I am so glad you are safe now. But I fear for the German people, especially the Jews and the gypsies."

Gigi is frowning as she relives the memory. Uncle A.R. will find her story useful—she gave me a glimpse into Hitler's psyche. It sounds like he is a drug addict—and his aides are able to manipulate him.

"Let's go back to the cottage now—I think a glass of wine by the fireplace is in order," I say. Giselle nods.

****

"Kat, come on in, we are curious to see what you found out from Giselle today," A.R. says, in a measured voice.

Billy Love and Parker sit in his office, close together, holding hands, looking relaxed following their long ride. I notice...I wish I could tell Erikray the whole story of Giselle, but I really can't. We closed the circle of people with knowledge of her escape from

Germany. Even Beulah Bell and Billy Love's sisters don't know. It has to be this way—to protect Giselle.

I sink into the chair and lean forward with my hands clasped together. "Giselle told me a sad story today—it seems Hitler is becoming deranged."

"What do you mean?" Parker asks.

"Giselle says he has severe mood swings—and a doctor visits him daily to administer injections and pills—sedatives and uppers, and who knows what else? It sounds like he is becoming a drug addict."

A.R. takes in the information, his face a mask, as he sucks his pipe—a cherry aroma wafts in the air. "Can I pour you three a drink before Kat goes on?"

He crosses the room and grabs the decanter filled with whiskey—he pours a finger into each glass, and delivers them to each of us.

I take a big gulp, and my eyes sting, but I go on. "Giselle shared that Adolf is unhappy that Germany is hosting the Olympics this summer. He is not really interested in athletes, and would rather put resources into building up the military."

"Then why didn't he just say no?" Parker queries.

"This is where it got interesting. Apparently, Paul Goebbels, the propaganda minister, pushed Hitler to host the games. Convinced him that the world would see Germany as this great Aryan race."

"Wow, so his aide essentially made the decision for him," Billy Love exclaims.

"Yes, indeed, his top assistants are able to manipulate him when important decisions are being made. Giselle also mentioned Henrich Himmler, the head of the SS, as an influence."

"Kat, great work. This information will be very useful," A.R. says, as he drains his glass, and puts his pipe aside.

"What will you do with the information?" I ask.

"Think of Parker and me as the gatekeepers—for now at least, you and Billy Love can't travel through that gate."

Fiddlesticks.

Last night, papa shared the whole story of Giselle's escape from Hitler with Billy Love and me. The four of us sat around a roaring fire in the cottage—with the flames licking the bricks—blankets piled on our laps as we listened intently.

As papa spoke, I couldn't help examining Giselle's porcelain, fine featured face. Remarkable—no one, not even close friends, would recognize her now. I noticed Billy Love staring at her too—she must have been thinking the same thing.

Giselle looked shocked, putting her hand over her mouth as papa described how he used chloroform and a morphine injection on the SS guard. She seemed unaware of the risks papa had taken to help her.

Today, Billy Love, Giselle and I chat animatedly about papa's scary, revealing story.

"I don't remember much about the first few days. Glen gave me strong sedatives and I was groggy—I slept a lot. Then, I had the surgery and the painkillers knocked me out for a couple more days. I gradually became more alert when we were aboard the ship to New York."

"Where was your plastic surgery done?" I ask.

"Truthfully, I don't know. Aunt Liz wanted me to know as little as possible. If by chance, I was captured by the Nazis, I would be unable to tell them. The surgeon may have been going by an alias—he introduced himself as Dr. Klein, but now that I think about it, I really am unsure."

"Aunt Liz and Glen really planned the whole escape in detail, didn't they?" I say.

"Oh, yes, looking back I am so grateful…the risks they both took. I am concerned that Liz, still in Munich, could be discovered, and something dreadful could happen to her."

Returning to the topic of the plastic surgery, Billy Love asks, "Giselle, what did you think when you looked in the mirror for the first time after the bandages came off?"

"The doctor peeled them off and then handed me a mirror. I still had some swelling, so I didn't look completely like I do now, but—it was such a shock I almost passed out—had to put my head between my knees and take deep breathes to get myself under control."

"My new face was surreal—I don't think my own family would recognize me unless they heard my voice; so, it was an adjustment, and the voyage on the ship gave me time to accept the changes."

"Was it difficult to go by Giselle Gregor?" I ask.

"At first, but then it became a bit of a game. I had to call Mood "Glen"…then he would practice calling me Gigi or Giselle."

"What was it like on the ship, in your new role as Giselle?" Billy Love asks.

"You have to remember that every aspect of me changed. My hair went from blonde to raven, I had a whole new wardrobe, my face was that of a stranger…I even lowered my speaking voice and changed my gait, walking at a slower pace. I pretended I altered my look for a movie role; that helped to get me through each day."

"Did you talk to other people on the ship?"

"Oh, yes, we sat for dinner each night with the same group of people and I strolled the decks each day. There were a lot of older couples traveling home to New York and some businessmen from Rotterdam. I believe they were diamond sellers, headed to Tiffany's."

"Any good-looking, young, single men?" I ask slyly.

Giselle looks a little startled at my directness; she blushes. "Why, the handsome captain joined our table for dinner one night."

"And?" Billy love says, leaning into Giselle's personal space.

"He was quite dashing—attentive to me the entire meal. I found him entertaining and he flattered me, calling me a beautiful woman—it had been so long since a man cared a whit about me.

185

Adolf was the exact opposite of him. No wonder I was so miserable. The captain helped me realize that charming men exist…that I needed to get out of the situation with Hitler."

"Did you see him after the dinner?" Billy Love persists.

"He came to my cabin and we walked the decks together, leaning against the rails, watching the sun set over the ocean. He asked for my telephone number, but of course I couldn't give it to him—and I had to lie to him about where I was going—I told him the state of Iowa, where I had relatives."

"Giselle, how romantic, I can picture him in his white suit and cap," I respond. "I bet it did feel uncomfortable to lie, but it was necessary. You are young, there will be other charming men," I say.

Giselle sighs. "Yes, Glen warned me to stay away from him; eventually, I listened. I stayed in my cabin the last night, said I had the stomach flu."

"So, you didn't see him again after that?" I ask.

"He saw me leaving the ship at the dock and yelled my name. I pretended not to hear him and continued to walk down the ramp with Mood. I cried a little and Mood put his arm around me—comforting me."

"Thanks for sharing, Giselle. We think of you as part of our family now—the wolfpack," Billy love says.

"I accept," Giselle says, smiling now, crinkling her eyes.

"Group hug," I yell, pulling Giselle, Papa and Billy Love into my arms.

****

It is Saturday night. Erikray and I are having dinner together at a high-end restaurant in Tulsa—Noah's.

I took extra time getting ready for our date; laying out my ensemble on the bed. The mid-calf length plum silk crepe dress, which hugs my body in all the right places - the matching silk jacket. The mink cape, just purchased today—divine. Diamond dangling earrings and a pair of gold kid shoes completes the look, along with a sequined black clutch.

My dark brown hair with streaks of red, is styled close to my head. My makeup is chic and understated, with a touch of pink color on my lips. Layers of black mascara frame my turquoise eyes.

I am the first to arrive at the restaurant. In the entrance, I catch a glimpse of myself in the full-length mirror. I look glamorous—it has been way too long—I have been spending most of my time on the ranch lately, clad in my uniform of dungarees and flannel shirts.

I peer into Noah's. There are white linen tablecloths set with bone china and sterling silver utensils. Low, multicolored flower arrangements accent every table; and tea lights shimmer, making the room romantic. Soft, classical piano music flows from the ebony baby grand in the corner.

"Madam, may I take your wrap?" the waiter says to me.

"Thank you, sir, I am waiting for my boyfriend, Erikray."

Erikray is meeting me here—he is coming directly from the ranch. I need to give him full attention tonight. I know he feels I have been ignoring him ever since Giselle came to live at the Ranch.

The waiter pulls out my chair and seats me. Every table is full of patrons, and the room buzzes with conversation. In one corner, a woman shows off her green turban, THE style for 1936. Frankly, I am not fond of it. Too severe and out of place.

I think about Giselle—and the rest of the family.

Erikray finally appears in the doorway. He is dapper, dressed in his double breasted, pinstripe suit, polished shoes and fedora, which he takes off and hands to the girl in the coat closet. His neatly trimmed hair is slicked back with pomade. He is handsome—heads turn toward him. The din wanes as people admire him.

I wave and he glides across the room, kissing my cheek before taking the seat across from me.

187

"You look absolutely gorgeous, Katerina. I think I will call you by your full name tonight. It is such a regal Russian name."

"Why, thank you, Erikray. You clean up pretty well yourself."

"I ordered us some champagne. Let's have a relaxing evening," I say, as the waiter brings over the fluted glasses and places the metal ice bucket and bottle of bubbly beside the table.

The waiter pops the cork and pours the liquid into the flutes. We clink glasses, smile at each other, and drain our glasses. The fizz pops in my mouth.

Of course, we order steaks—it's Oklahoma after all—Noah's specialty.

The conversation moves to life on the ranch. "A.R. is easier to be around these days. Earlier this fall, I contemplated quitting...nothing I did was right. He even criticized the way I herded the cattle and cleaned the barn."

"I agree completely with you. He changed when Giselle arrived."

Upon hearing Giselle's name, Erikray's tone changes, and his voice becomes louder. "When are you going to tell me more about Giselle? I know you and Billy Love are keeping a secret from me."

I shift uncomfortably in my seat and put my finger to my lips. "Shh, keep your voice down. I told you before, you will have to trust me for now."

"Katarina, for weeks I have trusted you, and all the while you continue to ignore me." He is shouting now, pushing away from the table and standing up. The patrons are all riveted, staring at us.

I put my hand on his arm but he flings it away. "We're through, and I am leaving the ranch." He stomps over to the coat check, grabs his fedora, and is gone.

My face is red and I burst into tears. What have I done? The love of my life—I sacrificed my relationship with him. I need to call Billy Love...she will know what to do...she always does.

Chapter 31

Romance

Oklahoma
Billy Love
1936

Kat called me, sobbing. I could hardly understand her—with her blubbering. She was in her apartment in Tulsa, alone, when she was supposed to be with Erikray, at dinner. Apparently, he became defiant and made a scene at Noah's, shouting at her for not telling him about Giselle's identity, and publicly breaking up with her…quitting his job at the ranch on top of it. I know Erikray was under pressure from father. It probably contributed to his behavior.

Kat wants me to fix the situation—she wants to tell him about Giselle's identity, but I can't, it is too dangerous for even one more person to know about her. What if they broke up again and he blackmailed us, somehow? It would be a disaster. Only family and Parker O'Rourke keep the secret, as far as I know.

It is ironic that Kat lost her love, Erikray, and I found mine in Parker. Never in my life have I felt the tingling throughout my body, just being around him. I hope he feels the same way—he hasn't said the L word yet, but I am certain he will—I am ready to lose my virginity to him. My parents seem to like him, although father seems a little uneasy about our relationship…my sisters adore him, especially the twins—Parker is always pretending to mix them up. I gave him the tip on how to tell them apart.

I love the thought that Parker has his doctorate and teaches at Columbia—yet, I still do not know the connection between Aunt Liz, Mood and father. How did father know to send him the train tickets? What does teaching economics at a university have to do with Giselle? One day, I will find out—for now, I am focusing on him as my partner—my romantic relationship.

Erikray came back to the ranch and cleared his things from the bunkhouse. He left a note for father, then jumped in his pickup truck and squealed the tires as he left. Kat returns today—I will console her, but hold firm on my decision.

****

We are in Kat's room, keeping our voices low: not wanting Giselle to hear us. "Please Billy Love, we must tell Erikray," she says, begging woefully, as tears stream down her cheeks.

"Kat, we can't and you know it. You signed on for this; we can't jeopardize Giselle. The more people who know, there are more chances for blackmail. He could threaten father to tell local authorities, or worse, contact the Nazis in Germany—to extort money in return for revealing her identity."

"It seems so unfair, but I will say that Erikray made a fool of himself at Noah's. His angry outburst took me by surprise…maybe I didn't really know him as well as I thought I did. He said he was sick of me asking him to trust me," she moans.

I take my hands and gently cup her cheeks, flicking away the tears; then, I pat her back. "We will always have each other."

"Billy Love, I am happy for you and Parker. I will get over Erikray…" she trails off.

"Yes, you will—as for Parker, it took me a long time to find the right partner, but from the first day I met him in his office, we had chemistry. He downright flirted right then and there—after he grabbed me and shook me."

"I can picture you being sassy with him. You do that when you are trying to act confident," Kat blurts.

"I hate to admit it, but Parker can be intimidating. He really grilled me about the train tickets and how I knew the names on them—finally, I told him about father and he settled down."

"He is returning to Columbia next week, right? Have you two made plans for the future?"

"Oh, I have a plan alright—to seduce him and lose my virginity," I giggle, and slap the fleshy part of her arm.

"Ouch, you and your mother have such an annoying habit of slapping people to make a point."

"Think of it as family tradition," I say, with aplomb.

"Some tradition…now getting back to Parker, how can I assist you in planning your sexual escapade?"

We both collapse backward onto the bed, laughing hysterically. "I think liquor will be involved," I suggest.

"Don't plan it for the haybales; too scratchy."

"Silly, I plan to take him to the apartment in Tulsa - nowhere near my parents and sisters."

"Sounds like you have it all arranged, does Parker know?"

"Not yet, but he will soon," I say.

"Let's go talk with Giselle now, I think she is lonely. Papa is never around for her," Kat says.

"What has your father been doing with his time?"

"He holes himself up in his bedroom. He seems to be writing, but is very careful not to reveal anything."

"I, for one, am not going to snoop anymore. There is more to the picture than we know. Let's just keep it that way."

"Ha, I know you too well. Your curiosity will get the better of you."

"Maybe, maybe not." I open the bedroom door and call out for Giselle.

"Billy Love and Kat, I am filming around the ranch today, do you want to come with me?" Giselle says, as she readies her camera.

"Sure, we have some free time," I say.

Kat walks out of the bedroom behind me. She nods in agreement.

"When will I get to go into the Tulsa? It has been six weeks in the America - I am getting bored…my English is improving, no?"

"Giselle, father thinks it is still too dangerous. There could be spies everywhere—I still suspect the two card players on the train might have been on to you. Father will re-evaluate, but the target is six months. With the dramatic change in your appearance and your increasing command of English, he thinks you will be safe to move around more, be out in public places," I explain, carefully.

Giselle makes a pouting face. "I am sad. I feel like I did in Germany, always locked away in my cottage, with guards surrounding me."

"Giselle, it won't always be this way; you are a young, beautiful woman…eventually you will have a full life in America," Kat says.

"Just, for now, it is difficult," Giselle replies.

"You are like a sister to us. We know it is troublesome, but it will get worked out. Now, let's go out filming—we have a new pony. Then, we can go up to the main house for mother's cooking. She is making beef stew with all the trimmings, oh, and fresh bread right out of the oven. I can smell it from the cottage, drifting across the lawn," I declare.

"Danka," Giselle responds, her mood improving now.

"You are welcome," Kat says, with an impish grin.

****

"Gigi and Kat, why don't we have a glamorous dress up night at the ranch? Kat, you can bring some of your sequined gowns and makeup from your cabaret shows. Then Kat, you can sing and I will play the viola. It will be fun, like the old days when we were in Germany together."

"Great idea, Billy Love. We can invite your sisters; they are old enough to experience a cabaret, with all its bawdiness and fun," Kat exclaims.

We are seated at the large walnut dining room table in the main house, eagerly taking in the beef stew, dipping and sopping our bread into its thick, red sauce. A large canter of red wine is passed around—its rich bouquet the perfect complement for the stew. I take in our family: father, mother, Mood, Kat—and now Giselle and Parker. Giselle and Parker may not be part of my biological family, but who cares, I think of them as part of my extended family.

"Billy Love, I like your idea to hold a cabaret here," Beulah Bell says. "It's about time we have some fun. A.R. what do you think?"

"This is just what we need—I am in agreement, let's get it on the calendar."

"Kat, I got the note from Erikray, giving me his resignation. What the hell happened?" father says abruptly, in a bellowing voice.

"Uncle A.R. I can't talk about it yet, but Billy Love has made me see it was for the best."

"Well, he was a good ranch manager, but there are other ranch hands who I can promote to manager. I will train them myself," A.R. brags, as he holds court.

I make eye contact with Kat across the table…we keep our faces still, but we think the same thing. Father loves to take charge of any situation.

"Mother, Kat and I will clear the dishes. Thanks for the delicious meal—you are a great cook."

"Thank you, Billy Love. Now why don't the rest of us sit in the parlor for a bit. Billy Love and Kat can join us after they clear the table."

"Beulah Bell, I have a headache and will go to the cottage to lie down," Giselle interjects.

"Now Giselle, make sure the bedroom is darkened and put an icepack to your head. Mood has medicine he can give you, right Mood?" Beulah Bell asks.

"Yes, let me escort you back to the cottage…I will check my satchel for pills. Finally, I can be useful."

The two of them don their heavy winter coats and depart, moving toward the cottage.

Parker and father light their pipes and plop into the overstuffed cabbage rose chairs. Mother sits primly in the straight-backed cane chair, trying to clear the smoke away from her, waving her hand in the air.

As Kat and I take the dishes through the swinging door into the kitchen, I hear the blare of the radio in the parlor—Parker and father are listening to the BBC, a daily habit. I am thankful Giselle returned to the cottage…there is no need for her to hear what the hateful Fuhrer is sputtering about.

"Billy Love and Kat, leave the dishes and come in here," A.R. summons us. "There is important news from Germany."

"What is it?" I say, as father abruptly clicks off the radio.

Kat and I sit together on the red love seat. "Hitler has invaded the Rhineland, which is a violation of the Treaty of Versailles. This is just the beginning—he wants to conquer the world—it is the start of World War II. He wants to strengthen his military capacity," A.R. complains.

"Yes, and the Rhineland butts up to France. France will no longer have a demilitarized area; they become vulnerable to an invasion by Hitler," Parker adds.

"Father, what is President Roosevelt doing about Germany?"

"As far as I can tell, nothing. He is focused on job creation and getting us out of the depression. He wants nothing to do with building up our military—he is an isolationist."

"Yes, and I understand there are pro- Nazi groups forming in the United States. They deny Jews are being mistreated and discriminated against—why, they even push back about the existence of concentration camps," Parker says with animation, setting his pipe down and wrinkling his brow.

"Why would they spread these conspiracy theories? I saw the discrimination everywhere when I was in Germany," I reply.

"Even Aunt Liz and Uncle Petrus were victims. When Petrus failed to give the Nazi salute to an SS they rifle butted him in the back," Kat says.

"Oh, dear," Beulah says, her voice quavering.

"What can we do to make President Roosevelt wake up? Simon has not heard from his brother Leon for months now. He is fearful

194

Leon has been arrested and sent to a camp or worse—shot to death," I say.

"For now, nothing. It is too dangerous for our guest. We don't want to draw any attention to ourselves," Parker asserts.

"But......," I start.

"No, Billy Love, chapter closed. I mean it," father says adamantly.

I slump back into the cushions. There must be something I can do.

****

Tonight, is the night. Parker and I are going to have sex for the first time—of course he doesn't know it yet. I am prepared. I purchased a box of the new latex condoms at the local pharmacy in Tulsa. I had to pretend to be married, of course, for they would not sell condoms to a single woman. Ridiculous. The condoms are tucked into the bedside drawer, ready in an instance.

He is allegedly coming to the apartment for drinks before we head to the latest Marlene Dietrich movie playing at the Tulsa Theater. Parker is quite interested that I am friends with Marlene and served as an extra in the western film a few years ago. He is eager to meet her. It just won't be tonight. I plan to take him there when I visit her in Palm Springs this summer.

I think about my plans for the evening. There will be drinks alright, just no movie, at least not tonight. All the action will be in the bedroom. I purchased a matching black bra and lacy underwear to wear under my floor length silk negligee. The clothing is neatly folded on the bed, ready for use.

I sit at the dressing table, applying light, Elizabeth Arden makeup. I rouge my checks, thicken my lashes with black mascara, and apply a deep red lipstick: then I spray a light perfume across my chest... just an hour to go before he gets here. I turn the lights down low and light tea candles throughout the apartment—the radio is on in the background, crooning Billie Holliday. Billie spelled the girl way, not like my boy sounding name.

I am dressed now, my dark tresses curled around my chin. The decanter awaits on the coffee table, full of Parker's favorite liquor, brandy. Two sniffers park beside the decanter, along with a silver bucket filled with ice.

I peer out the window. Parker is pulling up to the curb beside the apartment building. I admire his physique as he bounds up the stairs two at a time—square shoulders, narrow waist, the body of an athlete, not a bookworm. He wears a camel blazer with navy pants—I look forward to seeing him without the blazer and pants.

I step away from the window and wait for the knock on the door. Slinking across the room…slowly, I open the door.

"Welcome, Dr. O'Rourke," I say, in a husky voice.

Parker takes a step back, taking me in. "Wow, I think we are staying in tonight rather than seeing a movie," he says smoothly, guiding me back into the apartment.

"Plans changed."

"Let me look at you. Beautiful," he says, with a husky voice as he twirls me around so that he can see my every angle and curve. My lacy bra peeks out from the top of the negligee where my deep cleavage appears. Slowly, he runs his index finger down the cleavage as he kisses me several times on the neck. With the other hand, he cups and rubs my bottom. I am instantly wet.

Barely able to speak, I motion toward the couch where the brandy waits. He peels off his blazer and rolls up his shirt sleeves, then takes my hand to lead me to the couch. I feel as if I am in a dream. Parker pours us each a double. We click glasses and look at each other intently—our pupils are dilated; our breathing deep and heavy.

We drain the brandy. "Do you want another?" I ask. "Maybe later," he says, as he moves toward me. He sits me on his lap. I can feel his firm, large erection against my bottom. We lock lips as we push our brandy laced tongues into each other mouths. After several minutes, Parker pushes me onto my back and hovers over

196

me—taking each perfectly formed breast out of the cup of the bra, examining them, gently squeezing them in the palm of his hand. I thrust them toward him, knowing he is growing thicker by the second. My deep red areoles and nipples tighten as they are exposed to the air.

I moan as he bends down and takes my hardened nipple in his mouth. Simultaneously, he pinches the other nipple, just firmly enough to make me tingle everywhere. He unclasps my bra and throws it onto the floor then slides the negligee down to my waist. His large hands are spread over my breasts as he squeezes them together, rubbing the nipples with his thumbs. I squirm, anxious for more. I am starting to feel a strong pressure in my pelvis.

He is kissing my stomach now and has pushed the negligee into a puddle on the floor. All that remains is my lacy underwear. He releases me suddenly and commands "Stand up, I want to see you. Walk across the room, then come back," his eyes are glittering. I dutifully cross the room, then return, walking wobblily toward him.

He peels off my panties and picks me up, carrying me to the bedroom, where he gently places me on the bed. He practically rips off his shirt and starts to unbuckle his belt.

"No, I get to do that," I say, with emotion. "Come here." I sit up naked and unashamed, wild with desire. He kisses my neck as I pull down his trousers and free his huge erection which strains upward toward me. I start to stroke it firmly, but he puts his hand on my wrist and flicks my hand away.

"Not yet, I want to bring pleasure to you first, get you loosened up. Spread your legs widely and bend your knees." I comply; then he is hovering over me, the tip of his penis against my vagina. He alternates using the tip of his penis and his finger to stimulate my clitoris. His mouth is on my breasts. I can't bear the pressure; I buck my pelvis wildly.

"Oh, God," I moan-- the waves of sensation keep washing over me, again and again. It seems to go on for hours before I collapse beside him. He has just brought me to orgasm, even before we have intercourse. It was spectacular.

Parker is on his side, pushing his astray locks aside, grinning at me. "Ready to go again?" he asks, kissing me gently, but gearing up. The erection is still firmly in salute.

I reach into the bedside drawer and pull out the condom. "Parker, I can't risk getting pregnant, are you ok if we use one?"

"Of course, if you put it on me," he grins slyly.

I take it out of the box and scroll it down him. I caress his balls and stroke him simultaneously.

Pushing him onto his back, I climb on top of him. His hands reach for my breasts, as I inch the tip of his member toward the opening of my vagina. I start moving over him and he starts pushing. It is uncomfortable, but not painful. I am so wet; I am leaking.

"Push harder into me, it is ok," I say, to encourage him.

"Are you sure? I don't want to hurt you."

"Yes, I want you, now. I need you." Parker plunges into me with three hard pushes.

We both start is move, with Parker thrusting up and down, harder and faster. He is pulling my nipples hard now; I am highly aroused. The sensation of his sliding penis is making me swoon. I throw my head back with ecstasy: as I come again, Parker slams into me ferociously. He groans loudly, moving his hands tightly against my ass, until he is finished.

Exhausted, we are both quiet for a moment, then I roll off him and pull on a robe. Not bad for the first time. Not bad? It was superb. Parker is a perfect lover. He arises from the bed and saunters into the bathroom to discard the condom...I admire his taut buttocks.

Returning to the bed, he admonishes me. "No robe, I want you naked all night," he says, as he pulls the sash off and pushes it off my shoulders. I climb back in bed, nuzzle his neck, and smile. "Want to do it again?" I ask.

"You little minx, now that I know you like sex, you won't be able to keep me away."

"Let's have another brandy. I will be ready again in about an hour," Parker declares.

"Deal," I say.

****

Parker leaves for Columbia tomorrow. In the week since I lost my virginity, we have had sex every day, in every possible way. On the kitchen table, doggy style, even missionary once.

We used the entire box of condoms; another trip to the pharmacy is in order.

Today, I am helping Parker pack for the trip back to New York. The bedroom door at the main house is closed...we can't keep our hands off each other. Parker stops packing every few minutes. We kiss deeply and run our hands over each other's bodies. Even fully clothed, I feel the heat rise from my crotch and breasts—I grind myself against his erection—why, I could reach orgasm with my parents in the room next door. Parker pulls me away. "Shh, let's finish packing now. Tonight, at the apartment, we can go all out." I pout.

This morning, Parker said his goodbyes to everyone at the ranch, including Giselle, who thanked him profusely for his role in accompanying her from New York to Oklahoma.

We are at the apartment in Tulsa. I am melancholy, thinking about the distance between us, and the lack of physical contact that lies ahead of us for the next months. I pace the apartment in my red satin negligee, the deep neckline exposing my swelling breasts.

Parker approaches me and pulls my head to his chest, placing both arms around my shoulders. "Billy Love, it is going to work out. You can take the train out to New York every month until the end of the spring semester...then, I can come to the ranch for a couple of months before I go to Germany in August."

I gaze up at him, confused. "Germany?"

"Yes, I am giving a lecture in Berlin. All of the economists in the world are gathering during the Olympics."

"Be careful, Parker, and make sure you check on Aunt Liz and Uncle Petrus."

"Of course. Now let's take off this satin sheath. I want you naked so I can admire you."

My face is burning as I step out of my puddled gown. There is a deep longing on his face as he stares at my body.

We have robust sex, one for the road so to speak, then we sink into a deep sleep, naked together, spooning. It is morning—Parker departs in a few hours—we loll in bed, cuddling.

"Parker, last night was amazing. I think I came five times. Never could I have imagined so much pleasure—I am so happy and sad at the same time. Finally, I found someone who matches me in every way, physically and emotionally."

"And you are the lustiest woman I have ever met," he continues. "I don't know if I will be able to keep up with you, at least in the bedroom."

"You are the most sensitive lover, always making sure I am pleasured. When I come out to New York, I will be turning the tables on you."

"Looking forward to lots of hot sex, Billy Love."

"Let's get dressed and go to breakfast. Your train leaves in two hours."

Neither of us has said "love" to each other yet, but the strong sexual desire can't be denied. I get turned on when he enters a room--How am I ever going to wait a whole month for sex with Parker?

Chapter 33

Summer Games

Berlin
1936
Elisabetha

All spring, I traveled back and forth to the Berlin suburb of Grunau...watching the German men practice rowing together on the Langer See. My guise is that of a sports reporter from Darmstadt. I carry a notebook and fill it with descriptions and names of athletes and coaches. I know the difference between a coxswain and a striker, the importance of cadence and oar synchronization, with the bending and pulling together of the crew. If rowers are out of step, the boat slows.

The boat races at the August Olympics will attract large crowds. Hitler and his aides are expected to attend—and the Germans are favored to win gold in every event. I am particularly interested in observing the eight-man boat—the finesse and strength required is astonishing—I watch them slicing the oars methodically through the waters, in cadence to the calling of the coxswain.

One of the friendly oarsmen, Helmut Radach, seeks me out when he locates me sitting on the park bench overlooking the water where they practice. He answers all my questions about the sport... he also likes to gossip.

"Coach thinks we can beat the Italians, but I am not sure. I saw some of their times. It will be close," he concludes, as he plops down beside me, clothed in an undershirt and shorts. He has a sheen of sweat on his lightly freckled brow—the sun is beating down on the lake, which is churning and roiling...torrential rains last night brought the water to its banks. We peer out toward the four-man crew. They are struggling to keep the boat steady as the waves pummel the oars, throwing off their synchronization.

"What about the Americans?"

"Nah, they aren't any good. Barely could put a team together. Had to settle for a bunch of college boys who had never rowed before they got to the University of Washington."

"Well, I do want to talk to a couple of the American coaches. It will make a good angle for my story—I called Tim Miller, one of the assistant coaches...he agreed to meet with me when the team arrives in Berlin."

"Hey, would you like me to be part of the story? I could talk about crew from the German perspective, you know, living in Germany—from the Nazi perspective," Helmut says, with derision in his voice.

"Helmut, be careful what you say. I don't think that would be wise. The SS are everywhere."

"Well, let me tell you what is happening. I have a cousin who is a great athlete...we competed in crew together. He would have been chosen for the German team: one day he didn't show up for practice. I went to his house—there was a sign on the door— JEW—the whole family was taken away. I found out later that one of his grandmothers was Jewish. Just like that, a family ruined. And all because Hitler and his thugs want to have this pure Aryan race, whatever that means. Look at him with his dark skin and hair; that disgusting tiny mustache. Anyway, to this day, I don't know what happened to my cousin," Helmut rants.

"So, no Jews can participate in the games."

"That's right. Did you know that Hitler and Goebbels came to one of our practices? Had coach line us all up to be inspected, like animals: made comments on our physical appearances. Hitler told Hans he was too skinny—to put on some muscle. Goebbels stood directly in front of me and stared. Acted like I wasn't there, commented to Hitler that I was small, but sinewy, and looked Aryan...suggested that I might be trotted out as an exemplar German athlete. I wanted to puke."

"Helmet, I am sorry you had that experience," I say, with a measured voice, "but please, please, please don't share your thoughts about the Nazis with anyone else, especially reporters from other countries. It is far too dangerous for you and your family."

"I better go—the next round of practice is coming up," he says, jumping up from the bench. Thanks for listening…and for the advice, I guess."

"See you next time."

As I drive back to Munich, my thoughts wander to Tim Miller, the American coach—my contact. He will have information about the Nazi groups forming in America—I will have messages for him regarding the German resistance that he will take back to the states.

Petrus is reading in the living room when I arrive home. The phone rings and I pick up on the first ring. "Liz, it is Parker O'Rourke. I am coming to Germany August 11 to give a speech in Berlin. Can you attend?"

"Certainly."

"Plan to meet me for dinner. I will tell you where when I arrive."

I hang up the phone and pause before going into the living room. I better get my story straight before talking to Petrus. Parker will have news about Giselle and my family in Oklahoma. From the tone of his voice, calm and collected, the situation at the ranch is going well. I feel an immense guilt…lying to Petrus is not in my nature, but there is no choice now. I am embroiled in covert operations with the resistance. And Petrus and Fritz Braun can't be involved.

"Who was that?"

"The neighbor. She talks too much—said another family down the street was kicked out of their home by the SS."

"A terrible situation. I talked to Fritz today. He and Deborah are hoping that Eva is somewhere safe—it has been six months since she disappeared…it's like she just vanished."

"Well, my intuition about Eva is that she is secure, probably somewhere in Germany."

"I don't know how anyone could have gotten her out of Germany, through all the checkpoints."

"I agree with that thought. Let's go for a walk—it is a beautiful spring day. I will throw on a light sweater, and we can stroll arm in arm like we used to do...talking about Germany in its finer hours."

"Liz, we also need to talk about *The Garden*...I think we ought to sell it. There is so little business these days."

"Not tonight," I say firmly. "Only pleasant thoughts."

****

The American oarsmen and their coaching staff arrived in Germany yesterday, settling into the extravagant Olympic village, where the gateway slogan announces, "To the Youth of the World."

Pictures from the Berliner Tageblatt reveal Hitler and his top aides personally inspecting the village, noting its centerpiece, The House of Nations dining hall. Adolf Hitler, one of the great narcissists in history—and Paul Goebbels, the full-on propaganda bull-shitter, beaming as they visit the site of the pool and the airy gymnasium. In their full military attire and red swastika armbands, they radiate power. Disgusting.

I am headed to the Lager See to make contact with Tim Miller. He will surely have official Olympic credentials. So, I will be able to identify him easily. He doesn't know what I look like. Covert operations need to be air-tight. All Tim knows is that he is meeting an alleged German reporter.

I am dressed professionally—in a suit of khaki linen, the skirt falling midcalf. A straw bowler hat completes the look, along with my two toned flat shoes. I carry the notepad as I approach the dock where the boats are launched.

I scan the area. It is somewhat chaotic—I surmise the first day of practice is always a challenge. Spotting the Americans in their red, white and blue attire, I confidently approach the group of coaches and read their name tags. "Excuse me, Mr. Miller, may I have a word with you about the USA team? I am a reporter from Germany."

Tim Miller makes direct eye contact with me, surprised that I am speaking to him in English. He is a tall, thick-waisted, muscle-bound man, with a receding hairline. "What do you want to know?" he growls at me, making a menacing gesture. "We need to get our boats in the water; there is no time for idle chatter with a reporter."

"Sir, I will only take a few minutes of your time. I hear the Americans will challenge the German team. I want to get your take on the races."

"Alright," he says, grudgingly. "I will be back in a few minutes. Get those boats on the lake."

He takes my arm and marches me up the hill to the bench overlooking the lake. I take out my notebook and start to scribble. "You took me by surprise. I was not expecting a woman."

"You would be amazed…women can easily fit into the landscape. All of the men are being in scripted into the army."

"I don't have much time, so tell me what you know about Hitler and his plans."

"The situation with the Jews is much worse than is being portrayed around the world. The Nazis forbid them to go to public schools and take their jobs away. Every week, Jewish families vanish. I suspect they are being sent to concentration camps. Hitler and Goebbels removed all of the discrimination signs, but they will go back up as soon as the games end. Get the message to President Roosevelt—the German people believe he will not intervene, but we need additional allies here besides Great Britain."

"I will relay the information. What else do you know?"

"There are rumors that the German army will invade Poland soon, where there are many more Jews, especially in Krakow. Hitler wants to eliminate the Jewish race—he is crazy."

"We need something from you, Tim. Rifles, handguns, and bombs. Can you smuggle them into Germany? Here is the address—a barn south of Munich. Memorize it, then tear it up. There is more resistance to the Nazis than you might believe. We are moving forward."

"We?"

"I can tell you nothing more. Do we have a deal?"

"Yes, I will call you on the date the weapons are delivered. It will be on the guise of a follow up article after the Olympics are over."

"Thank you, Tim. And now, I really do need to have a story about your oarsmen. What are your thoughts?"

"Ha, they are a young team, but they work hard and support each other. Many come from logger backgrounds. A few were abandoned by their parents—their experiences as children make them hungry for Olympic glory."

I scribble the information about the team into the notebook on my lap and comment, "Hitler is obsessed with the Germany rowers. I have been watching their practices all spring. One day, Hitler lined them all up…made comments about each one, and not all complementary. He will be in the stands, along with thousands of spectators."

We stand up and shake hands. "Thanks for your time, coach," I say loudly, as members of the Italian team pass behind the bench.

"No problem."

"Good luck," I shout, as he runs down the hill toward the lake.

Closing the flap on the notebook, I stare out onto the water; the lake is still today, a deep blue-green. Boats are slicing through the water. I can hear the coxswains shouting… I spot Helmut in his red, black and gold uniform, methodically pulling and pushing the oars, his biceps and triceps bulging. He is a good person, but I fear for him.

Today went as planned. Next up, dinner with Parker O'Rourke. I will go home, put my feet up, and wait for his call.

****

206

Petrus is at *The Garden*, going over bills and taking stock of our liquor supply—I am alone in the house, replaying my conversation with Tim Miller. I need to get the information about the weapons drop to the Red Orchestra members…in particular, Dr. Harnack. Wait, of course, Arvid and Parker are both presenting papers at the economic conference tomorrow. I will speak to Parker about serving as a messenger at dinner.

We are dining at the Zillemarkt—and it is teaming with visitors. Lights are low and the room is smoky. Many patrons are smoking cigars, cigarettes and pipes. The dark wood paneling gleams; the sandy flagstone floors link together in a herringbone pattern. A long wooden bar takes center stage across the end of the room…liquor bottles line up in front of the large mirror, creating the illusion of an endless supply of spirits. Voices bounce off the hard surfaces. There is laughing and gaiety—not many soldiers tonight—Hitler is keeping them out of sight.

I spot Parker in the corner table, away from the other diners. He waves as I move across the room; he stands and we air kiss, then he pulls out my chair and seats me.

"How are you?" he asks.

"I am well, and you?"

Parker is clothed in a gray linen pin-striped suit—he is a strikingly handsome man. "Great, I present my paper tomorrow at the conference." We speak in generalities, while the waiter takes our drink order.

I order the wiener schnitzel, Parker the chicken stew. We clink our sniffers of bourbon together. "Cheers to old friends," Parker says.

I am antsy, anxious to hear about Mood and Eva. "Please, tell me about Giselle and Mood—how are they?" I lower my voice, so it can't be heard at the next table.

"Everything went as planned," he says softly, "except Billy Love and Kat uncovered the plot."

I gasp. "What, but how?"

"I can't go into that…suffice it to say, they are supportive of Giselle and happy she is out of her situation."

"They will keep the secret," he continues. "But, they have no idea the extent of our involvement, including that of your brothers Mood and A.R."

"Good." I look down at my bland brown dress. Tonight, I am trying to fit in as an average German woman. I don't want to stand out in any way.

"She has good and bad days, but she is rapidly adjusting to life in America," Parker says, speaking broadly.

"I am relieved."

"Yes, we all are. I have something else to tell you. Billy Love and I are an item. I have never met anyone like her. Someday, I will tell you the whole story. She stormed into my New York office and confronted me, traveled across the country by herself."

"You and Billy Love? My goodness."

Parker laughs. "She is one sex-kitten, Liz. Insatiable."

"Parker, too much information," I exclaim, feigning indignation.

"Ha, it's true. I am thirty-two and experienced in the bedroom, but Billy Love will try just about anything - she relishes it."

"I'm happy for you."

"She comes to New York once a month and we never leave my apartment—we order take out." Parker grins, "It's like I am the bull and she is riding me, staying on as long as possible."

I giggle at the metaphor. "Enough about sex," I say, dabbing my mouth with the napkin. The wiener schnitzel was superb.

"I have something for you," I say, as I pull a sealed envelope out of my purse. I hand it to Parker and he swiftly places it into his inner jacket pocket. "Deliver this to Dr. Harnack tomorrow. Don't read it—you are just the messenger in this case. Tell Arvid to memorize the date and place, then destroy the letter. We don't want any evidence to be discovered."

"Will do. And, I will call A.R. when I get back in New York— let him know you are safe."

"Thanks, Parker. Tell my niece I am happy for the two of you. Do you think the relationship will last?"

"Are you asking me if we will marry? I am in love with her, but it is too soon. Maybe in 1937?" Parker muses.

Parker pays the bill…we emerge into the street. "Let me walk you to your car."

"I am staying at the hotel tonight. The eight-man rowing event is tomorrow—I am covering it for the Darmstadt newspaper."

"Oh, really, you are a sports fan now, huh? I heard the Germans are favored."

"Yes, they are, but the Americans are the story here. I got to know one of the assistant coaches, Tim Miller," I say, with an emphasis on his name. Parker subtly nods. He clearly knows Coach Miller is part of the network.

"What does Coach Miller have to say?"

"He is a man of few words."

"But does he say the right words?"

"Of course. If you come to the final race after presenting your paper at the conference, I will introduce you to him," I say, slyly.

"It's a deal. I will meet you by the American team's dock."

****

It is a blustery day, in late afternoon, beside Langer See. The waters are choppy—the rowers will face strong headwinds. There are 75,000 spectators, most cheering for Germany. Hitler, Goebbels, and Himmler are seated in the center of the stands, surrounded by SS guards. Nazi flags, with their black swastikas, are draped on poles surrounding the finish line. The eight-man boat race will begin soon—it is the last event of the day.

I spot Coach Miller and approach him. He is bent over one of the American men…his brow is furrowed. I am quiet, waiting for him to finish tending to the athlete.

"Don, I understand you have been ill this week, but you are crucial to our chances of medaling, that you sit in the 'stroke oar' seat."

"Coach, I can do it. When I am leading the stroke count, nothing else matters. I can gut through it," Don says, with determination.

Tim slaps him on the back and pulls him up. "Go ahead and join your teammates, Don. They are getting ready to put the boat in the lake."

"Right away, coach. Thanks for your encouragement."

"Liz, I see you made it."

"Yes, is everything alright?"

"We will see. Don is the striker; he holds the team together."

"I wish you luck...the information we discussed has been delivered to the German economics professor. Be sure to call me when you receive the date and time."

"Very good."

"Oh, here is Parker O'Rourke, an American economics professor in Berlin to deliver a paper. We had dinner together; he is a friend of mine. "Parker, Tim Miller. Tim, Parker." It is clear that they know each other, as they shake hands. There is that certain comrade-look that men exhibit, a twinkle, a half grin.

"Parker, we need to get to the stands. USA is in lane six—Germany in lane one. It is going to be a battle."

The race is about to begin. Hitler stands and the crowd roars in unison, "Heil Hitler," while pointing their rigid arms in his direction. I pull my binoculars out and focus on the race. We cannot see the start of the race...there are bends in the lake, obscuring the racers. My stomach churns with heartburn as I anticipate the race. We hear the starter gun—the race has begun.

Coming into view, there are three boats in the lead, coming fast toward the finish line. Italy, Germany, and USA. The coxswains are blaring through their megaphones, the oarsmen strain and pull meticulously, in synchronous strokes. The crowd is roaring now. The underdog USA surges, at a seemingly impossible pace, and crosses the finish line. Gold! Italy is second, Germany third. I look up at Hitler—he is scowling, with his arms crossed in front of him. Bile fills my throat at the sight of him.

The USA men are stunned, yet jubilant, as laurel wreaths are passed over each one's head, to celebrate the victory. I glance over at the German boat—Helmut, my friend and confidant, is slumped over, dejected. Hitler and his entourage clatter down from the bleachers. They stomp out of the venue.

The German rowing coaches will be dressed down by Goebbels; probably fired—after all, the German athletes appeared weak to the world. The crowd is silent, except for a small band of jubilant Americans waving their stars and stripes.

"This is quite the story, don't you think, Parker?" I question, as I pull out my reporter's notebook. "Coach Miller will have a lot to say. Should we go find him?"

****

The summer Olympics are over. Germany is back to the business of harassing Jews and rooting out the dissonant…every day is dark.

Tim Miller delivered on his promise. Dozens of rifles, hand grenades and other weapons were delivered to the barn on the appointed drop date. Under the direction of Arvid Harnack, a dozen men in the Red Orchestra are practicing how to use the weapons. I volunteered to train, but Dr. Harnack wants to keep me exclusively in the surveillance and messenger roles. If captured with a gun, the Nazis would torture me until I spilled information important to the resistance.

Dr. Harnack is planning a major underground operation. I don't know what it consists of—yet, but I will.

At home in Munich, Petrus is starting to get suspicious…he's asking a lot of questions every time I get a telephone call, or leave the house for a Red Orchestra meeting. If he ever discovers the truth, I fear he will leave me. One day, if Hitler is defeated, I can share the saga of smuggling Eva out of the country…and he and the rest of the Braun family can be reunited, but not now. The chain of information must stay tight. Operations must remain covert.

Chapter 34

The Recordings

Oklahoma and Hollywood
1937
Kat

It has been months since Erikray broke up with me and hightailed it out of town—I am still moping, missing him. Billy Love and Giselle are doing their best to cheer me up, but so far, it's not working. The three of us gussied up one evening and put on a talent show...even that did little to alleviate my pain. To top it all off, the Tulsa lounge where I performed, let me go; the great depression affected their bottom line.

"Kat, let's put a record on the Victrola," Giselle says, one evening. "Who do you want to listen to?"

"I'm not in the mood, Giselle." I say, with dejection in my voice.

"Come on silly, Ella Fitzgerald or Billie Holiday?"

"Okay, Ella then."

Giselle glides across the room, lifts the Victrola's arm, and snugly places the record down...the needle lands on the lip of the record. A sultry alto voice emerges from the horn...pure, perfect pitch. I feel my mood lifting as Giselle and I sway to the music. Then we dance with each other as Ella croons 'Cheek to Cheek."

"Kat, sing along with her," Giselle says, encouragingly.

I start softly - then I match her tone exactly, with power and clarity: 'Heaven, I'm in Heaven and my heart beats so that I can hardly speak. And I seem to find the happiness I see; when we're dancing cheek to cheek.' My dictation and phrasing are spot on.

Billy Love quietly enters the room, leans against the wall and shuts her eyes as she listens to me sing.

'Come on and dance with me, I want my arm about you, the charm about you, will carry me through.' I finish the song, hitting the final phrase with relish.

"Kat, that was fantastic," Billy Love says, clapping and whistling.

"You are so talented," Giselle chimes in.

Even Papa is in the doorway of his bedroom, giving tacit approval, his face glowing.

"It did feel good to sing again, Gigi, thanks for pushing me."

"Kat, Giselle and I are visiting Marlene Dietrich in Hollywood this weekend. You are coming with us; Marlene knows the executives at Hollywood Records—and she can get you an audience with them."

"I'm not sure I'm good enough."

"Don't be ridiculous; of course, you are, and Marlene, being the pushy broad, will make sure you are seen AND heard," Billy Love interjects.

"I will ring Marlene up tonight and she can follow through by calling the secretary and making an appointment," Billy Love says.

"Gigi, this is your first trip to Hollywood, are you excited?" I ask.

"Very much so—no offense, but I am itching to get off the ranch, see what life is like in America's cities. I am quite bored with the rural life."

"I don't blame you. It has been almost a year since you arrived…and father has finally given an indication that you can mingle with others. You can fit into society without being recognized," Billy Love says.

"Kat, why don't you take Giselle into Tulsa tomorrow? She needs some glamorous clothes to go with a glamourous city," Billy Love says.

****

Marlene is currently in residence at her mansion. She just wrapped the movie 'Angel' and is taking time off to relax and entertain guests, including the three of us. Uncle A.R. insisted on driving us to Los Angeles—he is determined to keep Giselle under

214

his watchful eye, making sure she doesn't slip up and reveal herself as Eva.

"I am excited to meet Marlene. I idolize her, really, as she is vocal in her distain for Hitler and the Nazi regime. What a powerful woman. I should have taken a lesson from her…and left Germany and Adolf sooner," Giselle says, in practiced English.

"Gigi, your English is so polished. I am proud of you," I say. "However, never mention Hitler to anyone besides Billy Love and me. You can't risk revealing yourself."

"You are correct, of course. As for my English, what else did I have to do for the past year? Practice, practice and practice English and take moving pictures, right?"

Billy Love laughs. "Right. I see you brought your camera with you, Gigi.

"Yes, if Marlene approves, I want to film her mansion."

"I think she will be fine with it, as long as you don't sell it to one of those Hollywood rags," Billy Love comments.

"Never would I do that," Giselle says, with animation.

"Billy Love is just teasing you, Gigi."

Uncle pulls into the circular driveway as we arrive at Marlene's mansion. He honks the Duesenberg horn and puts the clutch in park. "Oh, my," Giselle says with wonder, as she gazes up at the impressive house.

I look at the three of us—brunettes styled in the latest fashion. I am wearing an emerald green, rayon crepe dress: it is belted and the short sleeves are puffed, then cuffed at the elbow. My matching hat is rimless, perched snugly over my riot of dark curls. Billy Love's silk dress is royal blue, collared, with shoulder pads that make her belted waist look tiny—her ensemble is complete with a straw hat, a blue ribbon encircling its base. Giselle's new dress, which we purchased this week, is stunning. Sun yellow crepe, with a large collar; there is shirring throughout the bodice, with billowing sleeves ending at the elbow. On her raven, curled hair is a white flowered headband. We all complement our looks with short white gloves.

Marlene spies us as and waves as she emerges from the mansion, dressed in her usual masculine-looking suit, topped with a soft gray, felt hat.

"My darlings, my beauties, here you are. Welcome," she calls out, as we hurry up the steps to the house, our heels clicking on the cement.

Marlene hugs the three of us simultaneously. "Now, who is this lovely woman?"

"Marlene, meet Giselle Gregor. She is staying at the ranch with us."

"So, good to meet you, Giselle. I understand you are a fellow German, like Kat and me."

"Yes, I grew up in Munich."

Uncle A.R. gives Giselle a warning look—a signal to her - avoid revealing any more information. Giselle nods, subtly confirming his message.

"Marlene, you take good care of my ladies. I need to return to the ranch. It's the busy season and I still have not promoted anyone to manager. I have to do everything myself—it's hard to find hardworking men these days."

Uncle A.R. is so full of himself. At least he is in better spirits these days.

"Oh, A.R., don't you worry about these ladies. I have plans for them, and it doesn't involve you," Marlene laughs, as A.R. scowls.

"Goodbye father, thanks for driving us. We are grown women, and we can take care of ourselves."

Uncle departs and Marlene turns to Giselle. "Kat and Billy Love are like little sisters to me."

"I am thrilled to get to know you, Marlene. I love your pictures, especially the one where Billy Love is the stunt rider. Oh, and by the way, Billy Love and Kat call me Gigi for short," Giselle gushes.

"Let's go into the house. Kat and Billy Love, make yourselves some drinks and relax in the living room while I show Gigi around my place."

"Miss Dietrich," I hear Giselle say.

"Just call me Marlene. Heck, Marlene isn't even my given name. I had to change it for the movies."

I think to myself…Well, Giselle and Marlene have something in common…they both changed their names.

As Marlene and Giselle move throughout the house, I hear Marlene chattering. Giselle is quiet, perhaps overwhelmed with the sheer opulence of the home and the presence of a movie star.

At the end of the tour, Giselle says, "Marlene, your home is magnificent. My hobby is filming—I brought my camera with me. Would you mind if I filmed your mansion? It would be for my use only."

"Girl, of course, now let's get you a drink. Kat and Billy Love are already on their second round. We can't be far behind."

The four of us clink glasses. "Here's to friends," Marlene says, with aplomb. "Gigi is hear-by my newest little sister." Giselle beams. The outing to Hollywood is going well. She is relaxed, with her feet propped on the iron coffee table.

"I want to know more about you, Gigi. Why are you staying at the Howling Wolf Ranch?"

I look at Gigi. She has a carefully rehearsed answer.

"Marlene, I met Kat and Billy Love when they visited Germany—I am an only child. My parents are elderly, and Jewish. When the Nazis began to crack down on the Jewish people, my parents lost their jobs and were persecuted. They decided to send me to America, and A.R. secured a Visa for me. My parents left Germany and are now in Paris."

"Gigi, lucky for you, your parents were alert and aware of the abuses of the Hitler regime. I, for one, refuse to return to Germany for any reason until the Nazis are overthrown. You know, they have repeatedly asked me to claim Germany as my homeland—to make films there. That is bullshit," Marlene says, starting to ramble. "By the way, your English is very good. I had lots of classes when I first arrived in Hollywood. It is difficult to get rid of that guttural accent."

217

"Thank you very much. Kat and Billy Love were a tremendous help. We conversed every day in English."

"Enough about me, I want to hear what you have in store for Kat," Giselle says.

"Yes, let's take care of business, Kat. I set up an audition for you tomorrow at none other than Hollywood Records."

"Oh, my goodness. I'm going to sing Cheek to Cheek—it is in my alto range and I am comfortable singing it."

"Marlene, I know Kat will be signed and recorded before we leave Hollywood," Billy Love proclaims.

"Of course, she will," Marlene says, as she gazes at me. "The producer can be intimidating, so don't let him get to you. Be confident—his name is Johnny Romani—Italian. Call him Johnny, not Mr. Romani. In his younger days, he was a cabaret singer, so be sure and tell him of your connection with cabaret. Try to compliment him on his voice."

"Will you come with me to the audition?"

"Yes, Billy Love and Giselle can drop us off at the record label studio. They can tool around and do the Hollywood tourist thing. Maybe visit my star on the Hollywood Boulevard?"

****

"Johnny, where are you?" Marlene calls out, as we enter the windowless, box-like recording studio. It smells musty, like it needs a good airing out.

"I am in the back room, setting up the equipment—give me a minute," he growls.

"Kat, remember what I told you. Be natural, but forceful with Johnny."

Johnny strides toward us…he oozes Italian features—thick, black hair slicked back with pomade, olive skin, coal colored eyes, and a commanding nose. He wears a white dress shirt with sleeves rolled up; black pants with olive suspenders complete his wardrobe.

218

Chomping on a cigar, he is directly in front of me, looking me up and down.

I take the initiative. "Hello Johnny, I am Katarina Wolf, but you can call me Kat. Thank you for the opportunity to sing for you."

He and Marlene air kiss. "Nice to meet you, KAT," he says, after blowing smoke out of the side of his mouth. "Marlene tells me you have a beautiful, sultry voice."

"I sang at a cabaret in Munich for several years before coming to America. The experience really helped hone my voice."

"Well, well. I agree, as I also performed in cabarets. It is that live, raucous audience that gets you going," he brags. You can almost see his chest expanding. I try not to react—Marlene has him pegged alright.

"Marlene have a seat on the coach. Kat, give the piano player your sheet music—it's 'Cheek to Cheek", right? Johnny says, as he fires off a series of commands.

I calmly approach the microphone…I shut my eyes, centering myself, as I wait for Johnny to turn on the recording equipment.

"Ready for you Kat," he says, signaling the piano player. The pianist commences with the introduction—the soothing music flows from the instrument.

I begin, softly, then building, every note nuanced. I am focused on my breathing, my phrasing, pulling in my diaphragm to power my vocal cords. My alto voice glides over the notes, as I come to the second chorus and finish… "when we're dancing cheek to cheek."

There is silence, then Marlene stands up, clapping and shouting "Bravo." Both Johnny and the piano player seem stunned.

"Miss Katarina Wolf, I have never before recorded a performer in one take, but you, my dear, have accomplished the impossible," Johnny says, beaming as he clicks off the recorder. "I am offering you a contract with Hollywood records—and I am not letting you out of the studio until it is signed."

I erupt, knowing I should be graceful, but what the heck, "Woo Hoo!" I yell, hugging Marlene tightly, almost picking her up off the floor.

"Kat, we will record several songs, then market the record to radio stations around the country. We might even record a few in German, to market in Europe. Can you stay with Marlene while we produce the album?" Johnny asks.

"Of course, she can. My mansion is huge, I rattle around in it…plus I enjoy Kat's company."

Billy Love and Gigi stroll into the studio, searching my face for clues…I break into a wide smile. "I got a contract and I am signing on with Hollywood Records."

"Your dad will be so proud of you. He has been so supportive of you from the beginning," Billy Love exclaims.

"Marlene, I just had an idea. Why don't you and Kat sing a duet and record 'Falling in Love Again'? People would buy the record because you are an established star—it would be a way to get Kat introduced to a wide audience," Johnny says, with enthusiasm.

"Johnny, what a marvelous thought. I have a few weeks off until we start production on 'Knight without Armor'. What do you say Kat?"

"I would love to record with you, Marlene."

"Good. Johnny, we will see you tomorrow morning." Marlene turns and moves decisively toward the door, motioning us to exit.

I try to humbly follow, but am unable to suppress my enthusiasm. I skip.

✳✳✳✳✳✳✳✳✳✳✳✳✳✳✳

The past week has been grueling, yet exhilarating. Johnny hired some orchestra members to provide background music…Marlene and I tackled the duet, nailing it in three takes. I recorded three other songs. Now, we wait for Johnny to edit the recordings, work his magic.

Tonight, the four of us are cuddled together on the large overstuffed couch, wearing colorful chenille robes…warming to the flicking flames in the stone fireplace, and smelling the fragrance of the burning logs. "Marlene, what happens now, once the record is complete?" I ask.

"Johnny will have copies made to sell here in Los Angeles—he will also give records to the largest radio stations and urge them to play them on the airwaves. Once a song catches on, other radio stations across the country will follow suit, and you will have a hit."

"Is it strange to hear your voice on the radio?" I ask.

"Yes, because you hear your own voice differently from everyone else. It can be a bit of a shock at first, but believe me, your voice is special." Marlene continues. "I expect you will be an instant sensation."

"Thanks again for all you have done for me."

"You are welcome. I am proud to introduce new talent to the world."

"Gigi, did you show Marlene your footage of the mansion?" Billy Love asks.

"Yes," Giselle murmurs.

"It is wonderful. You captured the essence of every room; maybe you should sell it to the rags, make some money," Marlene says, gleefully.

Billy Love and I laugh. Giselle smiles.

"On another note, Gigi was approached by a photographer today, as we were posing by your Hollywood star, Marlene. He asked to take her picture—said she was pretty enough to be in movies," Billy Love says, with measured words, looking directly at me, alarm showing on her face.

"I declined. Really, I have no interest in acting. I like being behind the cameras."

I jump into the conversation. "You definitely are gorgeous, Gigi, but I agree your talent lies in filming."

"Kat, you might be on to something. Gigi, do you have any experience using the large, bulky cameras we use in filming pictures?" Marlene asks, leaning back into the cushions.

"Yes, I do, when I worked in a camera shop in Germany—I was an assistant to a great film maker. We worked with heavy equipment every day. You need an assistant or two to move the cameras around; to get the right angle of the scene."

"It just so happens that one of the cameramen joined the army. We start filming 'Knight without Armor' next month. What would you think of me pitching you as his replacement?"

"I have been bored lately with my life…it would be a great opportunity for me. Thank you so much, Marlene."

"Let me ring Adolph Zukor, the head of Paramount pictures. He will want to meet you and make the final decision."

In an instant, Marlene veers off message. "Isn't it ironic that Adolph Zukor is Jewish and shares his first name with that scoundrel Hitler? Goebbels practically begged me to come back to Germany and make pictures for the German people—hah, no way. I am in process of becoming an American citizen."

Billy Love says, peevishly, "My father's given name is also Adolf. Why do you think he goes by A.R.?"

I observe Giselle. Giving nothing away about her connections with Hitler, she responds to Marlene, "Do you believe it will be a problem, because I am a woman, taking a job away from a man?"

"Of course not. Mr. Zukor came from nothing and built up Paramount into the premiere studio it is today. As long as you know your job and work hard, he will support you."

I laugh, in short snorts. "Gigi, if Billy Love can ride bulls in the rodeo, you certainly can roll cameras for a living, maybe even make some decent money."

"Oh yes, I remember the crap I got from those mean-spirited boys at the rodeo, especially when I stayed on the bulls longer than they did. Calvy Clare was the worst one. He had absolute distain for girl-riders," Billy Love interjects.

"It's settled then. How wonderful that Kat got a record contract and now Gigi has an opportunity. Ladies, I am going to read my script in bed. I play a Russian aristocrat involved in some sort of espionage with the Bolsheviks."

"My mother was Russian, so maybe I can help you run lines."

"Kat, that would be perfect. Now, goodnight all." Marlene climbs the stairs, script in hand.

Giselle yawns. "I am tired – you two are such night owls. See you in the morning."

Billy Love and I talk quietly. "Kat, you and Gigi are on the road to success. And so far, Gigi is hiding her identity well. I was impressed that she turned down the opportunity to have her picture taken. I still think that Hitler is looking for her, even though Goebbels told him to forget her."

"Why do you believe the Fuhrer is trying to find her?"

"Aunt Liz and Parker met up at the summer Olympics. She told Parker that Fritz was interrogated by Hitler, but, since Fritz was kept deliberately in the dark, he could give them no information."

"I am still scared for Aunt Liz—and convinced that she is involved in something beyond smuggling Giselle out of Germany. Things are getting worse. And Parker is moody, on edge since his return from the economics conference. I try to question him…he brushes me away. When I am in New York, he is on the phone at 2, 3 am." Billy Love says, placing her hand over her chest, knitting her brow.

"We are still mad for each other, though. The sex is beyond great—our clothes are off the minute I shut his apartment door."

"Billy Love, I believe your relationship with Parker is strong, and I have to agree with you; Parker, Aunt Liz and your father are involved in some plot well beyond Giselle. It has something to do with Hitler and the Nazis—eventually, we will find out."

"Yes, let's good to bed and sleep on it," Billy Love says. We climb the stairs together.

****

Giselle and Marlene are up early, eager to depart to Paramount studios, where they will meet with Adolph Zukor.

I hear Billy Love on the telephone with A.R. "Father, I have some exciting news. Kat received a record contract with Hollywood records…there will be several songs on the album. She even sang a duet with Marlene, Anyway, she will stay here in Hollywood at Marlene's mansion until the album is released and marketed.

Billy Love listens while A.R. responds.

"I will tell her congratulations for you—Kat will be making promotional appearances and singing in some lounges here in Los Angeles. The marketing process will probably take several months."

"There is something else I want to discuss with you—just hear me out before you jump to conclusions," Billy Love says, lowering her voice so that it is barely audible. "Giselle is doing extremely well; indeed, she is like a new person, all of the sulking and moping, gone. Marlene's next picture is set to film starting next week and Giselle has an opportunity to be behind the cameras."

"Father, calm down. We can't keep her at the ranch like a prisoner. She can stay with Kat at Marlene's. There is plenty of room…I will stay the first week to make sure nothing adverse happens. I can even chaperone her to and from the studio."

There is a long pause, then Billy Love continues. "It is only for one picture, father…yes, Kat and I will be extremely careful."

"Giselle makes her own decisions now, and with Kat and me to protect and oversee her, she is at minimal risk."

"I love you too, father. Thanks for listening."

Billy Love hangs up the phone, walks over to me and hits me on my upper arm with back of her hand. "By George, I convinced him to let Giselle stay. Let's celebrate and crack out the bubbly."

"At nine in the morning?"

"Why not?" Billy Love says.

Chapter 35

Warning

New York City
1938
Billy Love

Parker and I married at the Lincoln Hotel. It was a small, but elegant affair—Parker in top hat and tails, I, encased in head to toe white silk and lace, my mahogany hair swept into a chignon. Most of the family attended, except of course, for Aunt Liz and Uncle Petrus; they remain stuck in Hitler's Germany. Marlene and Giselle were absent, too, busy making movies.

I am happy for Giselle, as she proves herself in the camera world--her life regaining meaning, some semblance of normalcy. She has entered the Hollywood social world, dating a few minor actors and she created a whole new scenario for herself.

We are living in Parker's large, World War One apartment on the upper east side of New York City—settling into married life.

I am adjusting to life in New York City, a different world from the isolated Oklahoma ranch. I like the jostling on the streets, the vibrancy of city life. It is a new adventure and I am ready for it.

We are lounging in the kitchen, having a mundane conversation.

"Parker, I want to redecorate the apartment. It is so dark, with the heavy velvet drapes blocking out the sun. To top it off, the deep brown paneling snaking up half the walls is depressing. I want to paint the walls a lighter college and rip out the curtains."

"Billy Love, my beauty, of course you can do anything you want."

"I will get started next week," I say, as I put my arms around his neck and pull him in for a deep kiss. He responds immediately, in every way. We end up in bed, for the second time today.

I prop myself up on one elbow and watch as he pulls his trousers up over his thick muscled legs. He leans over and kisses me lightly on the lips. "I love you so much, Billy Love, and would linger, but I must go to the university and prepare a paper to be published in the Business Magazine."

"Did you remember that Giselle is coming to New York and staying with us?"

"Of course."

"She sounded good on the phone—said she is remembering more conversations overheard between Adolf and his aides; plans on sharing it with us when she gets here."

"Has she told anyone else?" Parker's smile fades, as he becomes serious.

"No, not even A.R. or Kat."

"Good. Are you picking her up at the train station tomorrow?"

"Yes."

"Bring her straight to the apartment. We can't risk having a conversation of this magnitude within earshot."

****

"Giselle, over here," I yell, as she steps off the train stairs. Every time I see her, I marvel at the change in appearance following plastic surgery. Eva Braun is completely erased, and replaced with Gigi.

Today, she is completely unassuming…wearing a drab olive-green cotton dress that falls to her mid-calf, sensible shoes, her face void of makeup. Her dark hair is captured in a bun at the nape of her neck. Even with her sensible look, though, she is beautiful: with her almond shaped, blue eyes, high cheekbones, raven hair, and long, thin neck—people swarming around her notice.

"How was your trip?" I say, as I take her suitcase from her, and we stroll toward the cabbie waiting at the curb.

226

"Uneventful, I am excited to be here, having only passed through New York City once," she says, knowingly. "Can we do the tourist scene while I'm here?"

"Most certainly. Parker is waiting for us at the apartment. I'll let you settle in, get you a bite to eat. Then, Parker will want to hear your news."

Parker has ham and cheese sandwiches ready for us. "Giselle, so great to see you. I just picked up the food at the Deli down the street. When you come to New York, you have to eat like the natives."

"Parker, let Gigi catch her breathe a minute, freshen up—then we can eat. Did you pick up the beer?" I ask, while setting the kitchen table.

"Yes, it is chilling in the refrigerator. Billy Love, did Giselle tell you anything yet?"

"No, silly, the cab driver was gabbing the whole time—it wouldn't have been appropriate, anyway. You know that—you said yourself, no one else besides us should have information about this."

"Okay, I am anxious to hear her story."

We finish our meal, and now full of deli goodies, sit in the living room. Giselle looks relaxed, but Parker is literally on the edge of his seat, his hands clasped together, looking intently toward Giselle.

Giselle begins her tale, speaking softly, in clipped English. "I tried not to think much of my time with Adolf...for a year while I stayed at the ranch, I literally blocked him out. But once I started working in Hollywood, the memories started flowing back. It was odd—I was getting ready for work, and suddenly there it was, vivid pictures of Adolf's Munich apartment." She pauses, and stares, as if pulling up the scene in her mind.

"Go on," Parker says, encouragingly.

"The doctor was there, administering medications to Hitler. He always gave me a sedative, too, which made me groggy. This particular day I pretended to take the pill. I wanted to be alert when Hitler's visitor arrived."

"Who was the visitor?" Parker interrupts.

"Parker, let Giselle finish, we have plenty of time." I say.

Parker leans back, exasperated, but stops talking.

"Heinrich Himmler, Hitler's general and head of the SS, an awful man...always got Adolf worked up. Anyway, I went into the back bedroom as I usually do, but I didn't shut the door."

"At first, they chatted and smoked cigars...then Hitler was screaming at Heinrich, telling him to get out the goddamned maps of Europe. I could hear the rustle of paper as they spread them out to study the terrain."

Giselle continues. "Adolf demanded the German army prepare to invade Poland, but Heinrich pushed back, reminding Adolf that Germany had a non-aggression treaty with the country. Hitler lashed out, told him that he could resign or start getting the troops ready for war - that Poland would be the first of many countries Germany will conquer."

Parker and I are stunned - Giselle just informed us that Hitler intends to take the world into war once again. This cannot be happening.

"At this point, Adolf was in a rage. He stomped throughout the apartment, and I heard his glass of bourbon shatter against the wall. He demanded an answer from Heinrich. He went on a tirade about how Jews were ruining Germany."

"Heinrich eventually agreed with Adolf, flattered him, and slunk out the door, like the low life he is."

"Did he come to you afterwards?" I ask.

"Yes, and he was rough with me. Pinned my arms behind my back and twisted them. When I yelped, he slapped me and told me to keep quiet. In that exact moment, I knew I needed to contact your Aunt Liz, Billy Love. Adolf had become too erratic—I had to get out of Germany before it was too late."

"Liz and Mood risked their lives to get me out; and I am forever grateful to them. Even today, though, I worry about Liz, still living in Munich."

"Rightly so. I have had no communication with her for a while now. Germany is pretty much cut off from the rest of the world," Parker says, sighing.

"It is clear that Hitler is unhinged and his top aides are not going to stop him," I say, putting my arm around Giselle's shoulder and pulling her close to me.

Giselle is pale as she finishes her story. "What will you do with this information?" she asks.

"I have contacts high up in the United States Government, including some five-star generals. You, Billy Love and I are the only ones who know the source of this information and we need to keep it that way. As it is, we have a President who is an isolationist. I don't know if he will act aggressively toward Germany to prevent invasion of Poland, but the Brits might if they knew about it."

"Now, Gigi, let Parker keep your secret—sweep it out of your mind. Let's have another cold beer, then we can hit the streets of New York City; have a little fun. We are too young to be so serious, right?"

"I agree - let me change into something fancy; I feel dull in this green dress."

Giselle trails off to the bedroom.

Parker and I look intently at each other, speechless. We just received invaluable information that could prevent a world war!

"I believe every word of Giselle's story. It fits - Hitler just annexed Austria, allegedly to unite German speaking people into one country. The Nazi party had heavily infiltrated that country...Hitler marched some troops in and easily overthrew Chancellor Schuschnigg."

"It makes perfect sense that Poland will be invaded next and I can't help but think it will be soon," Parker exclaims. "Himmler has had plenty of time to build up the German troops."

229

"I think there is another reason Adolf wants to take over Poland—more than three million Jews live in Poland—the largest Jewish population in Europe….to preserve his elite Aryan race, Hitler has a plan to deport as many as possible to concentration camps. That man has no moral compass."

"I agree, he is a monster," Parker says.

"Look what happened in Austria. Immediately after they annexed it, all anti-Semitic laws were applied."

"Parker, I can't understand why the United States refuses to issue visas to Jewish people in Germany and Austria…to help those being persecuted come and resettle here."

"President Roosevelt is focused on the New Deal; getting the American people work, growing the economy. He supports severe limitations on immigration. It's not right, but the president has agreed to send a representative to the Emigration and Evian Conference coming up in France."

"I am not hopeful, but it seems this is all we have for the moment, I say, without much conviction.

"What we heard from Giselle today could change our leaders' thoughts on Hitler. I am disappearing for a couple of days—will you cover for me? If asked, I am in California for an economics conference."

"You can't even tell me?"

"No, it is too dangerous. I need to deliver the message to the right people—and there are two distinct messages—Hitler plans to invade Poland soon, and he continues to oppress and purge Jewish people."

"Do you think they will believe you? After all, you can't reveal your source."

"I will convey the information, but protect Giselle's identity. She took a risk even telling us her story…it is all I can do. Now, you and Giselle have a great night in the big apple; when you get home, I will be gone."

****

230

"Gigi, let's treat ourselves - get our hair done at the salon in the Lincoln Hotel. After that, we can have lunch at the hotel and buy some evening clothes at Macys."

"Billy Love, that would be wonderful," Giselle remarks, clapping her hands together. "Just what I need."

We are back home after a lovely afternoon, preparing for the evening. Our dark tresses are elaborately coiffed, pulled back from our faces and pin curled into waves. My heavily beaded chiffon dress is draped on the bed; beside it is Giselle's metallic gold silk gown, with a low back tied together with cutouts. Silver and gold, elegant for the two of us.

Out on the town, Giselle and I travel to Greenwich Village, to visit the Café Society, the newest jazz club. Our mood is lighter than the somber spirit of our earlier conversation. We duck our heads and enter the dim stairwell leading to the basement club— where the air is thick with smoke and chatter. The alto saxophone player wails—we sip martinis, suck olives and blow smoke at each other, laughing.

"Billy Love, here's to us…friends forever," Giselle says, lifting her martini and tilting it toward me.

"Friends forever, and also, Kat is part of our inner circle."

"Dear Katarina, yes indeed."

"Kat and I may be blood cousins, but we consider you an adopted cousin; part of the wolfpack, as we call ourselves. We rely on each other, don't we?

"I would not be here today, in 1938, without you and Kat…so grateful. Come on, let's take advantage of the music."

We make our way to the dance floor, passing several tables of seemingly drunken men. "Now, there are two beautiful women," one calls out loudly. Another pinches Giselle's bottom…she shrieks and slaps his hand hard. "Now, now girlie," he slurs.

The men are dressed in a uniform, consisting of brown shirts and jack boots. I narrow my eyes as I recognize them—members of the American Nazi organization known as the German

231

American Bund: its goal—to promote a favorable view of Nazi Germany.

I ignore the men and continue toward the dance floor, but their table is so close, I can hear their conversation. "I smell some Jews in here," one says, "What do you say we take them out?" he says menacingly, putting his fists up as he looks around the room, allegedly trying to spot a Jew.

"Clarence, look at the guy over there," he continues, as he points across the room toward a small, dark-haired man. "I'll bet he is both a Jew and a faggot—a twofer." The men howl with laughter, as the music abruptly stops.

"Why, we have a Jew for a president...Franklin D. Rosenfeld. He got us the 'Jew Deal" alright," Clarence says, as the group peels with laughter. The rest of the patrons are silent now, aghast at the men and their lewd comments.

"Giselle, I can't keep quiet."

"Please, Billy Love, don't make a scene."

"I have to---"

Moving to the microphone, I place my trembling arm on its neck, "You," I shout, pointing at the group of men. "Yes, you, all of you...are a bunch of appalling scumbags. You don't deserve to be called Americans or even be allowed in this establishment. You need to shut your filthy mouths and slink off to mommy."

Two of the men stand up and stagger menacingly toward me. I stand rigidly, not moving...and then two burly security guards, with billy clubs in hand, are between us, pushing the sotted men back; one of them drops to his knees when he loses his balance.

"You men have caused enough trouble here for one evening and every evening from now on--you are banned from this club. Now get out," one guard commands sternly, as he moves them to the door, baton at their backs.

Ma'am, are you all right? Let me get you a drink...on the house," says the club manager, as he escorts us back to our table.

"Oh, Billy Love, I was so scared for you," Giselle says, with tears streaming down her cheeks. "Thank goodness for the security guards. Why do you always go looking for trouble?"

"I don't. It finds me. Anyway, I have a moral obligation to speak out. It's my nature."

"Parker will be so angry when he finds out what happened to you."

"Oh, no, Gigi, this will be our secret," I say, as the manager plops down a double shot of bourbon...I down it in one gulp. "Please, another."

"I am reluctant to keep this a secret from Parker, but I will go along with your wishes, Billy Love. Mark my words though...Parker will find out, he is good at investigations."

The jazz music resumes with a rendition of 'My Funny Valentine', and as the sultry tone envelopes the room, the patrons resume their conversation buzz.

"Billy Love, I don't understand the hatred toward Jewish people...even in Hollywood, I encounter it every day."

"What do you mean?"

"When you run the cameras, you are on set constantly. People don't think we pay attention, but we hear the gossip, and it is vicious. Did you know that Hollywood exports many of its movies to Germany, and that each movie must be approved or censored by Goebbels?"

"No, really?"

"If there is any plot line that makes Germany look bad or focused on the mistreatment of Jews, it will be censored. Goebbels even throws tantrums if the director is Jewish, which most of them are in Hollywood. He insists their names be removed from the credits."

"Oh, my, how did this happen in America?"

"The studios, including Paramount, do not want to lose the German business, so they cave. I have seen them cut so much out of a movie, there is no plot left."

"What does Marlene think about all of this?"

"She is furious of course—and very vocal, like you, tells people what she thinks. Why, Adolph Zukor himself is Jewish, as are most of the other major studio heads."

"I know Marlene refuses to set foot in Germany until Adolf is out of power."

"That is right. You know, Billy Love, it is not just Hollywood who coddles the Nazis. It is well known that the publisher of the Los Angeles Times cavorts with the German ambassador, and his hangers on, at the Embassy in LA."

"I did know that, Gigi. Father rails against some of the editorials he prints, which are generally favorable to the Nazi regime…and he visited Germany during the Olympic games, where he hobnobbed with his Nazi buddies."

"His name is Norm Chandler, a very arrogant and narcist man."

"Gigi, let's call it a night, grab a cab and head to the apartment. We have had enough excitement to last through your entire visit. Tomorrow, I promise we will stick to the touristy things, like the Statue of Liberty and a boat ride in the harbor."

"Deal."

Chapter 36

The List

Munich
1938
Elisabetha

A dark cloud hangs over Germany. People scurry through the streets, avoiding eye contact with each other, only leaving their houses when absolutely necessary. Food is scarce—rationed, but the soldiers have plenty to eat. There are a lot of rumors about the Nazis…and much uncertainty. Laws are passed every month that further persecute Jews; and recently, Jews were required to register their property.

I am depressed, and am finding it increasingly difficult to hide my clandestine activities from Petrus. He grills me every time I leave the house—there are so many excuses and lies, it is hard to keep my stories straight.

I have one more undercover operation, then I will retire from the Red Orchestra group.

Dr. Harnack insists that my work is done; others will carry on without me. I agree--the secret of the whereabouts of Eva Braun is enough of a burden to hold within me. Periodically, the SS hauls Fritz Braun down to Gestapo headquarters and interrogates him regarding Eva's disappearance: of course, he doesn't have a clue. It is pointless. However, I am just one step away from Fritz… if they ever get serious about the investigation, it could be over for me.

"Petrus, I am going out for groceries—I will be back in about an hour," I say, as I pull on a headscarf, long woolen coat and boots.

"Liz, with the rationing, do you think you can get sugar and flour? A nice cake would be nice for a change."

"I will see what I can do, Petrus. I hope the lines are not too long."

Petrus is gloomy, having been forced to sell *The Garden* for very little money last year. My brother, A.R., kept us afloat for several years, but it wasn't enough; and now, there is no contact with America. We will have to scrape by with what little we have left.

Slamming the door, I head toward a worn shed several blocks from my house. I yank the door handle, and pull on the string to lighten the room, then I wait. After several minutes, there is a coded knock on the door. "Come in."

Leon Hilfman slowly steps toward me—filthy and looking exhausted, with deep violet circles under his eyes, his hair shaggy, past his collar; his body odor rancid. The German resistance has taken a toll on him…it is time to get him out. The window of opportunity is closing as the rumors of further restrictions on Jews is getting chatter.

"Sit down, Leon," I say, pointing to the lonely chair in the middle of the shed. Leon limps over and plops himself down, slumping.

"You have done everything you could--now is the time to go. Otherwise, you will most certainly be arrested for distributing anti-Nazi propaganda."

I continue. "Your brother, Simon, visited the Hollywood director Carl Laemmle, of Universal Pictures. Carl is determined to help Jews who need to immigrate to America. He has a list and you are on it, thanks to Simon."

"What do you mean?" Leon says, blowing warm air into his frozen hands.

"Carl writes and calls the German consulate with a list of names, Jews, who he wants to sponsor. He pays their way to the U.S. and helps them settle in—even provides them with jobs if they need one. He is a millionaire, so he has the financial means to help many people. I understand he has already brought over 200 people to America, so he has political clout with the folks at the consulate."

"Uncle Carl, as they call him, has a visa ready for you at the German consulate. You leave tomorrow."

"But, what about my possessions?"

"You can take nothing but some new clothing, a clean-shaven face, and a haircut, which I have arranged for you to obtain at a private home here in Munich. Here is the address, memorize it and tear it up. Get a good night's sleep, and good luck." I reach for him and hug his scrawny body to me. He looks up at me, tears welling in his eyes.

"So many of my friends are dead or were sent to Dachau...for minor infractions. Why does God do nothing to help us?" There is anger in his voice.

"Leon, I ask myself the same question, almost every day. We do what we can to resist, but in the end, we may not be able stop the evil permeating throughout Germany. You have been very lucky...now is the time to put your head down, and live a new life in America."

"Dr. Parker O'Rourke will meet you when your ship docks— he will then take you to the train that leaves from New York. Simon will meet you when you arrive at the train station; you can stay with him and Lola Estelle until you figure out what to do."

"Liz, I am forever grateful, but I do worry about your own safety."

"This is my last job in the resistance, Leon, and I am proud to get you out of here. Who knows what will happen in the next years? I sense Hitler will not be satisfied with ruling Germany."

"You are right, Liz, we believe he is plotting to invade Poland very soon."

"World War II is about to break out, isn't it? For the life of me, I can't understand why President Roosevelt is staying neutral, an isolationist, really. And very few people in America are speaking out about the persecution of Jews. Look at you, Leon, the Nazis fired you from your government job and barred you from German citizenship. They treat you like you are sub-human."

"It is Hitler and his aides who are corrupt, amoral and sub-human, not the Jews," Leon says, forcefully. "I will continue my work against the Nazi regime from afar, but mark my words, America will eventually need to send troops to Europe to stop Hitler from taking over the world."

"Leon, have Simon take you to the Howling Wolf Ranch as soon as you get off the train. My brother, A.R., needs to know that Petrus and I are okay. In addition, quietly tell him about the activities you were involved with in the resistance, and what is happening with the Jews. No one else needs to know right now, not even Simon. When the time is right, A.R. will know what to do with the information."

"Thanks again, Liz."

"It is freezing in here. You need to get on your way."

"America, here I come, land of the free," he says, bitterly.

Leon jerks the shed door open and runs into the street, limping badly, on his way to the safe house.

I wait ten minutes, then emerge from shed, and head toward the hope of finding sugar and flour. My last operation is complete. I slump with relief, take several deep breathes, then march to the store. No more lies to Petrus.

****

"Liz, that angel food cake smells delicious. What time did you say Debra and Fritz are coming over for dessert and coffee?" Petrus calls to me, as I plug in the coffee pot.

"Around seven, Petrus. Aren't you pleased that I stood in line to get the sugar and flour?"

"I had just about given up on you. You were gone three hours."

"Well, the lines were worth it—now we have a sweet treat, a rarity these days."

"Yes, well worth it. It will be good to see Debra and Fritz—it has been months since we saw them last."

238

I slice the cake and place each piece on elegant flowered bone china. Fresh strawberries rest on the pale, yellow angel food-- I carry the plates to the large walnut table in the dining room, placing beside them sterling silver forks and red linen napkins. The cups and saucers wait to be filled with bitter, rich coffee.

As I untie my apron, I hear the persistent sound of the telephone ringing. "Petrus, I will get that. Debra and Fritz should be here any minute; settle them in the living room."

"Hello, this is Liz Braun," I answer.

A deep voice, one I don't recognize, speaks into my ear. I clutch the phone tightly. "Liz, it is done; he left this morning." I sag against the wall—no need to respond, I know he is talking about Leon. Relieved, I gently place the phone in the receiver—I am about to revert to the portrayal of the boring, old German lady everyone thinks I am.

I think about my brothers, A.R. and Moody. They, too, have each risked so much to help innocent people. We are loyal to each other—we are the wolfpack—and we stick together for the cause.

****

We sit at the dining room table, sipping our bitter coffee and savoring each bite of sugary cake. I take notice of Debra—her hair completely white, her skin pale, her face pinched. She is so thin, her collar bones just above the neckline of her dress. She must have dropped twenty-five pounds since we saw her last. Her house dress swirls around her, much too large. I feel the familiar guilt at keeping Eva's secret—but I must, even if it exacts the toll on Debra.

At first, the conversation is banal, as we discuss the latest music and fashion trends. "Have you heard Kat's album?" Petrus asks. "I was able to get one on the black market. After dinner, I will put it on…terrific, really."

"I knew Kat had a lot of talent. I am so proud of her," Fritz declares.

"Oh, Fritz, I remember the days when Eva and Kat and Billy Love would hang out together, even go roller skating; they were just girls, then," Debra says, with sorrow in her voice. "Liz, it has been two years since Eva disappeared. Where could she be? I am starting to lose hope."

"Debra, I am certain she being protected somewhere," I say, my tone bright.

"Liz, you don't know that. Maybe you should stop giving false hope to Fritz and Debra," Petrus says, sternly, as he glares at me.

I instantly retreat. "I am sorry, I just have a feeling, an intuition. I will stop mentioning Eva if it is too painful."

"I know you mean well, Liz," Fritz says.

Petrus clears the dishes and changes the subject. "Let's get comfortable in the living room, start a fire, and listen to my niece's album."

"Yes, let's," Fritz says, as he helps Debra from the table. "There are still some pleasures left in this world."

Chapter 37

Reunion

Howling Wolf Ranch
1938
Katarina

In the months since I cut my record album, I have traveled from city to city, radio station to radio station, and lounge to lounge. It is a non-stop whirlwind of activity—I am ready for a break, to rest my voice and my body; take off the makeup and high heels. Do nothing, if I choose.

Johnny checks in with me every week; he is thrilled with my success. Of course, he is, because fifty percent of the profits line his own pockets. I don't begrudge him, though, he gave me a shot and I got lucky.

Most of my appearances have happened on the west coast—Seattle, Portland, San Francisco, Los Angeles, and San Diego—I landed in Tulsa and Oklahoma City, in my home state, too, where the local turnout was tremendous. There is a mid-western and east coast tour planned for next year, followed by a new album Johnny will orchestrate. Even now, he calls me to discuss tunes that fit my alto voice. There is a lot of competition out there—Ella Fitzgerald and Billy Holliday among them—I need to up my game.

I think about Billy Love, married to Parker now…a beautiful match. They are crazy for each other. And Giselle, living with Marlene, making movies, consistently happy, for the first time in two years.

Papa is circumspect these days. We don't talk much, and when we do, it is about me and my career. I don't have a clear vision of what he is doing these days. Aunt Beulah Bell says he stays in his room most of the time. It is impossible for him to work as a chemist here in the United States. He has no proof of his education. I will try to spend more time with him when I see him next…we need to form a stronger bond with each other, and try to get back to that place when we were together in Germany.

I am in San Francisco for my last stop on the tour; tomorrow, I head to the Howling Wolf Ranch. A.R. and Beulah Bell are hosting a huge reunion for family and friends. Everyone is expected to be there—Billy Love and her sisters, Parker, Simon and Lola Estelle Hilfman, Marlene, my father and Giselle. Only Aunt Liz and Uncle Petrus will be missing--stuck in Nazi Germany.

"Billy Love, when do you and Parker get to the ranch this weekend?" I ask, on the telephone.

"The train gets in around seven pm. I haven't seen you in six months, Kat. How did we let this happen?"

"I can't wait to see you, Billy Love. We cousins feed off each other, and finish each other's sentences."

"Father said there is going to be a special person at the reunion. Do you know who it is?"

"Nope, Uncle A.R. is keeping us all in the dark."

"Well, father is known for keeping secrets and popping surprises."

"He sure is—at least he is in a better mood these days…well, most days," Billy Love continues. "It helps that my sisters are all out of the house, in college."

We reminisce.

"Certainly, the twins were a handful in their younger days."

"I would say they were wild in high school, too, trading boyfriends and pulling tricks at school," Billy Love declares.

"Oh, well, our lives haven't been smooth sailing either— instead, exactly the opposite, with your rodeo, bull-riding ways and me singing in smoky cabarets," I say, laughing.

"Kat, I need to go. Kisses," I say, making a smacking sound.
"Kisses back."

****

"Aunt Beulah Bell, it is so nice to be back on the ranch, so to speak. Although I am grateful for all of the singing opportunities, it was grueling at times. I love that I can relax, pull on some dungarees, a flannel shirt, boots and hat—become a cowgirl again."

"Kat, we are surely glad to see you…and are so proud to be relatives of a famous singer," she says, as she grabs me in a bear hug. "And thank you for helping me out with the food preparation. I think there will be a lot of hungry people at the reunion."

I am the first to arrive at the ranch, Billy Love and Parker get in tonight, and the rest of the clan arrive tomorrow. Uncle A.R. has some big announcement—I am excited to hear it one minute, anxious the next. What if he is sick or something, or maybe the ranch is in trouble? Then again, it could be something really great. Who knows?

"Aunt, can we go over the list of food we need to prepare today?"

"Sure, honey. Here it is—deviled eggs, cinnamon rolls, sauerkraut—that's for the die-hard Germans; Billy Love and her sisters hate sauerkraut, in particular—lime jello with pears, fresh green beans with bacon, prime rib rubbed with butter and garlic; for dessert, two different kinds of pie, cherry and lemon meringue."

"Wow, you are an awesome cook."

"I enjoy cooking, so it is not a chore at all. Now, the eggs are done and in the refrigerator as is the lime jello with pears. This afternoon we can roll the dough for the cinnamon rolls. I will get up early tomorrow to bake the pies; that way, they will be fresh. I will put the prime rib in the oven for a slow cook, while preparing the rest of the food."

"It sounds heavenly, I can smell it now," I say, making a sniffing sound.

"Let's get to work," Beulah Bell says, tossing me an apron.

I strap it on, wash my hands, and grin. Life is good.

Aunt Beulah Bell and I have finished our food preparation for the day…we are relaxing, sipping rich, red wine at the kitchen table. I hear Billy Love's voice ringing through the house. "Mother, where are you? The newlyweds are here."

"Kat and I are having wine in the kitchen, come on in."

Billy Love and Parker come into view, holding hands and gazing into each other's eyes. I can see they are deeply in love.

"Look at you two, all lovey dovey."

"Kat, be nice," Billy Love says, as she drops Parker's hand to run across the room and hug me and her mother. "Where is father?"

"You know, I can't keep track of him. I think he said something about going to get supplies in Oklahoma City today. He should be back soon."

"You and Parker sit down, I will pour you a glass of burgundy."

Billy Love keeps talking. "Oh, and mother, father said there will be a special guest tomorrow. Who is it?"

"Billy Love, your father tells me squat. He loves to keep secrets; then randomly, he will blurt the answers out. You know how he is…then he laughs with that heh, heh, heh. I don't know how I stayed married to him for all these years."

"Uncle A.R. has a good heart, you know that Aunt Beulah Bell."

Beulah Bell rests her hand under her chin and sighs, "Well, I am too old to get rid of him now. Old habits die hard, you know."

"Mother, you are our rock," Billy Love declares. "You keep the family together, and keep father in line."

"He is impossible," Beulah Bell replies.

"I am tired after our train trip. Billy Love, I will take the suitcases up to the bedroom. You and Kat can catch up—it's lights out for me," Parker says.

"Good night Parker…I love you," Billy Love says, kissing him on the cheek.

"I am getting up at dawn, so I am also retiring," Beulah Bell declares, as she heads out of the kitchen.

Billy Love and I snuggle up on the couch—she provides details of her wedding, and I chat about my singing tour. It feels so good to connect with each other again...I am content.

It is late; we both nod off—a commotion startles us. Uncle A.R. is home and he is livid, slamming doors, stomping and yelling.

"Father, what is it?"

"Goddamn it! Goddamn it."

Parker and Aunt Beulah Bell are at the top of the staircase, rubbing their eyes, trying to grasp the situation.

"Uncle, calm down. Come sit with us and tell us what is wrong."

"Get me a brandy, Billy Love, and where is my pipe?"

"Right away, father, and I will make it a double, just for you."

Uncle drains his glass and lights his pipe, puffing quickly. His face is still red, but he is calmer now, leaning back into the couch.

Parker and Beulah Bell creep down the stairs and take seats across the room; we are all impatient to hear what has upset him so much.

"Last night, there was a massive riot throughout Germany; supposedly it was spontaneous, but I know better: Goebbels directed it."

"Uncle, what do you mean?"

"It was yet another attempt to drive out Jews, to destroy their lives. Why, the Hitler youth and the SA destroyed over 200 synagogues by setting fire to them. The local firefighters did nothing to try and save them. Throughout the night, shop windows were shattered and looted—of course, they were all Jewish shops, over 7,500 of them," A.R. says.

"Father, where did you hear this?"

"It doesn't matter, there is more. Jewish cemeteries were desecrated, and as many as 30,000 Jewish men were arrested and sent to concentration camps. It was a deliberate attempt to punish

Jews and promote Aryan policy," A.R. says, his foot tapping with agitation.

"How horrible; surely now President Roosevelt will step in, at least impose economic sanctions on Germany," I say.

"I doubt that will happen," Parker chimes in, wide awake now.

I look at Parker…he knows something. His demeanor shifts as he interacts with Uncle.

"Look, Europe is looking the other way, and so are most of the citizens of Germany. Only England is concentrating on what is happening with the Nazis. It is astonishing that we could have two world wars in the same century," Parker says. He continues, "When I was in Germany for the economic conference, I saw signs of impending war everywhere: all you had to do was look around. But no, people are foolish…they only see what they want to see."

"Billy Love, get Parker a Brandy, and get me another one," A.R. bellows.

"Sure father."

Billy Love returns with the drinks, then rubs Parker's shoulders. I go behind the couch and massage Uncle's neck. It is full of knots. I press firmly.

"Ouch, Leave me alone, Kat."

I step back reluctantly, feeling like a scolded child.

Beulah Bell directs her gaze to Uncle and stands up. "Okay, A.R., enough for one night. We have company coming tomorrow and we need to get some sleep. Now everyone, go to bed."

She pulls Uncle to his feet, and pushes him toward the stairs. He swigs the rest of his brandy and plods behind her, reluctantly.

I hope Uncle can get it together before tomorrow. There is no need to ruin the family reunion.

****

Everyone is here at the ranch except for Simon and Lola Estelle…and everyone knows they are always late. The rest of the clan chats noisily, waiting for their arrival. Marlene spins stories about her latest movie—I talk about my singing tour.

"I wish Lola Estelle and Simon would get here. I am going to starve to death," Bitsie Love says.

"Bitsie Love, you can wait a few more minutes. Don't be so dramatic," Beulah Bell says.

"Bitsie Love is right, we could starve. My stomach is growling," Babe Love says.

"You girls complain about everything. I don't want to hear another word."

I study the twins—I still cannot tell them apart. They have grown up, but they have a long journey toward maturity; they were the spoiled babies of the family. Bobbie Love is as aloof as ever, separating herself from the rest of the group, not participating in the conversations around her.

Papa is reading the LA Times' account of the Nazi Night of broken glass. "Kat, come over here. Look how they watered down the riots—suggesting that the Jews instigated them—what garbage. The Times should be ashamed of themselves."

I look over his shoulder. "It certainly does not match what A.R. told us last night."

"It is horrendous what is happening in Germany right now."

"I agree, father, we just have to keep the pressure on Germany."

"Lola Estelle and Simon are here, and there is someone else with them," Babe Love says.

"Who is it? Bitsie Love asks.

I squint to make him out as he comes closer. He is a small, scrawny man who looks like Simon.

"Oh, my goodness, it's Leon, Simon's brother," I say.

I rush toward him as he enters the house and throw my arms around him. "You're safe, you're safe, you're really here in America."

"Yes, I will tell my story after dinner. But I want to say one thing before we feast. I send a message to all of you: Aunt Liz and Petrus are okay—they are making due with the Nazi occupation."

"That is such a relief. We have all been so worried about them," Billy Love says. "What about Debra and Fritz Braun?"

"They are getting along."

I notice Billy Love making eye contact with Giselle; Giselle gives nothing away, but I know her well enough to tell she is relieved.

"Come, everyone, it is time to eat, gather round, let's dig in," Beulah Bell says.

✱✱✱✱✱✱✱✱✱✱✱✱✱✱✱

We are all gathered in the living room. Billy Love, the twins, and I sit on the floor. Uncle A.R. stands before us, looking around the room, preparing himself to speak.

"Friends and family, I am hosting this reunion because it is time for me to tell the Wolf story. Over the years, I have been secretive. You all may have noticed that."

"No, really?" Billy Love feigns surprise.

Uncle put his hand in Billy Love's face. "To continue, there was a reason… which will become clear as the story unfolds."

"It begins in the early 1800s, when Napoleon occupied Germany. Our family had no fixed last name, so we were ordered to make a new declaration."

"This is boring," Bitsie Love says to Babe Love.

"Shhhh," Beulah Bell says, clamping her hand on Bitsie Love's shoulders.

"We chose Wolf."

"Why?" Babe Love asks.

"Later, now just listen. You can ask questions after I finish. My father, Johan, and my mother, Annen Wolf lived in Darmstadt, where they were politically oppressed. They were discriminated against and could not find work. They left everything, everything in Germany; even baby Elisabetha, our precious Aunt Liz, whereby mother's sister adopted her."

"My parents were fortunate to arrive in Oklahoma when they did, at the height of the land grab. It is ironic; they were oppressed themselves, yet they took the lands where the Indians once freely roamed. I was born after they arrived; and had no idea I had a sister and brother left behind in Germany. They told me when I turned twenty-one."

"Were you angry?" Billy Love asks.

"Furious. I didn't speak to them for weeks, but by that time I was helping father on the ranch and I decided it wasn't worth the fight. I did immediately get in touch with Mood and Liz, however, and we have been tight ever since."

Papa nods toward A.R., as Giselle and Marlene stare at us all, wide-eyed.

"I was sixteen when my parents left—old enough to work, so I stayed in Germany," Papa says.

"You all have noticed my hatred of Hitler and his regime. I followed his evil actions since before he came to power."

"We noticed all right, with your rant last night a prime example," Billy Love says.

Uncle folds his arms in front of him. He pauses dramatically. He is coming to the main point of his long story.

"You see, father was Jewish. He told me at the same time he informed me about Mood and Liz."

"Father, we are Lutherans, not Jews," Bitsie Love blurts out.

"Bitsie Love, your grandfather converted to Protestant—he never wanted his family to experience what he had in Germany. As Hitler became more and more anti-Semitic, he enlisted me to help get Kat and Mood out of Germany.

"Uncle A.R., are you saying that papa and I were all part of a giant plot? That my journey to Oklahoma was arranged by the family?"

"Yes, Kat, do you understand now why the climate in Germany was so fraught for the Jewish people, we all were determined to get you out? The Nazis have a whole group of people examining birth records; if only one grandparent is identified as Jewish, the entire family became targets of discrimination and destruction. Mood would have been stripped of his high position at Merck Pharmaceutical."

I nod, solemnly.

"But what about Aunt Liz?" Billy Love asks.

"She was adopted and her records sealed, so her Jewish roots are not traceable."

"Mood and I arranged for Kat to come over first, to sing in the cabaret in Tulsa. And we were able to get a false passport for Mood; he was Glenn to the German authorities. Mood essentially disappeared from Germany… and that's how we wanted it."

"So, we are Jewish, father. Did you have those nose jobs to try to change your looks?" Billy Love asks.

"Billy Love, even in America there is discrimination against Jews. Just read the LA Times, so, yes, in some ways I made the decision to have the surgeries-- right or wrong, I could make the case either way."

"The Nazi regime has implemented a law decreeing someone a Jew, if even one grandparent is Jewish. They are identifying people and deporting them to concentration camps, taking their lifesavings, and smashing their properties."

"Simon came to me and asked for help in getting Leon out of Germany. Leon was within days of being discovered as part of the resistance. He would have been arrested and shot to death."

"I am eternally grateful to you for your efforts, A.R." Leon says. "The resistance is growing weaker, as the SA and the SS are ferreting out plots against Hitler. Since I am a Jew AND a member of the Red Orchestra, they watched my every move. I was living in safe houses."

"So here we are today, with Germany poised to invade Poland. There will be another world war, I am certain of it," A.R. says. "The one small victory, the Wolf family is safe."

"Now back to the Wolf name, please, "Babe Love pleads.

"Our Jewish ancestors chose Wolf because it is the symbol for the Tribe of Benjamin."

"Huh?"

"Wolf means loyalty and spirit…to freely form emotional attachments, to trust our intuition, and most of all, the ability to control our own lives."

"And so, all of us become the 'wolfpack', working for and with each other," Billy Love says.

All of us strand in unison, and gather into a circle, silently holding hands.

It is 1938, we cannot know our future, but we can trust each other, and be strong together.

Resist.

Wolfpack.

Epilogue

1945
New York City
Billy Love

One week ago, Adolf Hitler committed suicide in his bunker, in Berlin. The newspapers blared—Eva Braun, his new wife, was also dead. I am incredulous as I read the supposed account of Adolf and Eva's deaths…the German propaganda machine lives on. For Eva has not stepped onto German soil since 1936, nine years, to make the point. And the high up German Nazi officials, duped as to her whereabouts, pretended that she was hidden away in Germany; allegedly, to protect her from the enemy.

Because Hitler's aides doused the bunker with gasoline and then blew it up, neither body was ever identified. There was assumption and speculation, but no factual information regarding Eva and Adolf.

Today, Germany surrendered. The war is finally over.

I gaze out our apartment window, onto the streets and the sparkling harbor of the Hudson River. Bedlam…horns are bleating, confetti is streaming from windows, catching in the hair of the celebrating patrons jammed on the sidewalks of New York. Windows open, I hear 'Bugle Boy of Company B, blaring at the highest volume. There are women dancing the jitterbug with each other; the dearth of men is obvious.

Parker is at the university. I must make my way to him, through all the chaos. Plans must be made for our introduction and announcement to the world.

I scurry down the stairs from our fifth-floor apartment and join the masses swelling the streets. I can smell the stink of body odor, yet, oddly, the floral scent of spring roses mixes with the smell and mitigates it. Some stranger pats me on the back and pushes me forward, cheerleading as she chants. Here is a sailor in his bleached white uniform. A group of men lift him to their shoulders and parade him through the streets: their new hero, a symbol of the great United States.

Although the throngs celebrating in the streets of New York are jubilant, the other news coming from Europe is devastating: Hitler's attempt to wipe Jews off the planet came close to achieving its goal.

I have a flashback to 1938, when President Roosevelt refused to intervene, or even sanction the Nazis for their treatment of my fellow Jews. Now, he is celebrated throughout my country as a savior. In my view, waiting until 1942, when the Japanese attacked Pearl Harbor--to declare war on Germany, was a travesty. Might we have prevented Hitler from invading Poland?

Pictures of the concentration camps reveal emaciated, naked bodies, people crawling on the ground, clawing their way toward the liberating soldiers, not even able to scream; their eyes vacant. The crematoriums are filled with human ash; bones are piled in ditches. It is a horror scene of amoral human destruction.

Over the years, many Americans, including its leadership, were complicit in denying the holocaust. There were German Americans who discriminated against Jews, and were actually encouraged implicitly by officials who looked the other way. The United States made it so difficult for German Jews to obtain visas, many, many were left in Germany and eventually rounded up and sent to concentration camps. Most perished there.

Because of Liz, Parker and father…Kat, Mood, Simon, and Leon obtained visas to America. After 1938, the laws tightened: very few Jews were allowed to leave, and no countries would allow them to immigrate.

So, while I am relieved the war is over, there is a pall that sheaths me, a deep, throbbing hurt. My Jewish roots are twisting together, tangling with anguish. I need to get to Parker… he is a great comfort to me.

I push people out of the way and stumble onto the green lawns of Columbia University…. I lean over and heave--bile comes into my mouth and I vomit thick, green slime onto the cement curb.

The taste of rancid meat spreads throughout my mouth. I wipe the lingering slime away with my hand, and make my way toward the bench in front of me. A young woman grabs my arm and settles me on the bench—she takes out a handkerchief and gently wipes my lips. She moves silently away. I dry heave. Then the tears start, like a torrential rain, pounding down my face, tasting of salt. People stare...I am awash with grief, pent up for years, as the celebrations surround me and continue unabated.

****

Parker cannot see me like this...I need to pull myself together. I enter a restroom in the basement of his office building and gaze in the mirror—I am a total mess. I dig in my purse and pull out a brush, to tame my hair. I rake it through my long tresses and twist it into a bun. I grab the bar of soap and scrub the black mascara off my cheeks, then retouch my lipstick. My touchup will have to do...I am presentable again.

I smooth my skirt and button my lavender cardigan sweater, then I head up the stairs to Parker's office, popping a mint into my mouth, with the hope it will lighten my breath. The building is full of energetic, young students shouting in delight. They, who have never experienced the horrors of war, the innocents. So many lives sacrificed for them—so that they can have promising futures.

There is no one at the front desk, so I proceed to my husband's office. I push open the door; he is on the telephone, but he motions me; I snuggle into his shoulder, as he talks with animation.

"Who?" I ask silently.

"Liz, I don't have a very good connection. Can you speak slowly and clearly?"

"Yes, I know it is bedlam in Munich. I think, though, it is best that you and Petrus go in person to tell Fritz and Debra about Eva. It would be too much of a shock for Eva to ring up her parents out of the blue, and say, guess what, I am living in Hollywood,

255

California. I think Fritz might have a heart attack. It has been nine years, for Pete's sake."

"Liz, start making arrangements for you, Petrus, Debra and Fritz to come to New York City. Billy Love and I will get the rest of the Wolf clan and Eva here next week—we will hold an international press conference."

"Okay, I will let you talk to Billy Love now." He hands to phone to me.

"Aunt Liz, it is so great to hear your voice. We feared for your safety every day of the war. I can't wait for you to get here—we have some family secrets to share with you; but that will have to wait; it is a long story, and the phone lines are all jammed now. Go share the jubilant news about Eva. We will be waiting to hear their response."

I hang up the phone and kiss Parker on the cheek. He can sense I am sad, but I am also resilient. There are many good times ahead.

"Billy Love, we need to call Giselle, I mean, Eva. It seems strange to call her Eva after nine years of Giselle."

"Parker, I think back about Eva's situation. It is a pure miracle we kept her secret, isn't it?"

"Very few people in the world knew about her situation—those that did, trusted each other. Remember the day we met and you confronted me about her? I was so alarmed that you, the spunky upstart, would reveal Eva's identity and spoil our covert operation."

"And I was prepared to dislike you intensely. Was I wrong."

We kiss deeply, and then pull away from each other.

"We need to call Eva, let her know that Liz is calling her parents. Let's go home, there are no classes today. If there were, the rooms would be empty," Parker says.

"Yes, it's been an emotional, unforgettable day. In so many ways."

****

"Liz called back, Billy Love," Parker says.

"How did Fritz and Debra take the news?" I ask.

"At first, Debra howled with rage and tried to attack Liz. She had long assumed Eva was dead.... And now to hear that she was living under an assumed name in America the whole time—it was too much for her to take in," Parker says, frowning.

"Oh, my goodness," I say, raising my eyebrows.

"When Debra finally calmed down, Liz was able to explain the whole story: why she didn't even tell Petrus. That it was kept secret so that the whole Braun family was safe during the war."

"Debra did tell Liz that she didn't believe Eva died in the bunker with Hitler, as the newspapers claimed. She was adamant—if Eva was with Adolf, she would have contacted her and Fritz."

"Parker, speaking of Eva, we need to get her out here to New York, to prepare her for the press conference. The intensity of the reporters will be glaring; and with the reunion with her parents and sisters on top of it all, she is going to need all of the support she can get. I am going to get Kat out here, too. We will take Eva to the salon, rinse her hair back to blonde, treat her to a facial and have her makeup done."

"You sound like a teenager again, Billy Love, with all your scheming."

"I am a little giddy. It is such a relief to share our story—what are you telling the New York Times in advance of the press conference?"

"I am keeping it vague: only that it is an important announcement regarding Adolf Hitler."

"Will that draw them to the event?"

"Yes, because I told them I was giving them the scoop. This news will be blared around the world within minutes of the announcement - Giselle Gregor is really Eva Braun, the Hollywood camera operator, hah," he says, smirking.

"So, the press conference is next week, on the steps of the New York Public Library. Who should be there, Parker?"

"Liz, myself, your family, Mood, Kat and you…and, of course, Eva."

****

I am in the apartment kitchen, boiling water, preparing to drop in the strands of spaghetti. On the stove, the meat sauce simmers; a delicious tomato smell permeates the air. I dip a spoon into the ragu sauce and take out a sample. It touches my tongue, and I savor the deep, harmonic flavor.

"Eva, taste this. It might need a pinch more garlic, but it is almost perfect."

"Billy Love, this is delicious. I can't wait to eat."

"Kat, can you uncork this red wine? We need a full- bodied wine to complement the ragu," I say, nodding toward the wine rack.

Kat reaches for the burgundy, presses down on the corkscrew and, with a loud pop, unplugs the bottle. She grabs three wide-bottomed glasses and pours the deep red wine.

"Here's to us, and nine years of keeping the secret," Kat says, smiling broadly.

"Cheers," the three of us say, in unison, as we clink glasses and sip the smooth, rich wine. We air kiss each other.

Parker is in the den, preparing remarks for the press conference. Tonight, is the last night of privacy the three of us will have for a long time. Eva's family arrives tomorrow. The press conference is the following day.

The table is elegantly set with sterling silver, bone china and shimmering tea lights. I study Eva in the glow of the candles…Her raven tresses are returned to golden blonde, cut soft and feminine, off her face. Her blue eyes twinkle, her bow-like lips are moist with deep red color. Even with all of the plastic surgery to her cheeks and chin, I can see Giselle Gregor falling away, with Eva Braun emerging to take her place.

258

I rinse the spaghetti and load up the plates…ladling the sauce on top of the spaghetti.

"Let's eat, I'm starved," I say, as we scrape the chairs away from the table and sit down. I put Kat's record on the phonograph. It plays softly in the background.

"Eva, how did your parents sound when you finally spoke to them?" Kat asks, before she digs into the spaghetti.

"Mother could not stop crying. She was pretty hysterical—father finally had to get on the line so she could pull herself together."

"Well, it would be such a shock—I mean, so many years, assuming you were dead," Kat says, with animation, waving her hands, almost knocking over her wine glass.

"I guess my sisters wouldn't believe I was in America the whole time. Aunt Liz had to tell them the whole story about how she and Mood smuggled me out."

"Your family arrives tomorrow, right, along with Liz and Petrus?" I ask, as I twirl my fork into the spaghetti.

"Yes, they are staying at the Lincoln Hotel in Manhattan. Parker is picking them up—he will bring them to the apartment. He wants me out of the public eye until the press conference," Eva remarks, sipping her wine.

"This ought to be the best family reunion of all time," Kat says.

"Indeed," I say. "Eva, what did you tell Marlene about your trip to New York?"

"I was mysterious…told her I was visiting you and Parker, but I also hinted at the press conference and told her to watch," Eva says, wiping her mouth with her cloth napkin, then smiling at us. She is having fun playing cat and mouse with people closest to her.

"Knowing Marlene, I am sure that didn't sit well with her. Did she poke around, try to get more information?" Kat asks.

"She sure did. But I was mum," Eva says, pulling her index finger across her lips.

"I am pretty sure you will be receiving a phone call, Billy Love, immediately after the press conference," Kat says.

We stack the dishes in the sink. "I'll do them later, let's go talk to Parker about the press conference," I say.

Parker comes out of the study, carrying a sheaf of papers. He is roguishly handsome, with his sandy hair side-parted and swept back in a small pompadour. He smiles at us, with his brilliant straight teeth. I love him so…the sprinkling of freckles across his strong nose adds to his charm.

"Parker, there is leftover spaghetti in the kitchen," I say.

"Thanks Love, I will get it later. Let's go over the press conference. Eva, I want to make sure you are comfortable with it."

Lately, Parker has shortened my name to Love—no Billy, just Love. I like it.

****

The Wolf family and the Braun family are gathered at the Lincoln Hotel, getting ready for the big reveal.

Last night, the Braun family gathered at our apartment to reunite with Eva. Parker, Kat and I went out for a leisurely walk in Central Park—to give them privacy. It was an emotional celebration, with a flood of tears, but also smiles. Debra Braun kept grabbing Eva's face, twisting it from side to side, studying the contours, trying to see her daughter.

"Kat, mother had doubts at first that it was me. She couldn't get over the change in my appearance. Daddy, though, the minute he heard my voice, he recognized me. My sisters clung to me and wouldn't let go, a far cry from how they used to treat me."

"How did Aunt Liz seem to you?" I ask, pulling on my silk stockings.

"She was quiet, she seemed pinched, tired," Eva says. "Maybe I was imagining it. Nevertheless, she was happy for me."

"The war really took its toll on her, and she had to keep your secret, Eva, for years. How was that possible?—quite a burden, I would say," Kat responds.

"Love, are you and the ladies ready to leave for the press conference?" Parker says, as he pokes his head into the bedroom.

We are, indeed, ready…a team of women in our early thirties. We are clothed in linen suits. Kat is in ivory, her dark tresses streaked with red, gleaming against the neutral color. Eva is in turquoise, reflecting her sparkling eyes, and I am in magenta, with matching pumps.

A little-known fact: magenta 'represents universal love at its highest level.' This is what I feel toward the Wolf and Braun families—the highest level of love. I grab my magenta pocketbook and head out the door. The reveal is finally here.

****

It is a cloudless New York summer day; a light breeze drifts across the library's veranda. The microphone stand is perched in the middle of the steps—Parker is testing the sound, as a large crowd is milling below on the dais.

Several New York Times reporters, along with a gaggle of photographers, watch our every move, desperately trying to unwind our story.

"Oh, Miss, what is your name? Why are you here? What can you tell me? Can you give me the scoop?"

Endless questions…we ignore them and stand silently behind Parker, as he begins.

The crowd hushes itself. "Hello, my name is Parker O'Rourke. I am a professor at Columbia University. We are gathered here today to tell a story—a story that happened nine years ago, that begins in Munich, Germany."

The crowd is expectant…all eyes on Parker…riveted.

"You see, the people behind me all played important parts in this story, risking their lives," Parker says, as he turns to each of us, acknowledging us.

261

"You are all aware that the evil Hitler perished in his bunker only weeks ago." The crowd nods furiously; many pumping their fists in the air, making catcalls.

"Well, the newspaper accounts were not accurate," he shouts, putting his arm around Eva, bringing her up to the microphone.

"Tell them who you are," Parker says, yielding the microphone. Eva's clear and calm voice rings out, stunning the crowd. "I am Eva Braun." She repeats in German, "I am Eva Braun."

The people below seem stunned as Eva continues, "The people behind me are my dear, daring friends. They smuggled me out of Germany in 1936, made arrangements for plastic surgery, accompanied me to America on an ocean liner, then escorted me by train to Oklahoma where I lived in obscurity for a year on a cattle ranch."

The people are murmuring, and then there is a roar of support, cheering for us. Bright pops of light spring from the cameras…there is bedlam, with reporters shouting questions, and interrupting each other.

Parked returns to the microphone. "So, you see, Eva was not in that bunker with Adolf Hitler. Adolf abused her and held her prisoner in her home. Again, these people behind me, rescued her from his grip. For the past nine years, she made a life for herself in America, with the support from the Wolf family.

Each of us approach the microphone, telling the press and the crowd about our part of the rescue. The crowd swells as the celebration continues for Aunt Liz and Uncle Mood, Parker and me; father and Kat.

Parker sums up the story, as thunderous clapping rings out. We join hands and raise them in the air… jubilant.

As we bask in the applause, someone elbows his way through the crowd. He is a stocky man, with a thick torso…On his ruddy face, round glasses are perched. He continues to make his way up the steps toward us. Who is this man?

I am bewildered. Why would he be at our press conference? It appears he wants to speak…Parker steps aside, after warmly shaking his hand. It is apparent that Parker knows him. Has Parker been keeping something from me? I peer at father, Aunt Liz and Uncle Mood. They are smiling at Parker and this man. They all know each other? Kat, Eva and I furrow our brows—confused.

The man holds a box filled with metal objects. He holds up his hand to quiet the crowd; and speaks in his deep, rough voice.

"I am J. Edgar Hoover, director of the FBI…I am here today to award the Shield of Bravery to four of our agents. This represents the highest award in the land."

Kat and I gasp. FBI agents? Our fathers and aunt? Parker? I well up--I taste the saltiness.

"Elisabeth Wolf Braun, please step forward. As an agent in Germany, you infiltrated the Nazis, helping countless people, many of them Jewish, to safe houses. You risked your life transporting people into Belgium, in the years before world war two. You helped Eva Braun escape from Adolf Hitler. For this, I award you the Shield of Bravery."

He steps forward, takes the metal pin and secures it to Liz's lapel. The crowd whistles and stomps their feet.

"Mood Wolf, you gave up your job as a chemist to accompany Eva Braun to America. As an FBI agent in Germany, you secured information about drugs manufactured in Darmstadt, and supplied to the Nazi army; your efforts helped the United States in strategic planning during the war. Your meticulous documentation of your time in Darmstadt aided our efforts to defeat Germany."

More clapping, as Mood receives his award.

"Dr. Parker O'Rourke, you served valiantly as an undercover agent, traveling often to Germany in the pre-war years, giving and receiving information, often from Elisabetha. You led the 1938 New York operation which culminated in the arrest of 33 German spies…they were charged with espionage and convicted."

Parker pulls me toward him and kisses my cheek. After receiving his award, he speaks. "I want to thank my beautiful wife,

Billy Love, for her bravery and support over the years," Parker says, emotionally. "Sorry, Love, I was obliged to keep my agent status secret."

"Finally, what can I say about A.R. Wolf? Come over here." He claps father on the back. "A.R. has been an agent since the mid-twenties. Under his cover as a ranch owner, he led an investigation into the Osage Indian tribe murders, revealing sinister secrets about the killers. He, along with his sister and brother, orchestrated Eva Braun's escape and provided Eva's information about Hitler and his top aides to the FBI. He helped shepherd many dissidents out of Germany. A.R. Wolf, you are a stellar star of the F.B.I., well deserving of the Shield of Bravery."

As J. Edgar pins the metal on father, I spot mother in the crowd. From her facial expression, I can tell she did not know…she raises her fist and shakes it at father, but I know her, she won't be mad for long.

My four loves stand side by side, as bedlam breaks out in the crowd. People lift children to their shoulders to view us. Car horns honk continuously, police officers blow whistles, and confetti rains down from the nearby apartment building windows. More reporters arrive—and try to push through the celebrating crush of people. It is a very good day…I beam.

✳✳✳✳✳✳✳✳✳✳✳✳✳✳

"If you call one wolf, you invite the pack!" Wolfpack, indeed.

About the Author

Jean Wolf grew up in a small town in Iowa, where she experienced a childhood filled with adventures. She made a yearly trek to Lake Okoboji, where she stayed in a cottage with her grandparents, and cavorted with some of her "Wolf" cousins. Her parents, grandparents, and cousins' personalities and quirks influenced the development of some of the characters in this novel.

Her grandfather was a column writer for a small publication in Lytton, Iowa. He was a prolific story teller, frequently gathering the grandchildren around him, spinning tales of his life. The decade in which this book is set, 1928-1938, was inspired by his adult experiences.

The story-line in the book was prompted by the author's research into her German roots. She discovered many generations of Wolfs lived in Darmstadt, prior to her great-great grandfather immigrating to the United States.

Jean has a Master of Arts in Nursing from the University of Iowa, and a Ph.D. in Higher Education from Iowa State University. She spent over thirty years as a nurse educator at Grand View University, where she used story-telling to teach the art of nursing practice. She and her husband, along with two adult children, live in Des Moines, Iowa. *Billy Love's Wolfpack* is her first novel. A sequel, *Billy Love's Forsaken Children*, is planned.

Coming Soon by Jean Wolf

Billy Love's Forsaken Children

Billy Love's Forsaken Children

By Jean Wolf

It is 1945, and Germany has surrendered to the American allies. Bedlam ensues throughout the United States, as its citizens celebrate the Nazis' demise. While there are widespread festivities surrounding the allies' victory, the Wolf clan is despondent regarding the fate of the Jewish people. Adolf Hitler had come close to his goal of annihilating the entire European Jewish population.

Germany is devastated after the war—its families are torn apart, its children, orphaned. Billy Love, her cousin Katerina, and her Aunt Elisabetha, once again become united, as changing the plight of homeless children becomes their mission. Eva Braun, Hitler's mistress, who was whisked out of Germany and cloistered in the United States during world war II, is granted honorary membership in the wolfpack.

The connection of four women, exquisitely intertwined, and their commitment to each other, leads them on a journey of hope and healing for the forsaken children. In a time when the American government seemingly turns its back on the plight of young German children, the wolfpack takes action.

Four orphans are central to the story. Renata and Ursula, sisters in Munich. Ruthie, found in an orphanage in the Bronx. And Wolfgang, a young boy living in Frankenstein's Castle. What will be their fate and how can the women help them?

This historical novel is a story of people working together—"linked in, informed, and educated, bringing peace and prosperity to a forsaken planet"—IsaBell Allende.

For the precious children.

Billy Love's Forsaken Children

"I can promise you that women working together—linked, informed, and educated—can bring peace and prosperity to this forsaken planet."

Isabelle Allende

Chapter 1

A Divided Germany

New York City
1945
Billy Love

I sat on the hill below the Statue of Liberty, and gazed up at her stony face and outstretched arm. I thought about the bedlam of three months ago, when we reintroduced Eva Braun, also known as Giselle Gregor, to the world. I was still trying to process the entire event, where it was revealed that my father, A.R. Wolf, my husband, Parker O'Rourke, my Uncle Mood Wolf, and my Aunt Liz were F.B.I. agents. How could I have been so unaware? There were more than enough clues. I should have known, especially with father. All of the trips he made to Oklahoma City, allegedly to buy supplies for Howling Wolf Ranch, all the while he was reporting to the federal courthouse for his next assignment. And Parker would disappear for days at a time, using the cover of his job as an Economics Professor. In reality, he only taught one class at Columbia University, which freed him up to do undercover work in both the United States and in Germany.

It was a clear fall day, Indian Summer. I pulled my knees to my chest and dug my bare toes in the lush grass. Parker was meeting me here for some quiet, getaway time. We have been besieged with reporters calling us from all over the world, wanting to hear the story of how Eva Braun was smuggled out of Germany and concealed in a ranch in Oklahoma.

When The New York Times conducted a follow-up interview with Parker and me, in addition to telling Eva's story, I criticized the newspaper for under-reporting the plight of Jewish people throughout Europe. I was adamant that the United States' isolationist policy played a role in letting the Nazi regime get away with their heinous crimes.

I glanced up and read the plaque at the base of the statue. "Give me your tired, your poor, your huddled masses." We didn't take in the poor and tired. Hitler's Nuremburg laws systematically took everything from the Jews. The Nazis took their jobs, their education, their source of income, even their pride—then, they shipped them to extermination camps.

The public was euphoric that the war was over, but I was still battling a deep depression. Aunt Liz called the other day. She said Munich was in disarray, and very dangerous. Rats were roaming the streets openly, and children as young as five were wandering aimlessly, picking through garbage cans for anything edible. Apparently, there were many orphans, their fathers killed in the war, their mothers' dead after the ammunitions factory was bombed. I sighed. I would try to be more positive, tossing away my ruminations—it would be difficult.

A shadow crossed the grass. Parker arrived with some Deli ham sandwiches and a bottle of red wine. He sat beside me, and unwrapped the waxed paper, then handed me the sandwich. As he uncorked the wine bottle, I took in the bouquet, a sweet wood. I swirled the wine, we clinked glasses and I tasted the rich beverage. We relished the tangy, ham hoagies.

I still found it hard to believe I was married to Dr. Parker O'Rourke, decorated F.B.I. agent. My heart sped up a bit in his presence, and today was no exception. He was casually dressed, with an open collared striped shirt, and linen pants. His light brown, wavy hair was tousled.

I spent extra time on my appearance this morning, rolling my dark locks into a long pageboy. Generally, I don't spend much time on makeup, but Parker and I have not had many moments alone lately, and I wanted to look a little glamorous. I applied a lashing of black mascara, rouged my cheeks, and splashed on a matte lipstick, called Heart Red. I was garbed in gray gabardine, high-waisted trousers and my light pink sweater set, a modern, post-war look.

"Billy Love, you look gorgeous today."

I grabbed his arm and leaned in to kiss him. "Thank you, Parker." I said, as I pulled away and resumed staring up at the statue.

"Why are you fixated on the Statue of Liberty?"

"I can't stop thinking about how the United States government let down the people of Europe."

"For one day, let's concentrate on something else. Let's bask in the silence, away from the chaos of Midtown Manhattan," Parker said, in a low voice, as he leaned back into the grass on his elbows. I laid my head in his lap and peered out at the water. It smelled fishy today.

"I will try for you, Mr. O'Rourke, but it won't be easy. What do you think about your F.B.I. retirement?"

"It's great, and Columbia plans to hire me as a full-time professor, starting this spring semester."

"Parker, wonderful, I am so proud of you."

We became quiet, but I could not relax. I felt the tightness of my neck and shoulders, as I contemplated Eva's journey since the end of the war. She was staying with us, in New York. It was too traumatic for her to return to Munich, where all her knowns would have become unknowns. Many of her friends' brothers were killed fighting for the Nazis. There was uncertainty how the German civilians would interact with her. Might they laud her for escaping Hitler, or would they taunt her, and hurl obscenities and worse, for associating with him? Then, there were the United States troops guarding every corner, waiting for any unrest. The soldiers were keeping order, but at the same time, the German people eyed them warily. Perhaps Eva's presence would disrupt an already chaotic environment?

Aunt Liz claimed there continues to be a severe food and housing shortage throughout Germany. Some women were turning to prostitution in return for scraps of meat and vegetables. It was an untenable situation for thousands of women, most of them widowed or single parents, trying to survive on a daily basis. Many considered their situations similar to when Hitler ruled the land.

I sat up and turned to Parker, with a quiz able look. "Tell me again how the allied forces divided up Germany. I am trying to picture it."

"You just can't let it go, can you?"

I frowned. "Please, Parker, I need to know."

"Okay," he said, reluctantly. "The British zone is north and runs up to the North Sea. It includes Hamburg and Cologne. The French zone abuts France on the far west and the Russian zone is in the eastern half of Germany. The United States occupies southwestern Germany which, as you know, includes Munich."

"Why would they divide Berlin down the middle, with the eastern part of Berlin controlled by the Russians, and western sector of the city occupied by the American, French, and British?" I asked.

"Berlin is where Hitler and the Nazis consolidated their power. It symbolizes the allied forces victory. They all want a piece of Berlin."

"Parker, it seems impossible to divide up Berlin and still be able to function as a city. What will the Russians do, put up barbed wire and shoot people from the eastern sector if they try to pass to West Berlin?"

"There are already rumblings about that very thing, Billy Love."

"Terrible. There was a report in the New York Times that the Russian soldiers raped the German women as they entered the country from the east. I am grateful that Aunt Liz is in Munich.

Conditions could be even worse if she lived in Frankfort, for example."

"Billy Love, I have been invited back to Munich to assess the effect of the war on the German economy. Of course, everyone knows it is in shambles, but the people need to begin to heal and move forward. I want you to come with me."

"Oh, Parker, thank you," I said, as I threw my arms around him. "What are we going to do about the orphaned German children? There is so little reported about them. Yet, Aunt Liz says they are everywhere."

"It's time to return to the bustle of the city." He stood and tugged me up to him, kissing me deeply. I tasted the wine, as I melted into him. "No more talk of Germany today, especially around Eva. She has enough to cope with right now."

****

"Billy Love, you know Marlene is mad at us for not telling her ahead of time about Eva/Giselle, right?"

"Yes, I know."

Parker and I rode the elevator to our sixth-floor apartment. Our doorman, George, with his pristine white gloves, stared ahead and ignored our conversation. The elevator jolted slightly as we reached our floor. George slid the cage open, and we stepped into the hall.

"Have a good day, Mr. and Mrs. O'Rourke."

Parker slipped George a dollar bill and the elevator glided back to ground floor.

"Let's invite Marlene to New York," I said, as Parker inserted a key and opened the heavy oak door.

We entered the vestibule of our large, three bed-room, World War One apartment. Over the summer, Parker encouraged me to transform the drab dwelling—and I could not be happier with the outcome. I gazed around the living room and took in the sophisticated palette of silvery grays and shades of amethyst. A tufted, soft yellow velvet chaise nestled with a glass cocktail table. The gray, rich wool sofa faces the floor to ceiling windows, with scattered knife-edge pillows adorning it. Dressing the windows were pale silver, satin draperies. The look was complete with two, deep-gray leather chairs with nail-head trim. They faced the white marble fire-place, which I had re-polished.

"Great idea, Billy Love. Marlene spent the summer resting and recuperating following her USO tours. Now she should be ready for some catching up and enjoying New York City."

"Parker, Kat is in Germany, getting Mood settled back into his Darmstadt home, but she is returning to New York soon. We should invite her, too."

"Agreed."

"Eva, Parker and I are home," I rang out.

"Wonderful. I will be out in a minute," Eva said.

"Parker, can you retrieve the large, crystal vase, so that I can arrange the dahlias I purchased from the street vendor?"

"I love the deep, violet color," Eva proclaimed, as she emerged from her bedroom.

I studied Eva's face. It had been nine years since her appearance was surgically altered. Some days, I recognized the former Eva Braun, but today, all I perceived was the extraordinary cheekbones, the narrow bridge of her nose, and her sharp chin.

Following the press conference, when we disclosed Eva, I received a phone call from Europe. The caller identified himself as Dr. Klein, and indicated that he had performed the operation. He was thrilled that Eva survived the war and was safely living in America. Uncle Mood had kept the secret of her eventual home, Enid Oklahoma, at The Howling Wolf Ranch. Dr. Klein did not reveal his current location, as Japan had still not surrendered at that point, but he did say he was not in any physical danger. Eva spoke with him briefly, but became emotional, and had to hand the phone back to me. I expressed gratitude to him, and assured him that, one day, the whole Wolf clan would meet him, to thank him in person.

Eva was dressed in a navy-blue, button-front dress with white collar and cuffs. The shoulders were padded, which was the style of the moment. The pads made the waist look narrow. The dress flared at the hips and ended at the knees. Her heels staccatoed on the hard wood floors, then, she perched on the edge of the chaise lounge.

"I like being a blonde, again," she announced, as she patted her rolled curls. "But, it took a lot of treatments in the salon to make me presentable."

"You are beautiful either way," Parker declared. "I am fixing us a cocktail. Billy Love, tell Eva our plans."

I took a seat in one of the club chairs next to the chaise and pulled Eva's hands into mine. "Eva, you remember how angry Marlene was when we didn't inform her about you in advance of the press conference?"

Eva nodded.

"Well, we need to make it up to her, invite her to New York for a week---Kat, too, when she gets back from Germany."

"Bitte," Eva said, "And the three of us can gossip in German. It is such a relief to be able to freely speak the language."

"Parker will translate for me, so you better not ridicule me," I laughed.

Our lives were, by no means, conventional, but then again, who wanted a drab life?